Riders Across the Border

Center Point
Large Print

Also by Jackson Gregory and available from Center Point Large Print:

Emerald Trails
The Maid of the Mountain

This Large Print Book carries the Seal of Approval of N.A.V.H.

Riders Across the Border

Jackson Gregory

CENTER POINT LARGE PRINT
THORNDIKE, MAINE

This Center Point Large Print edition
is published in the year 2024 by arrangement with
Golden West Inc.

Originally published in the US by Dodd,
Mead & Company.
Originally published in the UK by
Hodder & Stoughton.

The text of this Large Print edition is unabridged.
In other aspects, this book may vary
from the original edition.
Printed in the United States of America
on permanent paper sourced using
environmentally responsible foresting methods.
Set in 16-point Times New Roman type.

ISBN 979-8-89164-004-7 (hardcover)
ISBN 979-8-89164-008-5 (paperback)

The Library of Congress has cataloged this record
under Library of Congress Control Number: 2023946245

CHAPTER I

Rogue Madden was laughing. But then that was a way he had, to laugh when most men would have drawn long faces.

"Straight from the shoulder, you say? Then take it!" he sang out with a will, and launched as hearty and clean a blow as the splendidly co-ordinating muscles of a truly superb young body knew the trick of delivering.

The ornately uniformed border Mexican, a man stuffed with arrogance and outwardly embroidered with much tinsel magnificence, had made the old familiar gesture toward his hip as he surged up from the table. His gun was half-way out of its holster when the hard, golden-brown fist caught him square between the eyes and sent him crashing to the floor.

The other men in the room—there were five witnesses to the quarrel—hastily shoved back their chairs from a table made colourful in the lamplight with scattered cards and glasses of the rare dusky-red wine for which the Madden ranch was noted; they became in an instant a sober-faced crew staring down upon all that show and vanity which one lusty blow had put level with their dusty boots.

As for young Madden, he stood leaning forward a little, lightly dusting the knuckles of his right hand, and one would have sworn that there was less of anger in his shining eyes than of his own mad brand of mirth. Yet none failed to mark how savagely the blow itself had been struck.

"He asked for it and he got it," he advised them, and laughed.

"None the less, my friend," said one of the onlookers, Don Anastasio Escobar, with a shrug as he stepped toward his prostrate compatriot, "you have, as you *Americanos* put it, started something. For your sake I could wish that you had been a thought less hasty." He bit his lip and his jet-black eyes burned ominously as he added under his breath: "It is as though you had slapped the face of Mexico herself!"

For the Special Deputy just now toppled over like a man of straw had arrived during the afternoon in the fashion of one who marches to the fanfare of trumpets. He was, let the lesser world know, none other than the redoubtable Colonel Carlos Toroblanco. Formerly a guerilla and a bandit, with his picture in the papers and a price on his head, he did most of his prowling at night and was known as El Toro, the Bull. Of late, thanks to the latest revolution, he rode the highways. He had come this way to-day in the role of an agent of the Mexican government upon some matter of border banditry, a thing which none should know better than he. Those who met him for the first time had no difficulty in seeing in him a hard, cruel man, swollen with pride, an insufferable bounder clanking spurs and twisting moustaches, a sabre-rattler and a ruffian. He had swept into the adobe-walled courtyard with a good deal of dash and clatter at the head of a score of ragged desperadoes over whom he presided like a field marshal. Don Anastasio Escobar knew him and vouched for him; hence he was bidden by young Madden into the game which had drawn these others for a wild, free night under the Madden rooftree.

While the dazed Toroblanco lay sprawling, Don Anastasio's sallow face arranged itself to the perfect picture of horror at sacrilege. He murmured as if communing with himself:

"Had it been any man on earth rather than the Colonel Don Carlos Toroblanco!"

"Your Colonel Don Carlos Toroblanco turns my stomach," Madden told him pleasantly. "Nor am I over squeamish, at that!"

"Yet," continued Don Anastasio soberly, "there are the laws of hospitality, my friend, *no?* And in your own house, at your own table—"

"Look you, Anastasio," retorted the other with a humorous quirk of the lips, which kept on smiling as though this were all so much farce and thistledown, "twice you name me friend and twice you find fault with my way!"

It was not that he was by nature quarrelsome, though it cannot be gainsaid that when trouble sought him out it found him meeting it fully half-way—and it must be admitted that he brought a certain lively zest into the encounter. If therefore Don Anastasio felt any urge to take up his fallen countryman's fight, Rogue Madden was certainly the man to accommodate him.

But matters were to progress no further in that direction. For after some seconds of dazed inertia Toroblanco scrambled to his feet, his face livid with wrath, his mouth dripping with imprecations.

"He was down just nine seconds!" announced a voice earnest and eager. "He came just that close to taking the count!"

There spoke the youngest of them all, Johnny Bandini, deft-fingered, nimble-witted youngster whose rose-pink cheeks and violet-blue eyes gave him a specious air of innocence. Habit was strong in this Johnny Bandini, recently arrived at the ranch as asylum while a minor affair with the border police should be forgotten; as a man went down out snapped Bandini's stop watch. To clock an event of such sporting order was but to respond logically to the stimulus of the moment.

But while Bandini was speaking still another voice rang out, this one bristling with warning:

"Rogue! Watch him, Rogue!" The man who spoke, immensely tall and lean and leathery, crouched as if to spring. "He's all artillery under the gold braid!"

"When you strike me, you laughing fool," roared Toroblanco, "you cut your throat for yourself!"

But Madcap Madden was as watchful as any of them. He leaped forward, catching up a heavy wine bottle by the neck.

"Even money I can put you down again and to stay this time, before you can pull your gun, Bull Calf," he both invited and challenged.

The lean and leathery foreman, Long Corbin, gasped; there was crack-brained folly for you! A pleased ejaculation burst from Johnny Bandini; here was a rare sporting event!

"Even money," he repeated eagerly, "and I'll back Rogue Madden's play to the limit!"

Though it was only a wine bottle against the weapon for which Colonel Toroblanco had sped a nervous hand, still the colonel, looking straight into a pair of very bright, clear eyes not a yard distant from his own muddy orbs, altered somewhat his original intention. The hand which had slipped under his coat came back into sight apparently empty, but when he lifted it to his mouth the shrill, ear-splitting blast of the silver whistle which he had palmed cut piercingly through a moment of silence.

"*Mama mia*!" said Johnny Bandini bleakly, and down went the corners of his mouth. "He bleats for help! The bets are off, *amigos*. For once in his life the great Toroblanco passes out before a half bottle of wine!"

"It's a signal to his tatterdemalion cutthroats!" exclaimed Long Corbin disgustedly.

"But there are only twenty or so of them, you know," said young Madden frivolously.

"Ah," gibed Corbin, "that's so. Most likely he'll just be sending the lot of 'em off for reinforcements!"

"Just the same," said Johnny Bandini, "you guys got to remember that all Rogue's cowboys went skally-hooting off to the dance at Las Palmas and won't be apt to show up till daylight."

"If Toroblanco wants to start the next war," said Madden, brisk and expectant, "now's the time to see where we all line up! Who's for me? Who's for the magnificence of the Special Deputy? And who's for himself, a quick dodge through a handy door and a fast horse to most anywhere but here?"

"Speaking of doors," observed a man who had not spoken until now and who seldom spoke save to the point, "there are several to this room. If all were closed and barred the five of us, I think, could give Toroblanco's twenty a run for their money."

It was Cameo Risden making his suggestion where he lounged against one of the two fireplaces in the room, his thumbs in the pockets of his beflowered white vest. The oldest man among them and the handsomest, his softly modulated voice gave no hint of tension, his fine, clear-cut features were untouched by any shadow. A familiar figure among gatherings of so many roughs along the border, in lusty mining camps, at race tracks, wherever games were played for high stakes, he found it possible to ply the trade of a professional gambler yet to remain an arrestingly patrician figure standing apart, touched by a subtle elegance. His large, wide-spaced grey eyes did not smile often and seldom frowned. Clean-shaven, he wore his hair picturesquely long. That hair was like spun silver and was, as all men knew, Cameo Risden's pride. Or call him Silver Risden if you like. Both names fitted him.

"Thanks, Cameo," said Madden with a little nod. For the gambler had said: "The five of us."

The five were, of course: Rogue Madden himself; Long Corbin, his foreman; Johnny Bandini; Cameo Risden—and Joe Quince. Thus far Joe Quince had had nothing to say for himself, and it was only natural that all eyes should focus on him, a small, round-paunched, cherubic looking man with a puckered mouth.

"How about it, Joe?" asked Madcap Madden lightly. "The bold dragoons will soon be on us."

"Me, I'm for peace first, last and all the time," began Joe jerkily.

Long Corbin roared him down, naming him quitter and coward, and then forgot him, leaping across the room, running to get the doors shut and barred. Toroblanco blew the final frenzied blast on his whistle, then fell back against the wall, his eyes flashing glassily as they seemed to be everywhere at once. Suddenly little Quince grew nimble; before Long Corbin could get to the door opening upon the corridor he shot through, vanishing in the dark.

"Coward!" yelled Long Corbin after him.

"No, not that," corrected Cameo Risden coolly. "But—well, tricky."

"Anyway, there are four of us," laughed their host. "Not counting our friend Don Anastasio!"

"Oh, all Mexico as here represented," growled Long Corbin as he dropped a heavy bar into place, "will stand together for once in history."

As the last door was closed a discordant medley of sounds came from outside, a metallic clang which might have been caused by two gun barrels clashing, the excited muttering of voices, the pad of feet. Toroblanco's ragged following had been housed for the night in one of the outbuildings across the high-walled courtyard opposite the rear patio and were coming at a run. Don Anastasio cocked an attentive ear, then turned toward the Special Deputy. The two stood a moment looking steadily into each other's eyes, though what either could read there no American present could make out; it was like staring into pools of ink.

Don Anastasio indulged in a characteristic deprecatory shrug. The gesture accompanied by a slight, quick gesture of both hands protested that here was no situation of his making. He bowed stiffly to the colonel.

"I am sorry, Señor," he said simply. "Mr. Madden is my friend and I must stand by him."

"Why, Anastasio!" cried Rogue Madden, his eyes at once glad and surprised. The others regarded Anastasio Escobar with no less interest; Johnny Bandini's baby-blue eyes widened; Cameo Risden's supple fingers fell to drumming on his vest. Madden alone appeared deeply moved; he could only exclaim again, "Why, Anastasio!" Forgotten in a flash was the disaffection of Joe Quince, though that had flicked him with chagrin, in his pleasure at this staunch adherence of Anastasio Escobar.

"Lights out!" cried Long Corbin. "Every lamp but one. I'll take that. The guns are in the next room."

But Madden interposed swiftly, countermanding his foreman's order:

"Get the guns, Corbin, but leave the lights on. There's never a single crack in door or shutter that they can slip a bullet through. And the Commander-in-Chief of the besieging forces, once he unscrambles his wits, will realize that should his zealous army grow hot for carnage and fire a broadside, they're just as likely to pop him over as anyone. And so—" His eyes flashed up with a thought which pleased him, and he concluded casually: "It's your deal, isn't it, Cameo?"

Cameo Risden's noncommittal grey eyes regarded him gravely a moment; then the gambler nodded, sat down and began gathering the scattered cards. Long Corbin emitted a sound which was like nothing else so much as the snort of a horse, and went for rifles. Johnny Bandini looked nonplussed a moment, staring from Madden to Cameo to Toroblanco, harkening to the increasing uproar outside; he opened his mouth as though to expostulate, but ended by squinting up his innocent blue eyes and wrinkling up his little pug nose in his own original interpretation of a grin. He, too, sat down, though in his case taking a chair meant merely perching on its arm, poised to project himself swiftly in any direction. He divided an unstinted admiration between the young rancher for his recklessness and the gambler for his aplomb, and set himself no more enviable pattern than either. He cleared his throat.

"Joe Quince, being in a hurry, left the best part of himself with us," he said, and fell to fingering the stack of coins where Quince had abandoned them. "What say we make it a jack-pot for Joe's pile?"

But Rogue Madden made a wry face and

scooped up the coins and flung them into the fireplace.

"Let the white fire purify them before any man touches them again," he laughed, and took his own seat. Over his shoulder he asked cheerily: "And you, Anastasio, will you join us again?"

"With all the pleasure in life, *amigo*," said Escobar, and resumed his place at the table.

"How about Toroblanco?" grinned Johnny Bandini. "If the fire can purify dirty money why shouldn't a good clean slap in the face—"

Toroblanco drowned him out, bursting into a small thunder of rage. The present attitude of the company in which he found himself was unbearably like a second slap. By all the canons of border brawls these men should be cringing in fear of their lives; instead, though his following howled outside and began to pound with rifle butts, they laughed and played and ignored him. The first rumble of his wrath died away only to be followed by a stormier one. He shouted to his men, calling two or three by name, bidding them batter the doors down and come to their leader's rescue.

"Well, then," resumed Johnny Bandini, as though there had been no storm, "what'll we do with Toroblanco's stack? It ought to go in the fire too, but we'd get no kick out of doing that stunt over again. Let's put it in the pot and play for it."

Rogue Madden regarded the youngster with

high approval, and even across the leathery face of Long Corbin, just returning with the rifles, there flitted a hint of a smile.

"You're a young man of ideas, Johnny Bandini," said Madden heartily. "Jacks or better for openers and—Playing, Corbin?"

"Guess I better," grunted Corbin, "seeing how you boys dispose of other men's money. And with Señor White Bull's pile to play for, too! Four—five hundred dollars in it, looks like. Sure; deal me a hand, Cameo."

"Thieves!" bellowed Toroblanco and ran to a door opening on the patio, emboldened by the laughing indifference of men who seemed blind to the serious portent of the moment. But his hope to have the doors open, to let his men rush in, to watch a room grow murky with smoke while a pack of fools was slaughtered, was quenched in its infancy. Long Corbin snatched up one of the rifles he had arranged conveniently on a bench at his side, and in a few choice words made the situation clear. There was to be no opening of doors.

While Toroblanco, red and furious and impotent, stood glaring, a very curious expression stamped itself on Johnny Bandini's face. One who did not know him well would have supposed him grown peculiarly sober-thoughted. Madden, however, began watching him expectantly. Bandini lifted a hand to his face, taking the tip of an engagingly retroussé nose between thumb and forefinger and shoving it still further upward as though not satisfied with its natural pugness. In this position the palm of his hand completely concealed his mouth.

At that moment the brief silence in the room was broken by an ugly snarling and barking of such an order as to cause one who heard it to form a swift mental picture of a savage brute of a dog about to fly at the first throat offering itself. The sound appeared to come from a spot just behind the Colonel Toroblanco, and that worthy whirled and sprang agilely aside. But there was no dog there. Again came the snarl, more vicious and ugly than before, this time from the corner into which Toroblanco had leaped. He spun about the second time.

"That man's acting kind of funny," observed Johnny Bandini, looking profoundly mystified. Of a sudden he sprang up, crying sharply: "Keep him covered with a rifle, Corbin! There's something in his pocket! And he talks about thieves!"

Though the clamour in the patio grew more insistent with raucous voices shouting to their leader, Toroblanco was forced to raise both hands above his head, and from glaring at Johnny Bandini he fell to staring with round, protuberant eyes into Corbin's unwavering rifle barrel. The sweat ran down his face; he lost all power of speech as Bandini's nimble fingers ran over his person.

"Look!" cried Bandini. "Pockets stuffed! No wonder he wanted to be on his way."

Speechless already with the indignity he was forced to endure, Toroblanco was further stricken dumb with amazement as from his coat pocket Johnny Bandini began pulling yard after yard of white cloth. Before Bandini had done he appeared to have relieved the dumbfounded colonel of a large tablecloth. Nor was that all; from the wadded end of the cloth came pouring forth, glittering and clattering, a cascade of solid silver knives and forks and spoons in quantity to have equipped the long table for which the cloth was meant.

"Can you beat it!" wailed Johnny Bandini, his baby stare never so soberly wondering. "Who'd ever think a fine gentleman like him would steal the silver?—And what's all this?"

Toroblanco in his consternation forgot the rifle trained upon him and allowed his arms to drop lax at his sides. Johnny Bandini's hand shot into one of the embroidered sleeves; out came two bananas. (There had been bananas on the supper table.) After these were disclosed as having been concealed in the right sleeve, the left was swiftly made to disgorge a pair of silver salt and pepper shakers, a sprig of celery, the fried wing of a chicken and the final item of three packs of soiled playing cards.

In the patio rifle butts hammered harder than ever. Gruff voices and high-pitched voices shouted to their colonel, demanding to know whether all was right with him, should they burst down the door?

"It's sure a funny thing—" began Johnny Bandini.

Toroblanco's brain, which had been a blank for a moment or two, flooded to understanding. Such a rage as not even this bedeviled colonel of ruffians had ever known flared up in his breast and he made a bound toward his tormentor, meaning to crush the life out of him. To be mocked thus while his score of men, all heavily armed and none of them averse to blood-letting, were as good as in the room—to strike the tragic pose and get himself laughed at—to be knocked down like a common mestizo, then ignored, then turned into a speechless dunce, made the man heedless of every earthly consideration save the one of summary vengeance.

But Johnny Bandini was not to be caught napping; in a flash he was across the room where with both hands at his mouth he was rendering a very creditable imitation of a cat and dog fight.

Rogue Madden, of an infinite capacity for enjoying a moment like this one, threw out his arms and whooped with such laughter as went rumbling and echoing through the big sprawling house. And even Cameo Risden was seen to smile.

"Johnny Bandini," cried Madden between gasps for air, "I love you like a brother. From this minute your money troubles are over; you are on my pay roll; name your own wage and damned if I don't double it!"

"Are we to batter down the door then, Señor?" shouted the outer voices. "Are we to start shooting?"

"Your bet, Corbin," said Cameo Risden. "Jacks or better, remember."

"They are all mad then!" muttered Toroblanco, and mopped his streaming forehead. The discovery did not in the least aid him toward a solution of his own little problem.

CHAPTER II

Thus one of those situations had arisen which permitted Rogue Madden to live to the top of his bent, and to indulge in beer and skittles while the tempest howled. To sit at cards while thunderous blows rained on his doors, playing for Toroblanco's money under Toroblanco's bulging eyes, was so much sheer joy. For life itself, to young Madden, was a game; his ambition, his religion one might almost suspect, was to make the game a merry one. Hence there was an ever ready laughter in his soul for most occasions of anything less than tragic import; and for even those other odd moments which gave an inkling of the humour to stalk in buskins, he was seldom hard put to whip up such a gale of merriment as blew all black and gloomy shadows clean out of his sun-drenched little universe.

Toroblanco, from looking at him, fell into gloomy confusion. The card game before his eyes was real enough, with the five at table drawing, discarding, filling their hands and making their bets. The noise of his own men at the door was no less real and sweet in his ears. Yet the combination of these two antithetical realities could not fail to superinduce in the unhappy colonel a queer sense of uncertainty.

Were the bars but let down and the doors jerked open it would be an altogether different matter! But he did not dare take a step or lift a hand in that direction, for Long Corbin sat with a rifle across his knee and a watchful, unrelenting look in his hawk eyes.

Toroblanco shook himself violently, stiffened his backbone and opened his lips to make clear his commands to those fools outside. Long Corbin shifted his rifle significantly. "No more talking, Pomposo," he admonished crisply. And Toroblanco, looking about to burst with the restraint, held his peace.

"Any door's got to go down in time before all that battering," said Johnny Bandini, and added: "Raise you ten bucks, Don Anastasio."

"I'm proud of those doors," said Madden. "Seasoned oak, a good four inches thick. Put up in the Diaz régime; old Ramon Olivares owned the place, you know. He started out like the valiant Toroblanco, swashbuckler deluxe, but he was a man of parts and served under a great dictator, and grew to be the fattest land-hog in all this part of the country. Sorry for you Bandini *mio*, but I'm going to put just exactly fifty dollars atop your little boost."

Toroblanco's rabble grew briefly silent outside. Here was a mystification for dull wits. They fell to murmuring among themselves, fruitlessly asking one another where was the Colonel Toroblanco, and why the locked doors and why no further word from him. His hands clenched as he listened to their muttering; he could have choked the lives out of them! Why didn't they beat down the barricade and come surging through? He looked almost pleadingly at Long Corbin. The cattleman gave him no encouragement.

"Señor! Señor Colonel Toroblanco!" a stout voice began calling. "What is it? Are you a prisoner in there? Are we to start shooting? Are we to go get axes?"

The man had no answer because his colonel dared make none. But he was afforded further mystification. In the silence among his men he must have heard the unconcerned voices of the card players. Madden laughed; Johnny Bandini whistled through his teeth at the turn of events as Cameo Risden was finally called and put down the winning hand; they spoke back and forth across the table as a fresh hand was being dealt.

"I guess we were all just playing for fun—except Cameo," said Long Corbin a hint mournfully.

Cameo Risden had done playing "just for fun" many years ago. Gambling with him was not merely a pastime and equally not merely a trade; it was more than a business to be thrown out of mind after office hours as so many businesses are; it was a beloved profession. And to-night he had been winning before the trouble started, and now he continued to win. The stakes were worthy even Cameo Risden.

For Rogue Madden had sold a smaller ranch and had taken the money in cash, that cash amounting to some twenty thousand dollars. With all that money hot in his pockets he had sent a man flying on horseback, carrying invitations to the logical merrymaking. Cameo Risden had put other and lesser matters promptly aside to answer the summons; little Joe Quince, now vanished from their midst, a very jewel of a poker player and companion, had been equally prompt, and Anastasio Escobar had been a house-guest for some weeks. Three other likely fellows invited had failed to arrive, but Johnny Bandini chanced in and Long Corbin was always dependable. And for a little while it had looked as though Toroblanco had been sent them by the sweet goddess Fors Fortuna herself.

In any case there was a good deal more than twenty thousand dollars now offering itself to the man on whom the sweet Fortuna smiled—as Toroblanco knew, if his stupid rabble did not. Give him his chance now, it would be down Fortuna, and up Mars, with rough boots trampling, smoke eddying, fire blazing out and Toroblanco filling his pockets the while he satisfied his wrath and tossed pennies to his wolfish followers.

So, small blame to Madcap Madden if he found

zest in the hour. The most conservative, even one like Long Corbin, must concede its possibilities.

The rabble in the patio fell back; there was need for consultation among them. Of their number was one aptly called El Carnicero, the Butcher, a sort of sergeant to whom the others looked for orders in Toroblanco's absence. Now was the very time for this Butcher to use to advantage all the brains he had. There were two things to think about: The redoubtable Toroblanco, grown so suddenly quiet, might be alive and a prisoner; or he might be a dead man. So his next in command needed to scratch his unwashed head and to spit reflectively through his strong white teeth. If Toroblanco lived, then a rescue was in order. Thus came swift promotion, a captaincy perhaps, high favour and money to jingle. No doubt of that. But on the other hand, suppose Toroblanco already dead of a slit throat and therefore in no condition to feel gratitude and dispense favours? What use in such a case to put one's self into danger? (For of course this Sergeant Butcher knew nothing of the more than twenty thousand dollars!)

The word Compromise coins itself for such men. The thing to do now was to wait, and while waiting to listen at keyholes and try to get a glimpse of what went on inside the house. So he divided his command, sending a good half of his fellows to scatter and reconnoitre in quest of an open door, or at least a keyhole or a crack through which an expert eye might come at much information. Thus the card game went on undisturbed and, as Toroblanco was quick to observe, in dead earnest. Stakes were high, play was quick and in some quarters reckless. There were no chips; bets were made in gold, silver and American bank notes. The players, saving perhaps Long Corbin alone, appeared to forget the wrathful man who watched them; they gave no hint of any sort of awareness of Toroblanco's men outside. The tall clock in a corner marked off another quarter of an hour which, alas, brought the Butcher no jot nearer his captaincy.

Singly the men who had gone forth exploring about the house came sneaking back, dark shadows flitting about corners, dodging among the olive and orange and pomegranate trees. Their reports could add nothing; they had peered into many a room, kitchen, dining room and pantry; all empty, the Indian household servants having gone long before to their quarters in the outbuildings; but they had had no glimpse into the big room whence came the voices and the clink of money and ruffling sound of cards.

So the pounding at the door was resumed, but in altered tempo and with diminished enthusiasm; it was to call attention to itself, to request an ear, to prelude the spoken words which followed:

"Señor! Señor Madden! I am the sergeant

of these good fellows; so, when our most distinguished leader, His Excellency the Colonel Don Carlos Toroblanco, whom God protect, is absent, then am I the one to whom these good fellows must look for orders. Am I heard, Señor Madden?"

"Verily," said the Madcap, looking up from his cards, his eyes dancing, "I do believe there is someone at my door!"

"Cards?" demanded Long Corbin, dealing.

"Give me a fresh start, Long Boy. Five pictures. And it'll cost every man of you ten bones to draw."

The Butcher's pounding was resumed. His voice, louder now but no whit less uncertain, rose above the clink of coins.

"Is Colonel Toroblanco with you, *señores*? We heard his whistle; we heard his voice. What of him?"

"What of him?" chuckled Madden, eyeing Toroblanco humorously. "In a way, good sergeant, he would appear to be of our midst; yet why so silent and still? Is it that though the body lingers here, the spirit rises above—"

"You mean," gasped the Butcher, "that he is dead?"

"*Bezugo*!" roared Toroblanco, so beside himself with rage that he forgot all about Long Corbin and the rifle.

When curses failed him, when all epithets

in general vulgar use seemed inadequate, he always fell back upon "*Bezugo*!" Thus quite originally and with a truly fearful significance he named the anathematized one for that species of southwestern fish which he was not alone in deeming utterly unlovely, unimaginative and a degree below the recorded scale of intelligence.

A startled cry broke from the Butcher.

"My Colonel! You live! You are a prisoner!"

"Stow your gab, Torro," warned Long Corbin, leaping up.

But Toroblanco was blown away by his rage, snapping all bonds of caution.

"Break down the cursed doors! Burn! Slaughter! . . . *There are more than twenty thousand dollars in here!*"

"Jesus-Maria!" squealed the Butcher, and there came a fusillade of rifle shots as bullets tore into the massive woodwork, their intent to shatter hinges, splinter the oak itself, create such openings as offered them opportunities for coming to the rescue of their leader—and to the more than twenty thousand dollars.

"I couldn't very well shoot the old rooster down in cold blood," mourned Long Corbin apologetically.

"It was too good to last," said Madden. "Well, we can always play poker, and it isn't every night that we can pull a party like this."

"Save your hands," urged Cameo Risden.

They were putting their cards on the table, face down, when there came, sounding sharp and insistent above all the uproar, a knocking at another door, that through which a little while ago Joe Quince had taken his headlong departure. After the knocking, a voice, equally insistent.

"Why, it's Joe Quince come back!" cried Johnny Bandini.

"Then the devil take him," said Madden. "Let him stay where he is. He deserted the Alamo when he had his chance to stick."

"You big fool!" yelled Quince, shaking the door more vehemently than ever. "Open up, I tell you. These coyotes will be swarming all over me in a minute."

Cameo Risden went swiftly to the door and jerked it open. Joe Quince, his face redder than ever and streaming with sweat, tumbled into the room, and the door was slammed and barred again.

Madden stared at Cameo Risden angrily. The gambler shrugged and picked up a rifle.

"I've always had the suspicion," he said coolly, "that there's more in Joe Quince than meets the eye."

Quince began a furious mopping of his streaming face with a big red bandanna handkerchief. Cherubic-looking still, there was an expression of hurt innocence in his eyes.

"I ought to let you sizzle on your own gridiron," he said to Madden, shaking his head. "I'm just a soft-hearted idiot, I guess."

"That door's bound to go down, I tell you," cried out Johnny Bandini. "We ought to get some lights out."

"That's all right," said Quince. "Now, listen: Me, I'm a pacifist and you know it. About to take to headlong flight to save myself from scenes of bloodshed, I got going fast enough to overhaul a hunch." He turned his eyes on Toroblanco, standing very tense and white. "I've punctured all four of the Grand Duke's tyres," he said smugly. "I've spilled his gasolene, let the air out of his Zeppelin, scuttled his ships, knocked the spokes out of his wheels, pulled the runners off his sleigh, scrapped his propeller and torn up the track in general."

Toroblanco started. He seemed first of all to catch an inkling of the meaning in all this absurdity.

"Tell your boys to stop the music a minute," said Quince, "and you shall have all the sad story. Otherwise—I'm sorry for you."

"Cease firing!" shouted Toroblanco. Then, as a crafty afterthought: "If they dare lay hand on me or hold me prisoner, storm the place. All booty will be yours!"

Joe Quince explained:

"It's the horses! I ducked around to your

servants' quarters, Rogue, and routed out a couple of your houseboys. We gathered up all the saddle horses in the stable and corrals, yours and the Grand Duke's, and hazed 'em off into a good safe place where they're close herded this minute. That's all. But I guess it ought to turn the trick."

Rogue Madden's face, a moment perplexed, broke into a broad grin and he smote Joe Quince so mightily on the shoulder that the little man folded up and subsided on a bench.

"Joe, I'm ashamed! I beg your pardon, Joe. I might have known—Why, I believe Cameo did know all the time!"

Toroblanco's jaw dropped and he stared goggle-eyed at his captors. To be set down on foot here, many a weary mile from the border, was to be checkmated at one move. To trudge on foot mile after mile was to such as Toroblanco and those he led to stroll endlessly in purgatory, tormented by the hot sun, the thirst, the burning sand, the pack upon the back—the ignominy! And worse even than all that, Madden's cowboys would come riding home in the morning when it would behove Toroblanco to be a long way from the Madden ranch.

"Me," said Joe Quince, "I'm for peace all the time. We give Toroblanco his horses back—they're not worth stealing anyhow—and he forks 'em and gets t' hell out of here. That's the ultimatum, huh, Rogue? And we go on with our game."

"Give 'em their horses and who knows they won't come back and mop up on us?" protested Bandini.

"They dump their guns first," said Quince. "Later on if they get some more and want to come back, we'll be all nice and ready to take 'em on; Rogue can pull in a handful of his riders and—me, I can be somewhere else, you know, sitting under somebody's palm tree, watching a dove."

Madden swung about upon Toroblanco, eyeing him sternly.

"How about it, *hombre*?" he demanded brusquely. "Personally, I'd be glad to have you gone. You're a damned blackguard, you know, and though I don't draw the line at rascals, I do like 'em merry-hearted and not altogether filthy. Yes, I'd be glad to have you gone and the doors and windows wide open for some clean air."

No considerable meditation was required on Toroblanco's part. He had the superiority in numbers, and there his advantage ceased. These men were as snug as in a fortress; they were armed and he had every reason to judge them so many wild devils when it came to fighting. And, topping all other considerations, he himself was utterly in their power; a little shiver shook him as he turned to look into the grey eyes of Cameo Risden. He had the unpleasant feeling that that gentleman, if the evening were permitted to be one of bloodshed, would shoot him down as coolly as he would deal a hand at poker.

"Throw down your guns, *bezugos*!" he stormed at his men. "Withdraw a hundred paces. Await me there."

In the end, after some slight confusion, much muttering and cursing and its consequent brief delay, the thing was done. Toroblanco turned on his heel and with much dignity made his retreat. His last look into Rogue Madden's eyes promised nothing of good. He tarried a moment only to transfer his fixed regard to Don Anastasio.

"Your name, señor," he said haughtily, "shall go down to Mexico City, together with my full commentary."

Don Anastasio sighed.

"My part was a difficult one, and yet—"

"And yet," cried the Madcap warmly, "you played it like a man. When you call the roll of your friends, Anastasio, set my name down at the top of the column."

Cameo Risden, thumbs in vest pockets, fell to drumming with his fingers.

"Let's play cards," said Joe Quince. "Oh, by the way, Rogue, here's a telegram for you. Looks six months old. One of your Mex houseboys outside was just bringing it in; he'd just got back from

Nacional—Where's my money? You dirty bums stole it! Hey, there!"

But Rogue Madden was deep in the contents of the soiled and much worn yellow envelope. The outer appearance of the thing merely exaggerated a bit the age of the message. It was several days old.

The game was to go on, of course. But it no longer altogether held Rogue Madden. Again and again he had to be prompted to draw his cards or declare himself. Times were when he did not appear to know whether he won or lost. The others began to look at him for an explanation, wondering whether his thoughts were still dogging the departed Toroblanco or were ensnared by something in the Western Union communication.

"I've got a notion—" he exclaimed once, his expression that of a man who listens to a voice calling from afar. But he broke short off without telling them what his notion was.

The game went on. Attrition led to elimination and the tale was being told. Long Corbin made his last bet and arose from the table and stretched himself luxuriously—Thus even a defeated man may retain some luxuries!—trying to look unconcerned, lighter-pocketed by six months' wages. Johnny Bandini was wiped out and began practising sleight-of-hand tricks with a discarded deck. Joe Quince, reimbursed for his scattered funds by Madden, made an error in judgment in going after Don Anastasio, and sat back a wiser and a poorer cherub. The game leaped to new heights like a balloon lightened by these droppings out. Rogue Madden, Cameo Risden and Anastasio Escobar were borne along into a new swift brilliancy of play.

All of a sudden, apropos of nothing that had been said, Rogue Madden cried out ringingly:

"I'll do it!"

"Are we playing poker or having a spiritualistic séance?" queried Cameo in his cool and courteous yet strangely arresting way.

The Madcap subsided with a grin which told nothing. But it grew clear from his ever wilder play that he was impatient to come to the end. A familiar, yet baffling eagerness was shining in his eyes.

CHAPTER III

Cameo Risden regarded his young madcap friend critically; twenty thousand dollars was a lot of money for any man to toss to the winds of chance. So the gambler, not without a glint of approval in his hard bright eyes, frankly studied the loser.

"You boys wait a shake for me," said Madden. "I'll be back in a jiffy."

He was up and away without explanation, bolting from the room as though in some tremendous hurry; they heard his boots clicking swiftly over the tiles of the patio.

"It's something to do with that wire," said Long Corbin, and yawned. "He's been restless ever since he got it. What time is it?"

Anastasio Escobar and Cameo Risden pocketed their winnings. The game had ceased when young Madden's table stakes were dissipated. Escobar, richer by about four thousand dollars, appeared satisfied and without envy of Risden with his winnings of approximately four times that amount. Long Corbin looked toward the tall clock; most obligingly it chimed for him: Half-past two.

"He said wait, so I'll give him until I smoke one thin cigarette. I got a day's work coming up."

"Pretty fast work, the way he stacked into

Toroblanco," offered little Joe Quince sleepily, yet with reminiscent satisfaction. "The Mex generalissimo was kind of free with his tongue."

"Do you know," confessed Johnny Bandini, "I didn't quite get the hang of it all. Couldn't very well ask 'em to stop a bit and tell me all about it. Who was that guy they were talking about? I heard something of it when it happened; must have been a year ago, when I was trailing my luck down Juarez way. Firing squad popped him off 'way down in Sonora somewhere, didn't they? Some pal of Rogue's?"

None seemed in haste to answer. When he had finished and looked at one after the other of them, they remained silent. At last Long Corbin, stamping up and down as though to get the blood to running in legs which had gone to sleep, muttered bluntly:

"That guy happened to be Rogue's old man."

Johnny Bandini whistled softly, his eyes round. But here came Madden hastening back.

"I'll tell you boys something," he announced breezily from the door. "You can all trundle off to bed now and grab your few winks of sleep, but at the very first rap on your doors, you'll have to come alive, brisk and lively, to help me do the grand as the one and only real thing in hospitable hosts this side beyond-the-moon."

He waved his telegram; some suppressed excitement shone in his eyes.

"They're on their way and ought to be here in two or three hours. I just had a word with Felipe; he's the boy who gave this wire to Joe; picked it up in Nacional where it was growing whiskers, waiting for someone to fetch it down here. Here, listen."

He read the message, his hearers listening intently as each of them counted on having the explanation of Madden's rather odd eagerness.

ROGER MADDEN
NACIONAL
MEXICO

ARRIVE NATIONAL JUNCTION TUESDAY AFTERNOON ON SUNSET LIMITED NINE IN PARTY COMING STRAIGHT TO YOUR RANCH CHANCE MEETING WITH FRIENDS OF YOURS ON TRAIN SILVIA SAYS SEND LOVE MRS BUD SAYS NO IMPROPER TOMMY BEGS FOR GENTLE HORSE AM BRINGING YOU LOVELIEST SURPRISE

ABNER YORKE

Well? Here was a party of friends swooping down on the ranch; that much was clear enough. But, "What about it?" There was nothing in the least novel about that; frequently Madden's place overran with merry-makers. He kept open-house always; friends or even slight acquaintances were forever descending upon him, staying overnight or for a week or more at the time. He was a Californian; more than that he was very much the true descendant of his mother's people who had been big rancheros in California since men on running horses had marked out the wide-flung limits of the enormous Spanish grants.

"I know some of these people, *no*?" said Don Anastasio. "That Silvia who sends love; she is Miss Silvia Vane. The Tommy is Mr. Tom Burton. The Mrs. Bud is Mrs. Bud Brown, that charming little widow who says she was born to be a nice duenna. I do not know the Yorke, though."

"And the lovely surprise?" queried Joe Quince. "North of the border it might be a case of high-grade booze. Down here it could be anything."

"It's a fool parrot," grinned Madden, leaping to conclusions. "Anyway that's my bet. I couldn't figure out who the devil Yorke was, myself; then that loveliest surprise gave me an inkling. I just barely remember that a young fellow named Yorke blew in at the other ranch up on the American side of Nacional about two years ago. Nice enough kid, but he had an old rickety idiot of a parrot that was enough to drive any man mad. The silly bird gave me the creeps and he knew it and so did the bird. American money to Mex dollars says that's what the surprise is, with

Yorke planning on leaving little old Polly with me when they breeze on to L.A."

"Well, be that as it may," said Long Corbin as he clapped on his disreputable old grey hat and made for the door, "I'm going to bed. *Buenas noches*, gents; I'm sorry I met up with you."

He yawned and stretched and his spidery legs carried him on his way. Madden made a spill of his telegram and sped it after him, laughing at the last glimpse of Corbin's rueful face.

"The rest of you boys do what you please so long as you count me out," he said. "Until the party gets here you see no more of me. I'm busy."

He gave them a nod for good night and hurried out. One by one the others wandered off to other parts of the many-roomed, rambling old adobe. Anastasio Escobar was the last to go. On his way he picked up the pleated telegram, smoothing it with long slender fingers; he stood conning it long enough to have read it two or three times. In the end he folded it back into its former creases, dropped it carelessly, put out the last lamp and left the big room to its shadows and shafts of moonlight through open windows.

The full moon, whose southern languorous loveliness had won no tribute from the card-players who had elected for lamplight murky with cigarette smoke, had all the while made the outer night glorious. Adobe walls gleamed white;

billowing pasture lands were like a stilled ocean; far off in the east the high, broken country of the Sudden Mountains was etched cleanly against a clear sky in which big white stars flamed low. Many a man would name this wide sweep of country a harsh and ugly land by light of sun; in the moonlight it was clothed in a rare, silvery loveliness.

Though within the house all was purposeful stir and bustle as the awakened servants came trooping in to prepare for the expected guests, outside there was only slumbrous silence and a vast peacefulness. But presently a little sound came from far off, at first a mere suspicion of distant rhythmic whispering. Swiftly it grew louder until it resolved itself into the clatter and thud of flying hoofs. A splash of water shot gleaming and sparkling high in air where the hoofs splattered across the shallow creek among the willows, and a moment later the lively clang of iron shoes rang out in the courtyard as two hard-ridden horses, running neck and neck, were pulled up.

A figure had risen quietly from a bench in the patio at the first suspicion of a distant sound. At the moment there was so little resilience in the step, and the moonlight fell upon so grave a face that, though the figure was unquestionably that of Rogue Madden, it was a different Madden. Whether or not the moonlight played pranks he looked far soberer than most people had ever seen him, and oddly chastened. He ran a quick hand across his brow and put on his hat with a savage little jerk. As the riders came closer he dropped his eyes to the cigarette which he began making with slow fingers, after the fashion of a man who rolls a cigarette as a tiny cylinder in which to gather not so much his crumbs of tobacco as his thoughts themselves.

The riders as they came into the yard saw him, marking first the flare of his match, and swerved to come straight to where he waited. He settled his hat even lower over his eyes, gave a hitch to his suddenly squared shoulders and stepped out to meet them.

As the horses under taut reins slid to a quivering standstill one of the riders dismounted hastily, exclaiming:

"Hello, Madden. I'm Tommy Burton, and—"

By this time all gravity had vanished from Rogue Madden's face, replaced by his quick smile, and his voice rang out cheerily as he said:

"Hello, Tommy! This is great. And where's the parrot?"

"There's been hell to pay!" cried Tommy Burton excitedly. Then remembering his companion he muttered hurriedly: "Oh, I beg pardon—Miss Wynne, this is Mr. Madden."

"Miss Wynne?" Madden repeated with a rising

reflection. And then added as he extended a helping hand: "Light down and—"

"Bandits!" gasped the girl, spilling out of the saddle so hurriedly that she must have fallen had he not steadied her. "We've been robbed! And I am afraid the shock is going to kill Aunt Polly!"

"*Aunt* Polly!" exclaimed Madden, and looked sharply at Tommy Burton who was dismounting more slowly and much more stiffly. "Speaking of parrots or people?"

"I am speaking of my Aunt Polly," she answered swiftly and a hint indignantly, as though she sensed silly jesting at a time when she was in deadly earnest. "She is terribly nervous; our doctor has been greatly worried about her condition, fearing acute neurasthenia. That's the real reason she came with me, to escape all the noise and excitement of the city, hoping to find utter quiet and calm out here. And to have this thing happen!" She shuddered; the mere glimpse he caught of her uplifted face obscured by the disordered hair which her ride had shaken down over her brow and about her cheeks gave him an impression of alarm. "She was beginning to grow hysterical when Mr. Burton and I left to ride on ahead."

Madden whistled softly.

"Here's a fix," he muttered vaguely. And added after a sober moment: "She is really quite ill, then? And you think the shock of being held up and robbed is going to affect her dangerously?"

"I never was so afraid of anything in my life! That is why Mr. Burton and I rushed on ahead. I—I don't like to begin troubling you or your father—you are Mr. Roger Madden's son, aren't you?—at the very beginning with my affairs; but it is so important that we have everything in readiness for Aunt Polly's coming! You forgive me, don't you?" She bit her lip; he did not know whether it were to control her emotions, or because she found it irksome to be asking favours of a stranger. "I thought that if she could go right to her room? In a quiet part of the house? And if you would please let me run in now and have things the way I know she likes them best? I am sure you understand, Mr. Madden, that if it weren't an emergency—"

"Why, bless your heart," she got for quick and hearty assurance, "the house and everything in it is yours to do with as you please. Come ahead."

He caught the reins of the two panting horses and led the way back to the patio, shouting lustily as he went, "*Juan! Ernesto! Corre pronto*!" Two half-grown Indian boys emerged from the kitchen in what, for them, went for headlong haste; they caught the bridles, stared curiously and moved off to the stables.

"This way," said Madden, and led his guests into the house. They entered directly the main *sala* in which some three hours earlier they had played at cards and baiting Toroblanco; the room had been aired, the litter removed and fresh fires lighted in the two big fireplaces. What light there was came from the burning pine and from the moonlight glimmering on the windows.

"I have ordered rooms made ready," Madden explained. "But of course I did not know of your aunt. I'm sorry!" He seemed sincerely troubled.

"You knew we were coming then?" asked Burton.

"I got Yorke's wire only two or three hours ago. A moment, Miss Wynne."

He left them standing by a fireplace to which they had been drawn for comfort in an uneasy moment rather than for warmth, and hastened into another part of the house. While he was away Tommy Burton looked curiously and with frank interest at the girl who, for her part, stared with troubled eyes into the fire. Almost immediately Madden returned, bringing with him a very stout, almost black Mexican woman who in stiff starched white apron and cap was the nearest thing the country afforded to a wide and comfortable southern Mammy.

"This is Maria, Miss Wynne. She understands mighty little English—"

"I know a few words in Spanish. I'll make her understand—"

"Fine! I've told her to show you the rooms. You'll select for yourself and your aunt whichever seem best to you. If you need any help, either with your Spanish or otherwise, you'll let me know? Tommy and I will be just outside, in the patio."

She nodded her thanks and began striving to hurry the leisurely Maria. Madden stood looking after her with a queer expression in his eyes. Then he took Burton's arm and they went outside.

"The rest of your crowd is coming along pretty close, isn't it?" he asked. "We'll be out here where we can hear them and be ready to lend a hand."

"You're a cool one, Madden," said Tommy. "One would say there was nothing commoner in your young life than highway robberies! You haven't asked a word about it!"

Madden laughed quietly.

"And you're simply bursting to be first to tell the tale!" he chuckled. "Well, let's have it, Tommy. I judge there are no gruesome details, or I'd have had 'em first rattle out of the box."

"It was only a little way from here," Burton began hurriedly and with a little shiver of excitement. "Lord! Came all with a flash and a bang, you might say, taking us all in a heap by surprise. Three or four miles from here where the rocky road winds among the hills. Down in a dry wash, where the wagon wheels scraped the banks on both sides, in a darkish spot where some trees shut off the moon, just as we swung about a sharp turn—"

"Who, exactly, make up the party, Tommy?" demanded Madden sharply.

Burton, in full career in his recital, did not like being interrupted with so much to tell, and answered impatiently.

"Just the five of us; Mr. Yorke—"

"*Mister* Yorke?" For the Yorke whom Madden thought that he remembered somewhat vaguely was a mere youngster, at most in his earliest twenties, and Tommy Burton was no man of the formal and conventional kind to be tossing his "misters" around profligately. "Why the mister, Tommy?"

"Why not?" snapped Tommy. "What's eating you anyway, Madden?"

"Curiosity," grunted Madden. "Gnawing my vitals. How old a man is this Mr. Yorke of yours?"

"I guess he's sixty; may be older. Why?"

"Hm," said Madden softly. And then, "Go on. Who are the others? You spoke of a wagon, I believe?"

"Of course. Give me a cigarette. Whew! Well, the rest of 'em are Mrs. Yorke, Miss Wynne, her Aunt Polly and your most damnably disgusted humble servant."

"What of the others? Mrs. Bud and Silvia and that crowd?"

"They quit cold on us when there wasn't any word from you and nobody showed up to meet our train at the Junction. They blew on to Los Angeles." He groaned and hurled afar the cigarette which he had barely lighted. "I wish to God they'd been on some other train altogether!"

"Sounds tragically interesting but scarcely illuminating!"

Tommy clutched him by the arm.

"I'm ruined, man! Wiped out. Stepped on and squashed flat like a gob of mud under an elephant."

"You mean the bandit? You didn't carry all your earthly wealth in your jeans, did you?"

"Worse than that. It's Silvia. You know her, Rogue; always plastering herself with diamonds and pearls and emeralds and what not. She's been galloping around New York with a wad of money to spend, and you can take my word for it she spent it! And I was howling jackass enough to carry a little flat box affair for her that must have had more money, boiled down to jewels, than any fool woman on earth has any right running around with. Gone; gone, I tell you!"

Madden said never a word. He began stripping leaves from a pomegranate and dropping them one by one to the pool into which a fountain splashed murmurously.

"The dirty greaser that held us up," ran on Burton hotly, "sure did a bang-up night's work.

He shook us down in great style. Every one of us naturally had some money. Mr. Yorke must have lost a lot. He's one of those old-timers that always carries a roll. I saw him fish it out and hurl it; gosh, he was mad! I bet there was enough in it to buy a lot in Hollywood and put up a twenty-nine-room bungalow."

"Just who is this Mr. Yorke, anyway?"

"He's an old-timer; that's all I know about him. He knew Miss Wynne's father a long time ago when they were both eating beans out of cans and making the cans over into coffee pots. Oh, yes, he's a friend of your old man's, of course. That's how he's here."

"Then he didn't know—" Madden began quickly, and concluded more quietly: "So it wasn't to me that he wired?"

"No, of course not. But look here Madden, what are we going to do about this thing? Can't you rout out a bunch of cowboys and take the trail after the damned brigand that pulled this dirty trick? If you don't get that stuff back, I'll be all the rest of my life working for Silvia, confound her!"

Madden may have heard him and may not. At any rate he did not answer. But he did stop the stripping and dropping of leaves and stood very silent and motionless, looking down. So Yorke was an old friend of his father and didn't know, of course, of that gallant gentleman's end before a firing squad down in Sonora. Equally of course, Tommy Burton had not known; it must be a full two years since Tommy had been here at the ranch, and it was but little over a year since the senior Roger Madden had been shot down.

"Oh, the devil's in it!" exclaimed Burton. "When there was no one to meet the train I ought to have done what the rest of my own crowd did, and skipped along. But Mr. Yorke was set on coming; said no doubt the wire hadn't been delivered; swore it would be fun once more to scare up a team and tool 'em along out here. And there was the girl and her aunt to be delivered, and he felt that it was sort of up to him. And me, being what I am, a wrong-picker that has the same attraction for bad luck that a lightning rod has for lightning, why at the last minute I pile off the train and don't listen to what Silvia's yelling, just blow a kiss off my fingertips, and all the while I guess she's naming me a damn' thief, and that's just exactly what she'll know I am when I—"

"Whoa, Tommy!—Who the devil is Miss Wynne? And why did she have to be delivered here and—"

"Why, don't you know that, even?" gasped Tommy. "She's your father's ward. Her father's dead; he and your dad were friends a hundred years ago, or did I tell you that already or did you know it anyhow? Anyway, she's obeying her old man's death-bed commands and coming to live here with her guardian."

"Funny I didn't know a thing about all this," muttered Madden rather lamely.

"What's funny about it?" demanded Tommy Burton. "Old Jim Wynne and your father had it all cooked up between them long ago. When Wynne died he and his girl were knocking about in Europe. Then she was all in for a spell, I guess; then she went to her sister in Scotland; then to her Aunt Polly in Boston, then on here."

"You'd think she'd have had sense enough to write," grumbled Madden.

"Her dad wrote for her, before he cashed in," said Burton carelessly. "Got an O.K. from your old man; said he'd be sending his girl along in time and—"

"When did Wynne write such a letter?"

"Oh, over a year ago. Died right soon after."

And Rogue Madden knew then that his father had gone to his death with that letter in his pocket. For Madden, Senior, had told his son that he had had a letter from an old friend, now dangerously ill; that there were a couple of things he could do for that pardner of other days; that one of those things was to run down into lower Sonora and look at some mining property of his down there. Out of those mining investigations had arisen complications; the Mexican government became involved; a petty insurrection created one of the complications; some ruffian of the Toroblanco type had found congenial work as well as financial profit in shooting down the elder Madden and assuming responsibility of the mining properties in question.

"But look here, Madden; why go into all this right now? There's the other thing. I tell you I'm worried to death. And while the trail is hot—"

"You don't know what worry is, my boy!" cut in Madden curiously. Then, as he heard the rattling of dry spokes and the crunching of wagon tyres in the distance, he added sharply: "Run out there and meet the rest of your crowd; I'll be with you in two minutes," and turned and hastened back into the house. For he had heard also quick light steps in the *sala*, and knew that Miss Wynne was returning from her quest of suitable accommodation for her invalid aunt.

They met in a room which was well lighted now by several lamps and the two ruddy fires, and so for the first time they saw each other clearly. For a moment each was occupied with that appraising examination of the other which is so natural to strangers who realize that circumstances are to make something of them quite other than strangers.

Deft fingers had put the girl's disordered hair back into place; it was a soft, curly brown with here and there a bright coppery sheen. A little worried frown was like a shadow in her eyes;

yet those were eyes which would stand a deal of shadowing and still sparkle like stars in a gossamery mist. Vivacious, one sensed her to be, and full of fire; yet now vivacity, too, was cloaked by an obvious distress. And there was something else, dimly sensed; a sort of arrogance? Perhaps. She was the daughter, amazingly and thoroughly spoiled, of an old pocket miner who had known the day, as Burton said, when he dined from a tin can, and who had come to know the later days when he could have filled a lot of the old tin cans with gold. Finally, considering what Burton had said of guardianship, it was evident that she was not quite eighteen.

She saw a young man, straight and brown and gracefully muscular, who in a costume of soft shirt and trousers thrust into tall, high-heeled boots, made a picturesque note in the setting of a picturesque home. There was some sort of devil, imp or wild spirit that made its restless abiding place in his soul; it flashed out at her from his eyes. It, exactly like some of her own livelier qualities, just now cloaked itself thinly, yet it was ever there stirring restlessly.

"Your friends are coming," said Madden. "And if—"

He broke off sharply at a sudden queer look which widened the girl's eyes and stamped something akin to fear on her features. She leaned forward, scarcely breathing, to stare at him.

"You?—*You?*" she cried incredulously. It was as though some monstrous thought had suggested itself which she could not believe, something she would not believe because it was unthinkable. But an instant later he knew that she did believe. For, drawing back from him, hardly above a whisper she gasped: "It was you!"

CHAPTER IV

When Miss Wynne—when you know her better you'll call her Gipsy, as her father did with all her friends following suit—drew back step after step, breathless and frightened, and then flung her accusation: "It was you!" Rogue Madden's dark eyes narrowed and there came a perceptible hardening to his mouth. And that devil, imp or restless spirit making its abiding place within the depths of the man's soul peeped out of his eyes, come in a flash, gone in a flash—and Gipsy Wynne drew even further away from him, and suddenly subsided on a bench over which, else, she would have tripped. She was as startled and rendered as speechless as the man who caught a terrifying glimpse of the Bottle Imp.

She had not said in so many words, "You are the bandit! You are the man who robbed us!" All that was quite unnecessary. Her meaning was clear, her tone fraught with scornful accusation in which, though she strove to fight it down, was that flick of fear.

They heard wagon wheels rattling in the yard before either spoke further. Then he smiled. Slowly and tantalizingly the smile broadened.

"Here's a pretty how-de-do," he chuckled.

"My loveliest surprise—for you are that, aren't you?—swears I'm the very desperate desperado who plundered my guests a little while ago! To be sure, Tommy Burton describes the bad man as a dirty greaser! Small compliment to me, I'd say!"

He had stepped swiftly toward where she sat and leaned over her. She would have sprung to her feet but it was almost as though some powerful emanation from him laid strong, compelling hands on her and thrust her back.

"Will you come out with me, Miss Wynne, to welcome my guests?" he asked coolly.

"If I do—I shall tell—"

"Come then. By all means. Let's go tell your Aunt Polly!"

She sprang to her feet then, edging away from him along the wall. A few feet away she stopped to look wonderingly at him. Seeing her bereft of words Madden treated her to a very elaborate shrug, quite as gracefully managed as even Don Anastasio could have achieved, and turned toward the door. His movement galvanized her.

"No—no! Aunt Polly mustn't know! It would kill her! She mustn't come in here. You must let us go!"

"Go?" He raised his brows at her inquiringly. "Go just where, Miss Wynne? After a good fifty-mile drive from the border, would you turn square about and drive back? Or maybe you're just joshing about this Aunt Polly of yours being an invalid?"

"I don't know what to do," she confessed miserably. "If you'd only deny! If I might possibly be mistaken!—But I'm not! Oh, I'm not! It was you! And I don't know what to do!"

"We'd perhaps better get your Aunt Polly to bed," he suggested offhandedly, by now at the door and about to go out.

Just then another door opened; here came Cameo Risden, clean-shaved, fresh-looking, and altogether serene. The girl whirled toward him as though toward a saviour sent from on high.

"Mr. Cameo Risden," announced Madden. "Cameo, this is our loveliest surprise, Miss Wynne of Boston and Somewhere-or-Other in Europe." And out he went, leaving Cameo Risden bowing in an outworn courtly fashion, and Miss Wynne unrelieved in her uncertainty.

"Welcome all; welcome to the rancho!" she heard a glad voice calling. Had she made some terrible, unpardonable mistake after all? Was that clear-ringing voice, a voice to make pleasant little ripples go widening out through one's consciousness, the voice of such a villain as she had fancied their highwayman must be?

"No! It was no mistake!"

"I beg pardon?" said Cameo Risden. "You said—"

"Oh!" cried the distraught girl, "it is you who

must pardon me! I don't know what I said. I must hurry to my aunt—she is not strong—"

Cameo watched her interestedly as she fled, then strolled into the patio after her, and stopped there while she sped on into the full moonlight and to the wagon. Madden was making himself known, not waiting for the offices of Tommy Burton. The new arrivals were getting down now. Miss Wynne shivered as she saw Madden's arms lifted, and Aunt Polly coming down so serenely in them.

There was the inevitable moment of semi-confusion attendant upon stranger guests meeting host for the first time. The girl pounced on a little grey bundle which had slipped to earth from Madden's arms and which was Aunt Polly constituting the diminutive kernel surrounded by the outer husk of many wraps. Aunt Polly, as her niece's arms closed so strong and warm and tight about her, let out a nicely modulated squeal of sheer rapture.

"Oh, Gipsy! Isn't it *won*-derful!"

"Yes, Auntie; of course it is," said the girl hastily, peering down solicitously at what the moon revealed of her aunt's face. "And everything is all right, dear. You're not to worry about a single thing on earth, but you're to come right in and get to bed. Everything's ready."

"Bed!" wailed Aunt Polly. "On a night like this, and almost daylight at that? With the fun just beginning? Bed, your"—she bethought herself in time, pulled the girl's head down and finished it in a defiant whisper—"bed, your foot!"

Her niece led her away none the less, promising her that she should meet their host inside. Madden had shaken hands with Abner Yorke, a distinguished-looking old fellow who might have passed anywhere for a Kentucky colonel, except perhaps in Kentucky, and was presented to Mrs. Yorke, a tall, lean, angular woman whom it would take a good deal of effort to care much for at first sight. Then while Tommy led her into the house and the Indian boys came for the horses and bags, Madden and Abner Yorke had a few words together.

"Miss Wynne has told you of our adventure?"

"Yes," Madden answered. "Her greatest concern, however, seemed to be what effect the shock might have on her aunt. She seems all right."

"That woman," said Yorke in puzzled fashion, "is miles beyond me. If you ever saw a nervous wreck, she's it. On the train I thought she'd fly all to flinders a thousand times. And then—Well, I can't make her out. She may die on you in ten minutes, or go quite mad or—Looks like I'd helped pile up no end of responsibility on you."

"Everything's ready for her to be got to bed in a quiet end of the house."

"Well, I'd say bed's the place for her. By the

way, where's Roger all this while? Haven't laid eyes on the old boy for pretty near twenty years. You're his son, aren't you? He's not away, is he?"

"Yes," said Rogue Madden gravely, "he's away."

Yorke looked at him sharply. There had come a sudden gruffness into the young man's voice; there was something ominous in the way he bit his words off.

"He's away," said Madden very quietly, "on the long trail, Mr. Yorke."

Yorke grasped his arm, gasping:

"You don't mean he's dead? Roger Madden dead?"

"They got him one night down in south Sonora. A pack of damned outlaws."

Abner Yorke pulled off his hat; the moonlight silvered his hair and imperial. He stood silent, his face turned up to the sky, a man sunk deep in mournful meditation. Before he spoke he took out a handkerchief, ran it back and forth across his brow, then blew his nose vehemently.

"Abner!" called Mrs. Yorke from the house. "You'd better come right in. It's chilly out there."

"Coming, my dear," said Yorke. He clapped on his hat, stuffed his handkerchief into his pocket and fell to muttering under his breath. "Well, well," Madden heard him say; and after that, "Well!" And then, "Damn dogs!" He drove both hands fiercely into his pockets and fell to jingling his keys, about all that was left to him to jingle. "And so Roger's gone, too!—And old Jimmie Wynne dead.—There were the three of us, my boy. Young fellows, lusty, full of all the real life-stuff, full of dreams—My God, all that was a hundred thousand years ago!"

They moved along in step toward the house.

"When—when did this thing happen?" demanded Yorke.

"A year ago. He had had a letter—I've just decided it must have been from your friend, Miss Wynne's father—about some mines down in Sonora. It happened while he was down there trying to straighten things out."

"Well, well," said Yorke. "Well!"

"I'm sorry," said Madden, "that I had to spring such news on you the minute of your arrival. I haven't mentioned it to the others. There's no use—Oh, you understand!"

"Why, of course I do! It's no good pulling the long face; Roger himself would be the last one for that. If there ever was a man—Ahem!—By the way, I believe you're just like him!"

"Thank you," said Rogue Madden. "I'd like to be. Let's go in now."

"Why, Abner! What's the matter?" cried Mrs. Yorke, the instant her hawk eyes fell upon his face.

"He has every right to show some signs of wear-and-tear," said Madden hastily. "You folks have had quite a night of it, I'd say. Coffee's on; you can be sitting down to breakfast the minute you are ready. And could any of you do with a drink? Cocktail or whisky?"

Yorke looked at him gratefully. But before he could put an acceptance into words another voice did so, and thereby startled at least one of their number. It was Aunt Polly.

"I'm going to have a cocktail! I never tasted one of the things in my life, and so I suppose it's time I did!"

"Aunt Polly!" gasped her niece incredulously.

Aunt Polly's many wraps had been laid aside and she herself appeared as a thin, frail-looking little soul with very bright eyes and something oddly bird-like about her. She was dressed all in dove-grey from tiny suede shoes to severe little hat; her small face was pinched and pale to the verge of transparency; she was only in her fiftieth year and passed everywhere for a good sixty. Just now there were two hot red spots in her cheeks and an unnatural brilliance in her eyes.

Cameo Risden had come into the room with the others; at this moment Johnny Bandini entered. Madden made the necessary introductions before he went out to make cocktails; Johnny Bandini, after a swift survey of the newcomers, bore down upon Miss Wynne as straight as any marauding bold bumble bee to tilted flower. And the girl, quick to take in all that outward fresh guilelessness that was Johnny Bandini's, accepted him promptly on his face value, which was the last thing on earth to do with Bandini, and was really grateful to have him near her.

Meantime Mr. Yorke had followed Madden out of the room and to the little pantry where were cupboards containing various items to interest a man in Mr. Yorke's mood. Tommy Burton drooped somewhat dismally over the fireplace. Cameo Risden chatted with Mrs. Yorke. She, it would appear, was full to brimming with one subject. One would have surmised that that subject would be the unfortunate adventure of the night. It was not so. She had no thoughts for anything but Aunt Polly.

She must tell Mr. Risden all about her; he must be informed at the very outset that that woman was but a chance train acquaintance. She started out assuming the thin veil of pretext that she was speaking only through sympathy. She spoke in general of nervous wrecks. A dozen words tore the thin veilings all to tatters and left her intolerance stark naked. Mrs. Yorke was assured that people who affected "nerves" were just so many self-centred, selfish, egotistical folk who only wanted the eyes, ears and hearts of all other individuals devoted to them; they craved attention, of course mostly masculine attention. And if there was ever an individual of this general class who ought to be put forthwith into a cell—Mrs. Yorke did not specify whether of jail or madhouse and perhaps did not care—it was Miss Polly Comfort.

"If there's one thing I can't abide," confided Mrs. Yorke, and Cameo Risden felt quite sure that there were many things to come under that head, "it's plain hysteria. Hysterics went out of style a whole generation ago. *She* doesn't know that yet! If you could have heard her! Laughing and crying until you'd have thought she'd gone quite mad. Maybe she had! Simply shrieking with laughter at being robbed!—I'm sorry for the poor thing, Mr. Risden, but—"

When Madden returned to his guests, Abner Yorke remained a moment alone in the little pantry. A window was open; he could look out into the silver night. He lifted a brimming glass and drank like a man performing a ceremony; he hurled the empty glass from him through the window so that it crashed against the adobe wall, flying into a hundred sparkling bits.

"It's the long good-bye to you, old boy," he said softly. His eyes were lifted to the field of stars; they seemed for a while to be striving to follow some winding pathway up there. "So long, Roger. Luck!"

A board creaked under an oncoming tread. He whirled about, guilty and ashamed. It was Madden again.

"The rest are just going in for breakfast. Ready?"

At table the tale had to be told all over again

for those who had not heard it. Johnny Bandini, immediately he had grasped what had occurred, exclaimed:

"Toroblanco!"

"Think so?" asked Madden mildly, and turned to look at Miss Wynne.

"Who, or what, is Toroblanco?" asked Yorke.

The recital of the robbery was suspended long enough for Bandini to sketch the high lights of the evening here at the old home. By the time he had done and Tommy Burton had again taken up his theme and finished with it, the sun was shining in at the windows. But as they arose from the table it was for the new arrivals to trundle off to bed, heavy with sleep.

"May I see you for a moment, Mr. Madden," the girl asked, as she took her aunt's arm in hers, "after I have put Aunt Polly to bed?"

Aunt Polly patted a yawn, but her eyes were as bright as stars.

"I am having the time of my life, Mr. Madden," she told him, and shook hands warmly. "Gipsy insists on putting me to bed, but I feel like a colt—"

"Sh, Auntie. It's the cocktail!"

"I'll be right here," laughed Madden. And to Miss Comfort: "Cocktails whenever you want them, you know."

He watched them depart, then turned to Abner Yorke, who came seeking him.

"I hoped to stay two or three days, Madden," Yorke said musingly. "Now, I guess I'd better be on my way. If you'll let us, we'll run out and see you some other time. We'll get a few winks and if you can spare us a team I think we'd better head back to the railroad. I'm a bit disturbed over the loss of some papers which were in my wallet and which are gone, of course, with what money I had with me. No chance of getting anything back, I suppose. But I can minimize the trouble of the loss of the papers by getting to Los Angeles without delay. My lawyer will know how to straighten things out; but it's a case he'll have to act quickly on."

"I'm sorry," muttered Madden under his breath, then burst out: "Damn it all! If—" and then shrugged and fell silent.

He was all alone in the big room, staring out of a window, when Gipsy Wynne came back. Joe Quince and Anastasio Escobar had put in their appearances just as the others were quitting the table, and were now taking their coffee. Cameo Risden had strolled, cigar in mouth, to look at his horse. Johnny Bandini, having done his level best to monopolize the one pretty girl at hand, was now lounging in the yard, waiting for her to have her nap and then brighten the world again.

"Mr. Madden," she said, coming straight to the point, "you know why I asked you to wait!

You are going to restore the things you—stole to-night. You must do it now."

He stood looking at her soberly. He seemed, less than listening to her words, to be measuring her; estimating, perhaps, her courage, her intelligence, her volatile spirit itself.

"Did you hear me?" she was forced by his silence to demand.

"Yes. I heard you."

"What will you do?"

"I don't know that I'll do anything."

"You don't deny? You haven't denied this hideous thing!"

"You seemed to be so very sure—"

"I am sure! I know! When you rode down on us in that dry creek bed, you know how we were straggling along single file; Mr. Burton first, on horseback, looking for the place where the road climbed up the bank again, the wagon next, I following behind, looking at the moon. When you held them up, I didn't know what to do for a minute. Then you saw me and made them go on and rode where I was."

"Well?" he prompted her drily.

"You had a big handkerchief over your face, tied across the nose, just under your eyes. You had your big black hat pulled low down. But you came very close, just to frighten me, I think—and I know you by your eyebrows, Mr. Madden!"

Come to think of it, there is likely to be as much

difference between one pair of eyebrows and another as between the eyes themselves, or noses or mouths. And Roger Madden's brows were distinctive; very black and heavy, they arched with peculiar abruptness near the nose and then sloped downward and outward in jet black heavy lines which *almost* curled upward at the ends.

"You spoke like a Mexican; you hid your hands in gauntlets, even; but you let me see your eyebrows and have a glimpse of your eyes. And now—Oh, yes, I am very sure."

"You are not afraid to be talking to me like this? Alone?"

Her eyes flashed her scorn at him.

"No; I am not afraid. I have but to cry out. And, besides, I am going to give you a chance—for your father's sake," she said hurriedly.

"Just what chance, I wonder?" he asked, and she was not sure now whether he mocked her or not.

"But I have told you already! A chance to return what you took." She half turned away from him with a little shrug of distaste. "Perhaps you may arrange it without anyone knowing—"

He appeared little impressed. In fact one would have suspected that he began to discover certain humorous possibilities in a situation which was filling her with distress.

"To know a man by his eyebrows!" He taunted her with his widening grin.

"It only began with that! That was just the first hint, pointing toward you. It's everything now, your carriage itself, even your voice, though you disguised it. More than those things a—a *feeling*. Oh, that may sound ridiculous, but you know it isn't. There are certain people who somehow make themselves felt. Even in the dark, were they silent, you'd know—"

"Did our souls rush out to a meeting when first our eyes met in the moonlight?" he asked her most sentimentally.

She flushed up angrily.

"Will you take this thing seriously, or not?"

"Not if I can help myself," he chuckled. "God forbid that I should take anything seriously in this most comical of all worlds."

But she brought enough sober earnestness to the occasion to serve for both.

"I know it was you, from many things," she told him stiffly. "I had my first true inkling of what you are when I became acquainted with your friends on the train. Those precious triflers! Your Silvia, who is Silvia to everybody. The conductor called her Silvia the first day out from Washington! That impossible Mrs. Bud. The two other men, the Russian musician who pretends to be a prince or something of the kind; the fat, gross man with the toupee and the smirk! Ugh!"

"That precious crowd certainly made a hit with you!"

"And I have learned more since coming here. Mr. Bandini told me what had happened in this room just before we came. How you lost a fortune, playing cards. Having lost so heavily—"

"I dashed out and made up said losses by scalping my guests! You ought to be a Lady Detective!"

"You don't deny it?"

"No," he said slowly; "hanged if I do!"

"Then you do admit it?"

He cocked his head most impudently to one side, regarding her with gay and twinkling eyes.

"Well, then—Yes, Miss Wynne, between friends, I do admit it!"

She gasped. Even to the end she was hoping. For one does hope so often against all better judgment. Even now, one hope dead, another sprang up. He had confessed; that meant that the next step was to be restitution. She spoke with a new eagerness:

"Then you will return the things you took!"

"Whoa there! I didn't say that."

"You mean you won't?"

"I mean I can't!" He made a wry face and thereafter, being Rogue Madden, fell to laughing again.

"Oh!" How much eloquence a girl like Gipsy Wynne could pack into one little round syllable! Disappointment, disbelief, a hint of sorrow and a full measure of disgust. "Do you care to explain?" she demanded, very cool and aloof.

"Most gladly. Let us say, shall we, that I did intend to return the various trinkets and what-nots, but that subsequent circumstances over which I have no control, make said restitution at the moment out of the question."

She knew he sought to mystify her, and he knew that he had succeeded. That was why she frowned and he kept on smiling.

"You leave me but one thing to do, Mr. Madden. And that is to tell what I know."

He shook his head.

"No. You mustn't do that. In fact, I can't allow it."

Of a sudden he was very much in earnest. But she was no less so. She retorted crisply:

"First of all, I am going to your father. For he is not only your father, but my guardian as well. Where is he?"

He went to the window and stood looking out.

"My father, Miss Wynne," he told her gravely, "is dead!"

She stared incredulously. It was her first thought that he lied to her. But when he turned toward her she saw in his eyes that this was true.

Here was a shock which for a little while threw her into confusion. Mr. Madden dead? What business had she here, then, in the home of this rattling, roistering young man, whom she knew to be a highwayman and who might be much else beyond even that? For the first time she experienced a quick flutter of uneasiness at being alone in a room with him, and looked about her as though to break into flight.

"When—when?" she murmured.

"A little over a year ago."

"*Over* a year ago? When? Exactly when, please?"

He told her. She estimated swiftly.

"Why, Mr. Madden's death occurred—before my own father's! Fully two weeks before! Then—then I haven't any guardian and never did have. I should have written. I oughtn't to have come. I am going away, immediately!"

To Rogue Madden had come many a wild inspiration in his time, but never inspiration so wild as that which all of a sudden visited him now. Again a look leaping up in his eyes set her wondering.

In an instant he became most businesslike, crisp and curt and bluntly emphatic.

"Listen to me, young lady. Neither of us has any profound knowledge of law, but we both have common sense. Your father was a business man and had your interests sufficiently at heart to do what he did in shipshape style. Therefore, he had the guardianship papers legally drawn, of course. Let's think how they would read. They specified Mr. Madden—"

"Mr. Roger Clark Madden, of the Madden Ranch—"

"At the time when those papers were drawn, there was but one Mr. Roger Clark Madden, of the Madden Ranch! Your most humble servant, my dear! Also, your legally constituted guardian!"

"You—*you* my guardian!"

She tried mocking him with rather brittle laughter.

"Exactly," he said shortly. "I, your guardian. You, my ward! And, taking the first obvious step authorized by my legal guardianship, I forbid you to say a word of what has happened."

"You forbid!" she cried scornfully, and began hastily drawing back from him. *"You!"*

With a leap he was at her side, his hand tight on her arm, his face peering down into hers.

"You are to do nothing without my consent, Ward! You are not going to leave the ranch, either. Not until I say so.—Off to your room now; you need sleep. You'll find that down here in Mexico we are prepared to take the best of care of our most precious possessions, our womenfolk! Over every window are good strong iron bars, that the better we may guard our wives and daughters—and wards!"

She tried to break from him; then started to scream. He drew her closer and then put pure panic into her by placing a broad hand over her mouth.

"I'll show you to your room, Ward," he told her sternly. "You'd prefer to walk at my side? Or have me carry you?"

She scarcely knew which way they went or how they came to the remote room. Before he closed and locked the door she looked up to stare wildly into a face which was once more mocking her with a broad, good-humoured grin.

"Ever read *Jane Eyre*?" he laughed at her. "This guardian and ward business! Better take care, Gipsy!—And if you start screaming I don't think anyone will hear you. You might try; your Aunt Polly *might* hear!"

The door closed, the big key turned in the lock, his lively footsteps sounded farther and farther away. She ran to the barred window, pressing her face against the iron grill, not knowing whether to be more perplexed or angry or alarmed.

CHAPTER V

Once she had taken a long, deep breath, looking out into a field across which a string of white ducks waddled down to the pools among weeping willows and pepper trees, Gipsy Wynne realized that she experienced no particular fear. The new fresh sunlight being poured out over a peaceful and quiet world was of a most reassuring order; the flapping of a funny little bantam rooster's tiny wings before he emitted his shrill buglings was too homey and every day to encourage heroics. In fact, the entire setting was all wrong for tragedy.

Besides all this, Aunt Polly was nearby; Mr. and Mrs. Yorke (so she thought) were asleep under this same roof; Tommy Burton inconsequential and therefore all the more reassuring, was at hand, or so she believed. Then there was a rather romantic gentleman with the romantic name, Cameo Risden; and that round-faced, fattish cherub, Joe Quince; and the simple and guileless youth, Johnny Bandini. The saturnine foreigner, Don Anastasio Escobar, with mystery and bold admiration in his eyes, was less assuring; but he need not count among so many. It was all quite like being in the heart of a friendly crowd.

When she lay down on her bed to think things out, to dally with the impulse to scream and arouse the household, Aunt Polly included, she was given pause by the consideration of what another shock and so severe a one might have upon her aunt's nervous system. Pondering at length, she ended by going to sleep. She was tired and slept soundly and for hours. She awoke to a lazy sensation of well-being—and then sprang up in the wildest haste as fully re-established consciousness, freighted with recent memory, came charging back.

She ran to the window; it was so peaceful out there in the bright golden sunshine. She lifted her hands to the iron bars; how solidly sunk they were in the heavy oak sills of the deeply recessed windows! She hurried to the door; it came open as readily as any door ever opened!

She started through, then ran back for a look into the mirror. In her bright little bathroom she freshened up a bit, swiftly yet to some advantage. Then she went out into a corridor and began seeking her way toward her aunt's room.

She heard voices, subdued by many doors through monstrously thick adobe walls, and rising above the voices a really delicious trill of laughter, Aunt Polly's laugh, as serene and gay and musical as a lark's!

It was a long corridor, with doors all the way on one side and windows on the other, looking out into a garden, wherein flowers bloomed with a profligate abandon which made the gayest of crimson and yellow splashes of colour. The house struck her as enormous. All on one floor, it was solid and sturdy and old-world, with black oak beams supporting the red-tiled roof; with Mexican tiles under foot which clicked under heel taps; with deep niches here and there along the walls holding simple silver candlesticks or bowls of roses or bright books in red and blue bindings. Some doors stood ajar; she caught intriguing glimpses of old walnut furniture and flamingly bright rugs on oak or tiled floors. She encountered a couple of Indian servants in neat white ducks; they showed her the whites of their eyes and the white of their teeth as she sailed on by them. To her attentive ears came a second gurgle of delight from Aunt Polly. Passing through the big main *sala* wherein last night she had interviewed and accused her host, she emerged into the patio and came on Aunt Polly holding court.

Aunt Polly sat perched on the rim of the fountain, freely displaying her diminutive high-heeled shoes. She was twirling a sunshade; she had drawn about her shoulders an extremely vivid shawl which her niece knew she had not possessed last night on going to bed; she was dressed in her softest, summeriest, grey-and-lavender dress. And she was actually rocking back and forth, hugging herself in an ecstasy of glee.

The cause Gipsy Wynne was not long in discovering. First of all Aunt Polly was to be suspected of an over-fondness for male society; and not less than three males were gathered about her. The elegant Mr. Cameo Risden, the sardonic Don Anastasio, the guileless Johnny Bandini. And it was Johnny Bandini who, awaiting the moment when the day should be made bright by the arrival of Aunt Polly's niece, was entertaining Aunt Polly with the choicest bits of his prestidigitatorial nonsense. The girl was just in time to see him divest himself of his coat, lay it carefully aside, roll up a shirt sleeve, plunge an arm deep down into the clear water of the pool, and appear to bring forth a perfectly dry pack of cigarettes and a burning match. He applied match to cigarette end, sent out a big cloud of smoke and from the smoke itself extracted a couple of eggs which he handed to Aunt Polly with a bow and a flourish. Even Gipsy gasped—

He heard her and leaped toward her, catching her hand as though to lead her across the narrow stretch of lawn—and then looked the picture of amazement as he regarded that which it would appear he had taken from her fingers: the stub of a cigar, soggy and disreputable, but still sending aloft its thin wisp of evil-smelling blue smoke.

"Why, Gipsy!" cried Aunt Polly, striving valiantly to look aghast, laughing-tears in her eyes.

For an instant the girl was indignant and confused. Johnny Bandini, with muttered apologies, was handing the cigar stub back to her—

Beyond the wall surrounding the big square yard arose the clamour of hoofs; with a rush horse and rider came on, rising like some great bird, sweeping on and over the high wall. With a gay jingle of spurs Rogue Madden threw himself out of the saddle and bore down upon them.

"It only goes to show," he called cheerily to them, "that here in this magic clime of ours you simply can't believe your own eyes." He stood laughing at Gipsy Wynne; had she failed to catch the double meaning of his words, she must have understood from the look with which he accompanied them.—And, though but fleetingly, she did experience a flash of uncertainty. But that was gone as quickly as it came. No. She knew.

She knew that in the moonlight, made darkly shadowy in the narrow gorge, this man had robbed his own guests. Even he himself had acknowledged that. Yet it was so hard here in the sunshine of the patio, with Aunt Polly perched on the fountain and convulsed with mirth, with Johnny Bandini plying his nonsense and with the others looking on, to believe in anything so sinister.

"They are well on their way by now, I suppose?" asked Aunt Polly, dabbing at her eyes.

"Oh, yes," said Madden. "I rode along with them a good half dozen miles. Beyond the barranca where the hold-up was pulled off," he added, and appeared to be making this explanation to Miss Wynne.

"Who?" she exclaimed sharply, already with swift intuition of the truth. Somehow that clear, teasing look of his had already told her.

"The Yorkes," he informed her coolly. "Also Tommy Burton. They left their politest farewells. You see, Mr. Yorke has to hurry on to Los Angeles before the loss of certain papers upsets some of his plans; and Tommy having my assurance that I'd do all that could be done here toward the recovery of the swag which the Bad Man shook him down for, is off for a confession to Silvia."

"Your assurance!" burst involuntarily from her.

"Oh, I've a notion I could be quite a sleuth, if I set my mind to it. And if you'd only help me? Didn't I say the first thing that you had all the earmarks of a bang-up Lady Detective?"

She bit her lip and was silent. Despite the sunshine and inconsequential atmosphere holding here, she experienced her recurrent flick of fear. The Yorkes gone; Tommy Burton gone with them—she and poor little Aunt Polly alone here with strangers, a long, long way from the world which she knew.

She turned toward her aunt.

"I needn't ask if you had a good sleep; I never saw you look quite so well!"

"I've been wanting to come West for years," exclaimed Aunt Polly. "I have felt that I would never be quite splendidly made new and well and young again until I did." She looked brightly at

Madden. "You look just as though you'd come this minute, dripping wet from the spring that Ponce de Leon was always looking for. And I feel just the way you look!"

"Did you know the Yorkes were going?" asked Gipsy Wynne, striving to be casual and serene.

"Mercy, no! I knew nothing of it until they were on their way. I slept as though I had been drugged."

Drugged? Gipsy started. She, too, had slept unusually heavily.

How quickly Rogue Madden caught her thought!

"Maybe you were drugged?" he suggested.

She laughed as though it were a great joke. But she could not entirely keep the anxiety out of her eyes as they turned quickly from Madden to these other men who seemed so much at home under Madden's roof.

Madden saw the look and had not the slightest difficulty in interpreting it. For he had the clue to her thoughts, recalling how he and she had parted a few hours ago. He studied her curiously, all the while whipping idly at his dusty boots with the riding quirt slung to his wrist. Then he made up his mind swiftly, not being given to long periods of pondering. He turned, smiling, to Aunt Polly.

"Miss Comfort," he said lightly and yet courteously, "I understand that it has long been your dream to live in a good, free and wide-open country like this of ours, and I am pleased right down to the bootheels that to me is given the pleasure of initiating you into your dream-come-true. Will you come with me for a little, please?" He stepped closer and put out his hands to help her down. "I am going out to stable my horse; and I'll show you something there that you will fall straight in love with. You are to see it first; I know Miss Wynne will be dying with curiosity, but she'll have to wait."

Into Aunt Polly's ears he whispered:

"It's a baby-colt, and the prettiest little thing that was ever foaled to clean up some fine day on every race track along the border."

Aunt Polly was all eagerness to go with him. Her niece, all uncertainty, thought of a lamb being invited for a stroll by a wolf. She hesitated; then saw her opportunity here at hand to tell these other men what had happened and to demand protection of them.

Johnny Bandini saw his opportunity also to pay tribute to the one pretty girl at the moment decorating the bright morning. There were many things of interest on the ranch; he would follow suit, eliminate Risden and Escobar, and have the bright morning's brightest adornment quite to himself.

But Gipsy Wynne scarcely heard what he was saying to her. She saw Madden and her aunt start toward Madden's horse; saw them pause while Madden appeared to have a second thought which caused him to excuse himself to Aunt Polly, and watched him turn and run back to the house, going in at a far door.

He reappeared as hurriedly as he had vanished; he and Aunt Polly went through a gate in the high wall leading the saddle horse, and presently even their voices were lost to her.

She turned swiftly to look again into the faces about her. Three pairs of eyes were upon her expectantly as the three men sensed something in her attitude which silenced them and held them waiting. Now was her chance to speak out, without Aunt Polly hearing, a chance which she had thought to snatch eagerly. Yet she had found it hard to break through that crust of silence. For she could not but feel that the opportunity had arisen through no accident but that Roger Madden had made it expressly for her.

She looked searchingly at young Bandini and was encouraged, at Cameo Risden, suave and courteous and gentlemanly, and was further encouraged, at the dark, expressionless face of Don Anastasio Escobar with its flashing black eyes, reading upon their surface his bold admiration, glimpsing other things hidden under that surface yet flaring out at her like tiny flames beyond a curtain, and turned away from him.

"There is something," she began hurriedly, her

hands clasping nervously. "I—I don't know quite how to say it." She swallowed, hated herself for floundering, reddened and exclaimed with animation: "You all know what happened on our way out here. We were held up and robbed. Now Mr. and Mrs. Yorke, and Mr. Burton have been sent away. Aunt Polly and I—"

She started and turned, almost guiltily, as a door opened and the stolid Maria came out into the patio. At her back, advancing to range themselves in a line at her side, were two Indian houseboys and a second Maria. The two women folded their arms and stood watching her, listening for her to speak. The Indian boys stood grinning foolishly as they too watched her.

Don Anastasio spoke to them sharply; what he said was clear enough, though he spoke rapidly in Spanish and some of the words eluded her. It was Maria the placid who answered. And thereafter she stood her ground, as did the others, and Don Anastasio shrugged and turned back to Miss Wynne. He had asked what they wanted; Maria had told him; a shrug was all that was left him.

"What is it?" asked the girl sharply.

"You will tell us what you wished to say?" queried Don Anastasio politely. "Something about the robbery?"

When she began again it was only to experience further interruption. She found herself wondering dully how many people constituted the household menage here! Others appeared, boys and women, and emulated Maria's party. Long Corbin arrived, almost at a run, which was a queer thing for Long Corbin, coming from the stables. He came close, greeting the three men at the fountain, and was duly presented to Miss Wynne to whom he made a jerky bow, pulling at the brim of his battered old hat. After him came two cowboys whom Long Corbin himself made known as Curly Whipple and Do-Boy Edwards. There were further bows, bright looks of approval, and thereafter silence as a strangely augmented audience looked to her as though they expected her to make a speech, and were all ready for applause.

"What's the funny idea, anyhow, Corbin?" asked Johnny Bandini.

"Madden said to come," returned Corbin. "Said that Miss Wynne had something to say she didn't want her Aunt Polly to hear, but did want everybody else to know."

Never in all her life had the girl been so taken aback. She fell into fresh confusion as, striving to think clearly, she found herself in a blind maze. For one fiery-hot instant she envisioned herself the butt of some insane jest; she heard in advance the loud, coarse laughter of all these men and the derisive cackle of women and boys as she made her announcement. She felt the sudden desire to run away from them all, to hide her head.

Following confusion came swift anger. She had not imagined things! She knew what she knew and that was that Roger Madden had robbed his own guests, had coolly admitted the fact and had refused to make restitution. Worse than that, he had even laid hands on her, forcing her into a barred room, locking the door on her. And he had made all haste, while she slept like a fool, to send the Yorkes and Tommy Burton away.

She lifted her head defiantly.

"We were robbed last night—it was Roger Madden, who, with a handkerchief over his face, pretending to be a Mexican, robbed us! I recognized him; I told him so, and that he would have to return the things he stole, and to let us go. He put his hand over my mouth to keep me from telling. He locked me in a room."

What a varied lot of expressions greeted her hurrying words! But there was none of the raucous laughter she had dreaded.

Johnny Bandini's innocent eyes grew round with surprise. Cameo Risden lifted his brows slightly and fell to massaging his chin. Don Anastasio simply stared, giving no hint to his thought. Long Corbin looked at her wonderingly, mouth open; then dropped his head and began making a cigarette. The two cowboys, Curly and Do-Boy, shifted their boots clumsily under her regard; Curly wrinkled up his nose and began scratching his head, while his confrere fell to a soft coughing behind his big leathery hand.

"*Que dice*?" asked one of the Mexican women. "What does she say?" There were muttered explanations, then round-eyed staring.

Long Corbin completed his cigarette in a heavy silence. He looked rather helplessly from face to face, cleared his throat, then demanded bluntly:

"Anything else?"

"Isn't that enough?" she flared out at him.

"Yes'm; guess it is," said Long Corbin. Still he seemed uncertain. He met her accusing eyes in one long stare, then dropped his head again. "Come ahead, boys," he snapped, and spun on his bootheel. "If that's all, we'll be going."

Off they went with never another word. The house servants fell to nudging one another, whispering back and forth; then Maria turned and led the way and in a string they returned to the house for all the world like the waddling line of ducks going to the creek.

"Do you mean—" the girl began in a mere thin wisp of a voice, shrinking away from the nearest of the men remaining, this one happening to be Johnny Bandini. She couldn't get any further in words. Did they mean that, knowing this, not a man of them would lift a hand?

Among strangers, there was at least that bond of youthful sympathy between her and Johnny Bandini. Her appealing eyes went back to him.

"So Rogue himself was the stick-up gent?" said Bandini, not seeming greatly surprised now that he had pondered her words. But he was frankly concerned and perplexed; not so much, she was quick to suspect, with the event itself as with the resultant situation. "Gosh," he concluded lamely, "here's the devil of a mess!"

Don Anastasio stepped forward and bowed.

"This is, as Bandini says of it, not a nice thing. Of one thing, Miss Wynne, you can assure yourself; that is of my friendship." He made the second bow and, hat in hand, took his departure, saying as he went, "I am going to have a talk with Señor Madden."

Cameo Risden had not spoken. Now, before speaking, he looked at Johnny Bandini, and with a flick of his eyes and a jerk of his head, transmitted a signal to that young man which resulted in Bandini drawing slowly away, leaving the girl alone with the gambler.

"Miss Wynne," said Cameo Risden coolly, "you have just made a rather serious accusation, you know."

She tried to laugh at him, repeating with scornful emphasis:

"*Rather* serious!"

"But you are sure?"

"Of course I am! Mr. Madden himself admitted it."

"Ah," said Cameo, and then smiled. It was not

a pleasant smile, but hard and cold and showing her something of a hard and relentless man under a smooth surface. "The truth, then. But just what, may I ask, did you expect to gain from speaking of it?"

"I was foolish enough to hope," she burst out, "that there were men among you."

"Why, so there are," returned the gambler equably, and still smiled.

"You say that, and tolerate such a condition?"

"We, like yourself, are guests here. We are men who do not make a habit in interfering in other men's affairs—"

"Even though those affairs be highway robbery and the restraint, against their wishes, of two helpless women?"

He shook his head.

"Last night we played cards. Roger Madden lost twenty thousand dollars as you have heard. Perhaps he could not afford the loss. We do not pry into his affairs, I have told you. We know nothing of his needs, of his financial condition."

He spoke as though that might very properly explain everything. If a man lost money, needed money and went out and got it at the point of a gun, Cameo Risden for one appeared to see nothing in the act to criticize!

"Are you all thieves?" she flung at him passionately.

He merely lifted his fine brows at her.

"We're perhaps an odd lot, take us as a whole," he said quietly. "What you might call a downright rascally crew. And if you want my personal opinion, Miss Wynne—and I hope you'll accept it in confidence, as I'd not particularly care to be quoted in the matter—why, I believe that the very least rascally of the whole lot of us is Rogue Madden himself!"

She shrank back from him. He made no step to follow her but stood watching her as a man may regard from some great distance an object in which he has only the most superficial and passing interest.

"God help us then!" she whispered.

He inclined his head gravely. It was as much as to assure her that, were help to come, it must be from without; from on high rather than from anyone here.

But there was Don Anastasio! He had proclaimed his friendship.

And yet it remained that she felt instinctively that Don Anastasio Escobar was a man whom she could never trust.

From beyond the high wall she heard a sudden burst of joyous, boyish laughter. That was Roger Madden. She sank down on the rim of the fountain, grown faint, her face in her hands. The sunshine of the southwest was all about her, pouring down in golden glory upon her, but she felt chilled and afraid.

CHAPTER VI

"It was all so *real!* I never knew anything so thrilling, so dramatic!—Rogue Madden, you are a positive scallywag!—I hope you don't mind me calling you Rogue? It's so much nicer than Roger, and suits you wonderfully!"

Rogue Madden, startled to begin with and puzzled at the end, looked down quizzically into Miss Polly Comfort's laughing face.

"I'd hardly stick at the 'Rogue' and swallow the 'scallywag,' would I?" he asked for want of something better to say.

Miss Comfort sighed.

"I seem to have lost all restraint, don't I? They wouldn't know me, back home! It's all the fault of the West!"

They were strolling slowly back from the stables where she had gone into raptures over a truly remarkable colt, mostly legs at first view, then fine spirit looking out on a new world through soft intelligent eyes.

"You set a fellow wondering," Madden confessed, still at sea.

She treated him to a delicious trill of her ready laughter. She had not laughed like that in Boston.

"Oh, I am not as green as you thought I'd be, Mister Rogue," she laughed at him. "If it hadn't been for Sam—Well, I do suppose I would have curled up and died."

"Sounds interesting. Sam, you say? Do I know the gentleman?"

"Remember how the low-comedy clown used to say, 'Oh, she wasn't a lady; that was my wife'? Well, speaking of Sam, he's just my brother. And he ran away when he was a boy and squandered his years in wild disgraceful rioting in your own West. And he told me all about you."

"About me?"

"About you-in-general. You Westerners. Tenderfeet do come out of the East yet—and you show 'em, don't you, Rogue Madden?"

More and more she mystified him, though in his mind there was that proverbial moment of dark before day.

"You think—"

"I know! I was prepared for it the minute I got on the train and started West. Sam prepared me. He said that you Wild West boys felt under obligation to put on a show for the tenderfoot. He said you'd no doubt shoot our bootheels off, just for fun. He knew I'd had a nervous breakdown—as though there were any such things as nerves out in this gloriously sleepy land of yours. Oh, I love it!"

"Well," muttered Madden, "I'll be—"

"I laughed after it was all over until that silly Mrs. Yorke wanted to choke me. Hysterics, that's what she said to her husband. But it was really the most thrilling thing—"

"You think that the hold-up was all a joke, then?"

"Why, I know it! I knew it all the time. I tell you I'm not as green as—as I would have been perhaps but for Sam. Was it you yourself, Mr. Madden?"

He took his time in speaking, and when his slow words came there was question rather than answer in them.

"What if I said that I was the man?"

She clapped her hands.

"I'd congratulate you on doing the thing delightfully!"

"What if I told you that your niece has already accused me of the robbery?"

Her face fell; she looked positively disappointed.

"So Gipsy guessed too? Oh, that's quite too bad. I was so sure that she was taken in." The fun seemed all spoiled for her.

"But if I went on to add that she sees no joke in it? That she thinks I am a real bandit and demands that I make restitution or vows she will denounce me?"

Back with a rush came all her bright delight.

"Oh, better and better! Gipsy thinks she's such a wise little know-everything! Don't tell her—"

"But wait a minute! What would you say to this:

That I told your niece that I couldn't return the loot, even if I wanted to; that she was determined on immediate exposure; that I laid hard and brutal hands on her, told her that as matters stood she was really my ward; locked her up in her room, and kept her there until the Yorkes and Tommy Burton had gone!"

"You did that?" she gasped.

He was afraid that he had gone too far; a look of consternation was in her eyes. He began cursing himself for a fool; if he brought back her acute nervous disorder—

But he had never heard Aunt Polly Comfort laugh as she did now. For that matter, no one on earth had ever known she could laugh like that. She could scarcely speak.

"Why, *why* did I wait so many years to come West! Rogue Madden, you're more than a scallywag. You're a positive genius!—And you actually got away with that? You actually made Gipsy think it was all in earnest?"

Madden, thinking swiftly, added the hurried information:

"She's afraid for you; she is in a terrible dilemma. She doesn't dare let you know that you are in the very stronghold of the bandit himself for fear you might experience a shock too great for you."

"The darling," murmured Miss Comfort. "The little goose," she added gaily.

"But she has told everyone else, I'm pretty sure," said Madden, watching her curiously.

"They didn't know already? You didn't tell them what you were going to do?"

"No one knew," he said. "But it looks as though—"

"Oh, it was too good to keep! But now, I suppose the fun is all over? You'll just return the money? I can guess, of course, that that was why you rode part way with the Yorkes; to tell them."

"Let me ask you one more question," said Madden thoughtfully. "What if I told you I did play highwayman just for the lark of it; and that I did mean to return everything after the laugh was over; and that, on my way back here, some other gent had the same bright and shining idea—and stuck me up? What then?"

She had a way of tipping her head to one side when she regarded anyone interestedly. She seemed for an instant now almost to believe him; then all Brother Sam's warnings began chiming in her memory, and she was swept on to new heights of delight.

"Maybe you can fool Gipsy with that sort of thing," she laughed. "Not your Aunt Polly. Why, man alive, I don't believe that there has been a real old-fashioned, honest-to-goodness bit of highway robbery in this sleepy country for fifty years! Listen to me; I've had a long talk with that most amusing boy, Johnny Bandini. He is the most talented boy! Why isn't he on the stage? He'd make his fortune—you are all made for the stage, do you know it? That handsome Cameo Risden, why he ought to be one of the Barrymore family!—Well, Johnny Bandini told me the *wildest* things! About a terrible affair here last night! About a picturesque and most thrillingly evil Toro-blan-co, and a tremendous game of cards; twenty thousand dollars!" She paused to wipe her eyes; she had difficulty in going on. "About a room barricaded, assaulted from without by a horde of ruffians, bent on slaughter, no less! Brr!"

"Johnny Bandini told you all that?—I wonder what you said to him?"

"He's far too nice a boy to call a—what he is. But I did tell him that he's a most unconscionable fibber."

"I see," muttered Madden.

Then all of a sudden had come that joyous burst of laughter which Gipsy Wynne had heard beyond the high adobe wall. Here was a situation made for Rogue Madden; made by him, too, as far as that went, but running on into such intriguing phases as he could never have foreseen. Truly it promised to be the very devil of a mess, for into all the merry-madness of it the devil was thrusting a finger. Why, if Toroblanco, in his blackest mood, showed up and took Aunt Polly by the throat and threatened her with death itself, Aunt Polly would only thrill anew! Oh, she would know just what to believe—thanks to her brother Sam and her own amazing innocence.

So she and Rogue Madden made a merry duet of their laughter; though Madden, had he been less the hare-brained madcap that he was, might have found infinitely more to frown than to chuckle over in this situation of his own and the devil's brewing.

They were aware of Anastasio Escobar approaching, regarding them sombrely.

"That man!" whispered Miss Comfort. "He has the very face of a villain—in melodrama! So I shall be much surprised if he does not turn out to be a great philanthropist or something like that."

Don Anastasio drew near and made them his bow.

"I dislike to interrupt. But might I have a word with you?" he said gravely to Madden.

"Why, speak, man! There are no secrets between us here," Madden grinned at him.

"If it has to do with highway robbery, brutal kidnapping and the like villainy," cried Aunt Polly, ecstatically, "speak on, Sir Bearer of Dire Tidings!"

Don Anastasio lifted the black line of his brows at her.

"You know, then? It was the fear of your niece—"

"Shucks," laughed Aunt Polly. "What is it, Don Ana-statchio?"

Don Anastasio shrugged. So this woman, then, knew? There was nothing to fear, it appeared, from a shock to her nerves.

"I am informed," he said stiffly, his moody black eyes once more on his host's face, "that these two ladies are held here against their will. There can hardly be truth in that, I hope? Eh, my friend?"

"The man is going to be a spoil-sport!" murmured Aunt Polly under her breath. "Setting up to be a squire of dames!"

"Squire of dames?" grunted Madden. All of a sudden he appeared to forget Escobar and whirled triumphantly on Miss Comfort. "I've got it!"

"Got what?" she asked eagerly.

"Why, the name for my ranch! It's always been called just the Madden Place, you know. Your 'Squire of dames' just put me in the frame of mind for a christening which comes slam-bang out of the old Arthurian yarns.—You see, Miss Gipsy Wynne is my ward. No getting around that; it's a legal and established fact. Ergo, I'm her guardian. Jolly glad, of course, so I become her Joyous Guardian! And thus these wide acres"—and he waved both arms, flourishing—"shall be known henceforth as—the Rancho of Joyous Guard!"

"Bravo!" cheered Aunt Polly. "A name to suit

the very rollicking atmosphere of the place. Why, it's in the air! Didn't you hear me call him Sir Bearer of Tidings?"

"I do not understand this," said Escobar, making himself as stiff as any ramrod. "If there is truth—"

"Miss Comfort will tell you everything. Everything! She knows it all," Madden sang out, and was off at a run. Not alone to escape Anastasio Escobar in a sober mood; also for a word with Cameo Risden whom he saw through the gate, smoking his cigar in solitude.

"Where's Miss Wynne?" asked Madden.

"Just gone in," returned the gambler. "If I am any good at mind-reading, she's going to find out for herself if there's such a thing as a telephone."

"While she's finding out that there isn't, give me two minutes." He shoved back his hat and rumpled his hair; Cameo Risden saw signs of some considerable perplexity in him. "I've dug myself into a most damnable sort of hole, Cameo."

The gambler shrugged.

"Ah! Not the first time, is it, Rogue?"

"And maybe not the deepest hole, but I swear it's deep enough!"

"Miss Wynne has been telling us that you were the robber. And that you finished with playing kidnapper."

"Oh, it's true enough." Madden made a wry

face. "Of course it was a fool thing to do—"

"Naturally," was Cameo's dry admission.

"I got the hunch when the telegram came. I didn't know just who were in the party; I made a wrong guess, as it turned out. I saw the fun of staging a hold-up and hopped to it. As it happens, I did a bigger business than I had ever hoped. Tommy Burton was heavy with swag; a lot of idiotic jewels of Silvia's. And there were all kinds of odds and ends; Miss Wynne and her aunt, even, were loaded to the guards. I wouldn't be a bit surprised if I had lifted anywhere from twenty to fifty thousand dollars off those folks."

"That would pay your poker losses," said Cameo idly. But his eyes were just about as idle as a pair of gimlets boring through soft pine.

"Damn my poker losses!—Look here, Cameo, the devil's in it!"

"Naturally," remarked Cameo as before.

Madden grinned, but grew serious again.

"Shut up, will you? I made my killing, and hotfooted for home, laughing myself pretty near out of the saddle. Know where the little arroyo is about two miles out? The grove of pepper trees makes it dark in there; you'd never know there was such a thing as a moon. And here I go, thinking about anything but what was just about to happen, riding right into it. Bang! A shotgun, my boy, and hot lead sprayed close enough to curl your whiskers. A voice then, sort of an ugly whisper right at hand tells me in a fashion that makes a man take notice, that unless I drop my swag and mosey on, the next charge of buckshot will tear me all to pieces. There wasn't any argument about it that I recall now. I had my choice of dropping the boodle, or being wafted out of this merriest of all merry worlds on a handful of buckshot.—And that's the sad tale and the whole general hell-of-it."

"I see," said Cameo Risden.

He seemed unmoved, but that was characteristic of him. He was a most excellent listener. He could hear a man through, in the telling of any wild tale, and add nothing to it. That was all right and that was Cameo Risden for you.

But Rogue Madden knew him well, so well that though Cameo's words went no farther just then. Madden was swift in trailing his unspoken thought for a step or two.

"Good Lord!" exclaimed Madden sharply. "You don't believe a word of it!"

Cameo's unchanging eyes regarded him, while Cameo's lips rounded themselves softly to shape a series of very pretty smoke rings; the eyes briefly watched the rings float away on the quiet air, then, and still without change in them, returned to a level meeting with Madden's.

"If it is your wish that I should believe you—why, certainly!" he said accommodatingly.

Madden glared at him.

"I tell you, man, it's the truth! I did rob those folks, just for fun. But before I even got back to the house some other night-blooming jasper shook me down. And I'm therefore in a fine sort of jam."

"I see." Cameo nodded with an affectation of thoughtfulness. That seemed about as far as he cared to go just now. And if there was anything whatever to be made of his expression, it hinted perhaps at polite boredom. He didn't yawn but one sensed a struggle with the muscles of his jaw to refrain.

"You think, confound you," grunted Rogue Madden, "that I stole the stuff meaning to keep it?"

"It wouldn't be any of my affair if you did. I told Miss Wynne that."

"But I didn't!"

"No," said Cameo. "Of course not." His white fingers caressed his clean-shaven lip as though stroking an invisible moustache. "And someone held you up? Hm. With a shotgun?—Toroblanco?"

"Who else?" demanded Madden eagerly. "Of course; it must have been Toroblanco. Don't know that I'd blame him much, at that."

"It's quite clear," drawled the gambler. "So extremely clear that I really shouldn't start up questions. But the thought does not suggest itself:

If Toroblanco had a chance like that, why didn't he finish the job?"

Madden looked blank.

"I hadn't thought of that! Why didn't he? Why there's no reason! He had the chance of his life. He could have got away with it as simply as he could knock a jack rabbit over."

"Naturally," nodded Cameo. "Of course the others may not think of that. And I shouldn't have spoken of it."

From Rogue Madden's face one could not have told with any degree of certainty whether he was going to laugh or cry. The facial muscles appeared to be in utter confusion. In the end his true character won, and the little muscles fell into line and yanked the corners of his mouth up—where they belonged.

"Just the same it was Toroblanco," he announced, as one who was done with mystification and saw the light shining just where he knew the light should be. "And I think I'll be able to figure out a reason or two why he should have refused to fall into temptation and blow me apart. Ever hear of the goose and the golden egg, Cameo? Me—I'm the goose."

"I never doubted it," Cameo assured him. "But the golden egg?"

"It's somewhere in the straw under a deal I have on with Anastasio. I don't altogether see it, but I know it's there. It's got to be! Otherwise it couldn't have been Toroblanco at all. You've got to have some explanation why he should just strip me of my booty and let me go galloping on."

"Perhaps for the joy of seeing you in a peck of trouble? Afoul of the law, arrested for stealing the stuff that he himself gets away with. What they call poetic justice, isn't it?"

Madden considered. "That would be a nice little situation—from Toroblanco's point of view!"

He turned thoughtfully toward the house. Cameo called softly after him:

"There's just one other thing you'd better think of, Rogue. Where do you suppose Toroblanco got any shotgun? Wasn't carrying one in his boot, was he?"

Madden came to an abrupt dead halt.

"You don't believe it was Toroblanco at all, that's clear. I'm hanged if I know whether you believe a word I've said. It's true, just the same. And if it wasn't Toroblanco, then who was it?"

Cameo studied his cigar, found it burning properly, returned it to his mouth, and observed around it:

"It could have been any of us here. Any of us, mind you. As far as possibilities go, it could have been myself! Of course I'm not saying that it was—"

"You're a great help to a fellow," Madden told him with due emphasis.

"Where to now?" asked Cameo. "Looking for Toroblanco?"

"The devil fly away with Toroblanco." And here all of a sudden Rogue Madden's rare good humour came back to him. There was trouble ahead, but praise heaven there was also a bit of joy, and it was toward the pleasanter aspects that he preferred to look. "I'm off for a word with my new ward. I'm her guardian, and I've a notion that girl needs a guardian who'll take his job seriously; putting in long hours at it, you know. I'm going to teach her to call me papa!"

CHAPTER VII

Cameo Risden was right; a telephone had suggested itself and become the object of Gipsy Wynne's search. It should be so simple to establish communication with some constituted border authority; to call with calm assurance upon constable or sheriff, chief of police or customs officer or even a fire station. Once that were done, she needed but await the big hand of Uncle Sam thrust out to her rescue, brushing aside all minor obstacles, such as Roger Madden and his entourage of rascals and vagabonds.

Such were her thoughts until she came to the bleak understanding that the commonplace, mighty and little appreciated instrument which she sought had no place here. She had searched thoroughly throughout the house, getting lost a time or two in the long corridors, and at last came to the room in which, had she known the house better, she would have begun. It was a cozy chamber, adjoining the big living room. Here was Madden's "office," could you call it that; he at times named it the sweat-shop. In the general mismanagement of his business affairs, he came here infrequently to struggle with bank books which would not balance to suit his needs; he once in a great while picked out with two fingers on a rickety old typewriter a letter which was no great triumph either in composition or spelling. A long table was littered with papers and account books and the like. There were, however, the redeeming features which brought the atmosphere of coziness among these unrestful articles; a couple of enormous comfortably-old chairs; a cushioned window seat where you might sprawl at full length and look across billowing fields studded with oak trees which grew long greyish beards of Spanish moss; there were things to smoke; and in a corner was a couch whose coverlet showed signs of dusty boots. To her the place was neither office nor yet merely den; the lair, rather, of the beast that irked her. And here, as a last hope, she looked expectantly but in vain for the telephone.

She did not know when he came in. She had not consciously heard him; no board creaked under the heavy carpet. But of a sudden she saw him lounging in the doorway, his hat on the back of his head, his hands in his pockets, a cigarette in his mouth and one eye half closed against the invasion of the little blue wisp of smoke. He looked amused, interested and downright impudent.

But when she turned, he did take off his hat; he even flipped his cigarette into the fireplace.

"Hello, Ward," he said jovially. "I was looking for you. We're going to have our talk now."

She intended to pass out of the room without answering him. There were two doors; she moved quickly to the one across the room from him. But he caught up with her and set his hand lightly on her arm. She shook it off indignantly.

"If you'll sit down a minute, like a good little Ward," he told her, good humouredly, "I won't have to hold you."

She sat down and looked at him with the air of one who, though occupied with matters of importance, consents to humour an idiot. He sat on a litter of papers on his table, caught up his knee between a pair of brown hands, leaned back and upset a bottle of ink to which he paid not the slightest concern, and regarded her with a semblance of profound gravity.

"You're going to be a responsibility, I can see that," he said, and shook his head dubiously.

She merely clasped her own hands in her lap and showed him the faintly resentful face of one resigned to await the end of an ordeal.

"As if I didn't have my hands full already," he sighed, and went on shaking his head. "Of course, being a kid of a girl, you won't have any more business sense than a jack rabbit. Well, lucky for you, I'm a reg'lar business man."

The resentment shadowing her piquant face grew into a less vague scorn. With an effort she remained silent.

"I'll take matters up in their logical order," said

Madden ponderously. "There are your mining interests down in Sonora. I'll have to look into them right away. I'll start a boy down that way to-day, telling the superintendent that he's fired."

"You—you—you—" Really she couldn't think of the words she needed.

"I happen to have seen that bozo," continued Madden contemptuously. "Just remembered him and what he looks like when I saw his name among your papers—"

"My papers!" she exclaimed angrily. "What do you mean?"

"Oh, of course I went through your bags while I had you shut up in your room. Seeing my duty straight ahead of me, am I to shirk it? You might have asked my consent," he thought to say reproachfully, "before making yourself my ward. You see," he went on serenely, "girls nowadays, so they tell me, are all hard at it sowing their wild oats. One never can tell when a new girl breezes along. How'd I know, until I looked, whether you had a gun in your bag, or at least a flask? I did find what strikes me as a trashy novel; I'll read the thing and let you know whether it's fit for you or not. You'd better get into the way of coming to me for advice, my dear."

He saw a tremor shake her from head to foot; it was the icy shiver of a towering rage, illy suppressed. Her clasped hands were clenched hands now; she actually grew pale. She had understanding enough to know that he had set out to tantalize her, but she could not know what deeper motives might lie under the superficial one. To have any man even in jest—if it were jest now!—so much as suggest that she was not to have her own way in everything, was to prompt in Gipsy Wynne a really arresting display of what she termed independence, and what ordinarily went for blazing temper. The most thorough job of old Jim Wynne's life had been the spoiling of his little daughter. She had no haziest recollection of the early days of poverty. By the time she was six, Jim Wynne's money started rolling in, and the waves of it grew bigger and bigger, the golden tide swelling to mighty proportions; and on that sparkling tide came floating in all the bright argosies of her and old Jim's dreams. Before she rightly knew a nickel from a dime she had vastly more money to spend than is supposed to be good for the very young. When Jim Wynne had done his noble best toward spoiling her, his millions kept right on with the good work. He had named her Gipsy when she was little and brown and lawless, burning-bright with eagerness which trampled on conventions because convention spelled restraint. Later when she sparkled into girlhood, he had remarked with a dry chuckle: "I'll have to change all that—you're a Queen of Sheba now. Sheba! How's that for a name, huh?" And she told him warningly: "Look out! I'll call you Solomon-in-all-his-Glory—and all those fortune-hunting old hens will marry you."

Just now she was Gipsy for that hotly burning-brightness, Sheba for that regal quality in which, as from a great height, she looked down upon a mere sunbrowned rancher named Madden. She contended with a tremor which went rippling through her, and very painstakingly moulded her lips into lines of her scorn.

Madden did not seem to note; he appeared preoccupied.

"That fellow, now, that I'm going to fire: Why, he's got eyelashes like a girl, and a little fuzzy yellow-brown moustache that looks like a confounded caterpillar—Consider me your superintendent of mining interests *pro tem.*—By the way, what salary was he pulling down?—Never mind. I'll be making readjustments, most likely."

"Are you an utter scoundrel?" she blazed out at him. "Or just a fool?"

"Is that your idea of the respect due a guardian?"

"Are you willing to make amends for the crime which you have committed?"

"I told you that I couldn't. You might have asked why—"

"I did, and you put me off."

"Well, I don't mind telling you. I've just been explaining to Aunt Polly—"

No chair could hold her at that; she sprang to her feet on the verge of panic. For her love for Aunt Polly who had long stood as mother in her life, was sincere and deep; and her fear for her aunt's health suddenly overshadowed all concern for her own affairs.

"Aunt Polly! Don't you understand that it would kill her? Or do you care? If you have let her know—"

"Your Aunt Polly, mine too by adoption, knows—everything!" He breathed the final word dramatically. Then, chuckling again, he ran on: "Oh, she's all right; you don't need to worry about her. She's my ideal, if you want to know, that little mite of an old lady. I only wish she were about sixty years younger; I'd marry her sure."

"If Aunt Polly were sixty years younger," she really snapped at him, "she'd have to wait about ten years longer to be born."

"Good Lord! You mean she's only fifty? Why that's just the coltish age for maiden ladies! I put her down for seventy."

"Aunt Polly has been aged by illness," she told him tartly. "In her present condition I suppose this thing which you have done will kill her."

"Kill or cure is my motto," grinned Madden, having no slightest fear for Aunt Polly. "And rather than bring her to a sad and untimely end, I'll bet you anything you like that this is going to make her fat. What she's needed all her life is a good laugh, and that's just what she's getting."

"But she doesn't know—she doesn't guess—"

"She's the best little guesser I ever knew! And I assure you she knows everything, even the end of the story which I was about to tell you—how, when I started home with my swag, lifted off my oncoming guests, some other hombre shoved a shotgun at me and asked me to say which I loved best, my money or my life. Since it wasn't my money—"

"And Aunt Polly believed that?" she demanded scornfully.

"Not a blooming word of it," he admitted cheerfully. "She thinks we're an awful lot of liars out here."

"Let me go! Quick!"

"Just where?" he asked her.

"To my aunt. If, when she fully understands—Oh, it will be you who have murdered her!"

"I told you, kill or cure's my motto. But I'm betting you what you like, both my big ranches against that curl over your left ear, that instead of killing her we're going to make her young again.—You've been stifling a rare spirit in her!"

"Can I go now?" she begged almost humbly.

He jumped down from the table, exclaiming approvingly:

"Now that's fine! You bet you can go. And as soon as you learn to adopt the proper filial attitude toward your guardian, you'll find him most anxious to humour you. In the small things, of course—"

She did not even look at him as she sped from the room. Already she had learned that there was no single weapon in her armoury, which had always before this been quite ample, that was of any slightest use against Rogue Madden.

He watched her depart, then returned to Cameo Risden whom he found chatting with Johnny Bandini.

"Cameo," said Madden briskly, "I've got a job on my hands. I'll be starting out this afternoon and I may be gone all night. Maybe longer; *quien sabe*? Meantime, will you take my place here? I don't want Miss Comfort or her niece to leave until I get back. And I do want the best of care taken of them. That fool Toroblanco, for all we know, may be good and sore; he's an unreasonable devil; he may even come back with his litter of pups at his heels, making trouble."

The gambler appeared to reflect.

"This job of yours?" he asked. "Going out looking for this same Toroblanco?"

Madden nodded. Johnny Bandini looked alert and intrigued.

"There are others here who can take your place,

Rogue," said Cameo. "I'd like, if you don't mind, to ride along with you."

"Me, too!" cried Bandini. "Make it the three of us, Rogue! You and Cameo and me—we'll Three-Musketeer 'em!"

Madden ignored the boy, saying curtly to Risden:

"But you don't even believe that Toroblanco robbed me!" Bandini cocked up his ears; here was news for him! "You don't believe that anyone did!"

Cameo smiled.

"What I may believe or disbelieve has not the slightest bearing on the case. I'd take all the joy in life, seeing you shake down this blustering Toroblanco. If I might have a hand in the process, so much more the joy!"

"You're a weird old brigand," grunted Madden, yet looked pleased—and brightly expectant.

"How about me, Rogue?" pleaded Johnny Bandini. "I'm working for you, remember. And who knows, if we clean up on this bunch, I might make a couple o' dollars."

Madden laughed and clapped him on the shoulder.

"Get ready for the fun then, you birds. I'll round up Long Corbin and some of the boys to ride herd here while we're gone. Only don't tell anyone what we're up to."

In the late afternoon, not waiting for dusk,

the three rode off across the billowing fields hoping, if luck rode with them, to come up with Toroblanco and his men at a certain likely spot among the rocky hills.

CHAPTER VIII

Rogue Madden knew his Toroblanco. At least knew him well enough in a general way to feel pretty sure of finding him at an early hour of the evening, and such knowledge sufficed for the moment, beyond which it was not Rogue Madden's way to seek to probe. That full-panoplied ruffian, Toroblanco, had drunk hard and long last night; else he had not been tempted into the sort of talk which resulted in his crash to the floor and his subsequent rage. Thereafter he had his choice, expelled from the Rancho of Joyous Guard, of forging on to the fifty miles' distant border, or bivouacking in the little rocky hills not over seven miles from the ranch. There was a hill ranch which would appeal to him at this time; the place of the half-breed, Vidal Chavez, half-brother to Toroblanco's own sergeant, the Butcher. It was there that he was confident he would come up with his man, counting on his having slept through the heat of the day. If Toroblanco rode northward at all, it would not be until after nightfall.

From the instant Rogue Madden and his companions shoved boot into stirrup, they rode at a rattling gallop; not a horse of the three but could do the seven rough miles handily in a half hour, not a saddle animal in Madden's stables that was not better than a "five-hour horse." The term was Madden's own, who swore he'd own no saddle horses that couldn't carry him the full fifty miles to the border in five hours. Beautiful animals, always in the pink of condition, they were their master's pride and an essential factor in his joy of life.

"I'll show you the place where Toroblanco made a monkey of me," was the promise lightly tossed to Cameo Risden and young Johnny Bandini, after the latter had heard the tale of the robber robbed.

"Another thing," Cameo reminded him, in quite the same tone as he had employed in the patio, and exactly as though that earlier conversation had run on uninterruptedly into this one. "You forgot to explain how it was that you didn't tie into him. Have you thought of that?—It might be, of course," as though he himself were suggesting an excuse, "that you didn't even have a gun on you."

Madden glared at him, but the dusk was already too thick for one man to make more than a grey blur of another's face as they swept along. Then of a sudden his mad laughter unleashed itself; his horse, startled, leaped to a fresh burst of speed. It had been said of him that here was a man who was practical in nothing on earth save in his jokes; but, to give the devil his due, at least he could laugh at his own predicament.

"Cameo, you four-flushing, double-decking card sharp, you, you're good for the soul! You've stood so many a time on a pair of deuces when you knew the other man had jacks or better, yes, by Glory! and stolen the pot, that you see a bluff in the honestest gesture a man ever made. Here I go hell-bent for Toroblanco, and you tell your sweet self, 'All bluff!' Nothing I could think of doing will ever convince you; the longest day you live you'll bet a man that I've got the boodle stuck away in some safe place right now!—And the funny part of it, Cameo, is that I *didn't* have a gun on me! Or the same thing; I grabbed up an old-fashioned Colt forty-five that had been hanging on a peg for twenty years; cylinder jammed and no bullets—and that's what I did my hold-up stunt with! Imagine me fighting it out with Toroblanco's shotgun!"

"I see," said Cameo. And his tone was polite and pleasant, yet remained the tone of a man who thought that he did see.

But Madden only laughed. To be sure Cameo held that he lied—but here was Cameo, just the same, riding along with him, straight into trouble, no doubt, letting no such flimsy things as his own suspicions stand in his way. There was a friend for you; what more could any man ask?

The first big star flashed out; the sky from leaden grey had turned a soft misty violet; a little evening breeze, sweet with the breath of sage, fanned their cheeks. The two miles to the arroyo where the pepper trees made a dusky glade were tapped out swiftly by the rhythmic pounding of hoofs; the three men pulled their horses in.

"Right there, it was," explained Madden. "I came along the trail there and—"

The horses had been restive from the moment they felt the tightening reins; now they began snorting and rearing and finally plunging wildly.

"It's right yonder," said Cameo coolly. "In the trail where you pointed. A man, I think."

Madden slipped from the saddle, giving Bandini his reins to hold, and went forward hastily on foot.

"It is a man," his hushed voice came back to them over the noise of restless hoofs. "Dead, I think."

They saw him go down on his knees. A match flamed out and in its small circle of light they saw his face in silhouette, and the face of the man on the ground.

"Dead," he repeated. "Shot through the head—"

"Not a shotgun?" said Cameo.

"No. Rifle or revolver. It's one of Toroblanco's men; I noticed him when that crowd came to the ranch. A sort of boss, under Toroblanco, of the rest of the gang."

It was El Carnicero. The Butcher. And all the promotion which was to be his in this life had come to him from a pistol ball. He had been dead some hours; the blood on his face was a black, dry smear.

Madden yanked off his own coat, spread it over the quiet face turned up to the stars, and swung up into the saddle without another word. He was puzzled; the shock had come and gone; men like the Butcher ended thus; in this particular case, though Madden knew nothing of the details of the man's existence, he was really too foul to live. There would be no weeping for him by any hearth in the wide world. But after shock, puzzlement remained. Coincidences have no rightful place in any logical scheme of things. Why was the Butcher dead here and now? Why shot at this particular spot? One wanted to establish some connection between his tragedy and Madden's own adventure under the pepper trees, yet what earthly connection was there?

There were five miles still to be ridden to the hill ranch of Vidal Chavez, the home of the half-brother of this murdered Butcher. They rode the five miles in almost unbroken silence. Each man of them was content with a still tongue and busy brain; Johnny Bandini strove now and then to peer into the faces of the others and guess at their thoughts, while they looked straight ahead. But then Johnny Bandini was very young.

From afar a ruddy glow above the rounded shoulder of a hill gave them first word of

Toroblanco. Riding closer they saw a crackling blaze in the pasture below the barn; it was a campfire about which motionless or slowly moving shadow shapes were Toroblanco's men. The moon had not yet risen but in the starlight other groups of shadows were the horses.

The three riders stopped under a wide-branched oak. From the campfire they looked to the ranch house, a squatty little affair of stone and mud walls with three big oaks standing over it. A pale, sickly light made a rectangle of a single window.

"Toroblanco will be at the house," said Madden. "Let's ride around to the far side."

They made a wide circuit, keeping to the shadowy folds among the hills and succeeding in putting the house itself as well as the barn between themselves and the campfire. When they drew rein again it was in the shelter of a tall mesquite thicket some two or three hundred yards from the lighted window. From here, leaving his friends with the horses, Madden made his swift way across the field to the squatty house under the oaks.

He feared little from any watch which might be kept, and made a bee-line to the lighted window. Only when he came quite close did he drop from a run to a tiptoe walk; he wanted no noise made now. The window was open; a couple of candle ends stuck into bottles gave a sufficient light; he heard voices distinctly. The arrogant and truculent voice of Toroblanco himself rose above the complaining whine of another man whom he discovered to be the rancher, Vidal Chavez.

Toroblanco's heavy spurs, bespeaking his readiness to ride, clanked noisily as he ranted up and down in the small room; Madden, at the side of the window, got a glimpse of him; his hat was on and he was whipping at his thigh with a gaudy pair of gauntlets. Vidal Chavez, looking cowed and terribly afraid, crouched in a corner.

Toroblanco named Chavez "*Bezugo*!" That was the final epithet with Toroblanco; hence it was to be inferred that his storming at his frightened host was not at the beginning, but rather at the very crashing crescendo of the finale. He had exhausted himself of all the vilely picturesque vocabulary of the border ruffian; Madden had come only in the nick of time.

And why all this foam and fury of the great Toroblanco directed against the poor little futile old Chavez? Because, it appeared, Chavez had the misfortune to be brother to a certain El Carnicero, the Butcher; and because this same Butcher had been sent forth by his chief on some errand, and now delayed everything on earth by failing to return!

So, then, it had not been Toroblanco who had shot the man? Perhaps not; quite as likely, yes. For if there is one supreme accomplishment germane to the Toroblanco breed it is the quality of dissimulation, of casting themselves for heroic parts in dramas of their own invention—in a word, of carrying the trade of the common or garden variety of liar into the precincts of a high art. You listen to a Toroblanco; to form any opinion of your own you must first forget every word he uttered.

Rogue Madden set his elbows on the low window sill and leaned into the room, shoving a revolver in front of him.

"Never a bellow out of you, Bull Calf! Never a single bellow!" he admonished softly.

Vidal Chavez, who had borne about all for one day that he could stand up under, simply settled down in his corner quite as though his leg bones had melted. Toroblanco, mouth open, hair bristling, nostrils aquiver and face a hot brick-red, grew as still and gave the same impression of ineffectiveness as an electrical man with the current shut off. And Rogue Madden snorted, whether in disgust, disappointment or satisfaction it would have been hard to say.

But it was expecting too much to ask of Toroblanco to hold his tongue altogether and for long.

"Now, Bull Calf, don't bellow," said Madden warningly, and then ran on pleasantly and quite as though the task of the moment were but a bit of frivolous merrymaking—as for him in a way it was—announcing lightly: "That was a very pretty thought of yours, to hi-jack me back there under the pepper trees—By the way, while I think of it, this Carnicero that you're missing and waiting for is dead back there, in the same little arroyo of the pepper trees. Someone shot him; wonder if it was you?"

Toroblanco's brows went up sharply; his black eyes rounded. Still that might be his play-acting; you never could tell. As for Vidal Chavez, he looked interested, though not in the least surprised and not particularly concerned. If his half-brother were indeed dead, that meant nothing to Vidal. For there were no legacies to expect, and there was no cause for grieving. But, after a moment of reflection, he did bethink and cross himself.

"To return to the question of the new game of rob-the-robber," continued Madden. "If it works once, why not twice?—Your hat, Toroblanco. Pitch it to me."

Toroblanco would have argued the matter, and small blame to him. But Madden made very clear that there was to be no foolery of that kind; odd how emphatic the little sound of a click of steel can be when it is just the faint clear note as a revolver is cocked! Toroblanco sent his broad braided hat spinning to the window; Madden caught it deftly with his left hand.

"I don't suppose I am going to find anything in your *sombrero*—that I'm looking for," he admitted cheerfully. "But time is limited and I'm making a methodical search. You know how it goes. Your coat, Toro."

Toroblanco, having already arrived at "*Bezugo*!" was minded to begin all over again, but once more listened to reason. It looked as though the veins on the man's forehead would burst as he drew off his coat. It, like the hat, was hurled at his tormentor. Handicapped as he was, Madden made a swift search and found nothing of interest to him, allowing various negligible odds and ends to drop to the floor. In the end he flung the highly ornamental coat out to follow the gold-braided hat.

"Boots, Toro," he commanded.

Toroblanco looked for all the world as though about to burst into tears. But the boots came off, were examined and thrown far out into the field, one east and one west. Madden was grinning broadly by this time.

"And now—Wait a minute! Maybe that's what I want; that buckskin bag hanging to your belt. Fork it over."

"Robber!" fumed Toroblanco.

"Certainly, only you needn't bellow, I keep telling you; first robber, then robbed, now robber again. The buckskin bag, Toro *mio*. And lively; I see there are holes in your socks and toes coming out for air, and I know you wouldn't want your toe nails shot off, would you? The little buckskin bag."

It was weighty, and Toroblanco would have hurled it at Madden's head, hoping to stun him, but did not dare. He tossed it as gently as a Mexican girl could toss an orange to her little sister.

"I know what you're thinking about, Bull Calf," laughed Madden. "How you've got twenty men just the other side of the barn, but they might as well be in jail down in Mexico City! Also how you'll skin 'em alive when I'm gone! But think, too, how they'll laugh. Behind your back for the next ten years. You *would* rob me, would you?"

"It's a lie! A cursed Gringo lie. You know I have robbed no one. It is you—you—"

"You're foaming like a mad dog," Madden warned him, though still pleasantly. "Look out you don't blow out a boiler. Now—your breeches, Bull Calf."

Toroblanco cast a wild look about him, gathered himself as though to spring—and suddenly a long windy sigh gushed from him, and he appeared to collapse like a pricked balloon as he subsided on the raw-hide-bottomed chair. He was driven to the crumbling brink of desperation; yet he held back; he was afraid of the man who laughed at him yet kept so clear an eye and so ugly a weapon trained on him.

"I gave you the money," he expostulated weakly.

"I haven't time to look into it at the moment; it may be all right, but I think not. I don't believe that this is all that you robbed me of. Come, your pretty pantaloons, Generalissimo."

Toroblanco shivered, braced himself, got one trousers leg off and sat staring moodily. Laughter welled high up in the mercuric soul of Rogue Madden. He fought it down, fought it hard and valiantly and victoriously. He made a little gesture with the revolver; Toroblanco yanked off his trousers, thus denuding himself of the last remaining vestige of his swollen dignity. Vidal Chavez's eyes grew rounder and rounder; a flick of contempt came into them. Pluck even a bird of paradise and you have no better than a plucked crow. Gone, utterly vanished, was the great man, Toroblanco. In his place stood a ridiculous ruffian, in faded bluish cotton drawers, with holes in his socks, with a nondescript and none too clean shirt.

Even now Rogue Madden had no business laughing, as he was not out of the affair by any means. Yet no longer could he contain himself. His shout of laughter burst from him as naturally and as inevitably and uncontrollably as any flash of lightning from surcharged clouds. He and Toroblanco's gaudy trousers vanished; the echoes of his delight he left behind him.

As though all Toroblanco's activities were so much black powder touched off by that laughter, the Special Deputy bounded into action. He roared curses and commands and threats; men heard him even above their own noise beyond the barn and came running. He dashed about looking for his revolver; he kicked poor little Vidal in the ribs and ran on. He found his weapon and charged back to the open window, beginning to fire through it before he saw anything whatever to shoot at. Vidal got up and crawled away; the room poured full of men.

Rogue Madden, from the first jump, ran like a deer straight across the field toward the two men waiting under the oak. They saw him, heard the sudden uproar, and came racing to meet him. While his horse, led by Bandini, was still running, Madden swung up into the saddle.

"Out of this, boys," he called cheerily, and the three streaked south "hell-for-leather."

There was all that hubbub which Rogue Madden anticipated; shouts and running and the wildest disorder as Toroblanco's men scurried back to the corral for their horses. These were moments of confusion since there was no chemist's trace of military order in anything which this rabble did: one man got another's saddle and an argument started; Toroblanco boomed curses and commands in his own inimitable fashion, yet held back himself until somehow he could improvise such clothing as permitted him displaying himself. Little Vidal Chavez, alas, had never so much as an extra pair of overalls to his name; besides, Toroblanco could never have stuffed himself inside garments of a size to fit Vidal. Beyond the barn, though men made what haste they could with saddling, none the less they laughed guardedly at their leader's predicament. Those who had seen him storming about in his undergarments told those who had missed the show; they grabbed at saddle and bridle and weapon, yet tarried to poke one another in the ribs, enraptured with the vision of Toroblanco plucked of his feathers.

When these men at last burst out of the corral, mounted and armed, they made a long straggling line charging southward. The starlight brightened the rolling fields and save for a drowsing steer here and there the fields were empty. A man somewhere in that uncertain line fired off a gun; another answered; they lifted threatening voices, shouting. And they rode on. But there was so little knowing whether to bear straight on, to turn right or left. Further, already a whisper was going about: It had been more than one man tonight; the Man of the Laugh had had other men with him. How many? No one knew. Also, their sergeant, El Carnicero, was dead; murdered by this same Laughing Fool. It was not pleasant to be dead; it was wise to ride warily when one passed the open fields and plunged into the creases and hollows and dark barrancas of the rocky hills. Finally,

Toroblanco had not yet caught up with them to goad them along.

So Madden and Cameo and young Bandini sped along undeterred, their fleet horses away from the first jump with a comfortable lead, and widening the distance between them and pursuit with every rushing second. At times Madden waved over his head, like a captured banner, his trophy of the encounter. And, between gasps of delight, he managed to explain.

Even the grave Cameo smiled. Johnny Bandini caught Madden's infection and was convulsed with it. Only, he regretted presently, Madden had hogged the fun; he should have let them in on more of it.

"Recover the stolen goods, Rogue?" asked Cameo, but not until they were in sight of the white walls of Madden's hacienda.

"Part of it, I guess," was the answer. "We'll see."

They pulled their horses down to a walk, and Madden poured the contents of the buckskin bag into his palm.

"It's coin of the realm, all right," he muttered. "Yet that's just the devil of it! Coin of Mexico! About two hundred bucks, Mex. Not the stuff he took off me at all!"

"Anything in the breeches?" asked Bandini.

"I hate to put a hand in his pockets," said Madden in a tone of disgust. "Yet a man mustn't be squeamish, and thank God for hot water and green soap!"

He made his hurried investigation. He found tobacco and cigarette papers; a pocket knife and a few matches. That was all.

"What made you think he'd carry the stuff on him?" asked Bandini.

"What else could he do with it? Of course he'd carry it. It must be somewhere in Vidal's shack; in the room where Toroblanco was. He wouldn't have had it out of sight."

"I suppose," said Cameo carelessly, "that you've figured out what's going to happen?"

Madden looked at him questioningly. Cameo shrugged.

"He's going to visit us real soon, you know. If he doesn't shoot the gang of us up and burn you out before morning, why, it'll be just because he can't."

Madden, of course, should have realized that before he even set forth on to-night's jaunt. But as a matter of fact he had done nothing half so obvious and sensible; he had been occupied only with that part of the nocturnal adventure which had already taken place.

"Why, I never thought of that!" he exclaimed. He whistled softly and then fell to frowning. "It wouldn't matter; I wouldn't give a hang, would you?—if it wasn't for the womenfolks! Great Scott, what a mess!"

"And you hadn't even thought of it!" jeered Cameo Risden.

"Confound you, Cameo, I hadn't! Why in blazes didn't you tell me?—You think of things."

"I guess you made him mad, all right," mused Johnny Bandini. And added with a sudden thought: "Say! You didn't see the man that robbed you, did you? What if it wasn't Toroblanco at all? What if you jumped the wrong man to-night?"

Here was a thought to give some men pause. Not Rogue Madden. He found in it only the most intriguing possibilities. Last night, over the poker table, they had disposed so gaily of a good part of Toroblanco's worldly wealth! To-night Toroblanco had been held up for another hundred *pesos* or so; stripped to his last *centavo*—if he were by any chance the wrong man and did not have the loot of Madden's guests to fall back upon!

So, when they dismounted in the home corrals, Rogue Madden was laughing again.

"They're apt to be on us in fifteen minutes, you know," said Cameo, lighting a cigar with his customary care. "I wouldn't mention it, only—only there are times when you really don't seem to be looking very far ahead, you know."

"I'll be ready for 'em," retorted Madden, and was off at a run for the house. But over his shoulder he called back gaily, "Only it'll be longer than that. First off, their horses are not in it with mine. Next, it'll take Toroblanco more than fifteen minutes to make himself a pair of pants out of a saddle blanket or a tablecloth!"

CHAPTER IX

Much may happen in a few minutes, when a driving force is hard at work. It may have been noted that in less than half an hour battles have been won and lost, ships have been sunk, empires have tottered. Time, after all, doesn't amount to much; it is that which is crowded into it.

Rogue Madden burst in upon Aunt Polly, her niece and Anastasio chatting in the living-room.

"We're off for a ride, so get ready!" he sang out as they turned expectantly at the noise of his hurrying boots. "Gather up your traps, everything you have; pack your bags. I'll send Maria in to help you. We're going to my other ranch; across the border and back into the good old U.S.A., and long may she wave!"

Gipsy Wynne sprang to her feet, her eyes lighting up. Back into the States! Out of bondage! For the high hand of this young brigand must change in a moment to a meek hand of supplication there. Aunt Polly looked at first disappointed; it was so romantic here in Mexico! Then she, too, brightened. There was some wild lark afoot, never doubt it. Why had their host been gone so long to-night, if not to prepare some other zestful affair for them? Of course. And she was ready for it, eager for his next dramatic effect. He might fool Gipsy, never Miss Polly Comfort. Through Brother Sam's lessonings she had arrived at pre-visionings. She, too, jumped up, beaming.

Both would have asked questions, but Rogue Madden was no longer in the room to answer them. They looked to Escobar; never did shrug stand him in better stead. He knew nothing; if Madden meant what he said, they were to make a hasty preparation for a more than fifty-mile ride. Escobar's eyes narrowed speculatively.

"Come along, Gipsy," cried Aunt Polly, snatching her niece's hand. "There's fun afoot, my dear!"

"Aunt Polly!" Gipsy could not make her aunt out; such an explosive summons as this should have set all that dear lady's nerves jangling and, if precedent were of any significance, put her to bed for a week. But evidently precedent was not to be relied on.

Madden came running back; he had darted through dining-room and kitchen, giving brisk orders right and left, and was on his way outdoors again. Aunt Polly stopped him with an exclamatory:

"What on earth is that you're carrying, Rogue Madden?"

Madden looked at what he still held in his hand; he had forgotten.

"It's the trophy of the chase," he grinned,

and tossed the things from him. “Toroblanco’s pantaloons! I had intended having a boy climb a tree and hang ’em out there at the top for a banner! I won’t have time now.”

Escobar gasped. It was true, what Madden said: he recognized the resplendent garment. And now he had a clue: There had been an affair with Toroblanco, and more was to be looked for from it; hence this hurried departure.

Outside they heard other orders being given, as Madden ran here and there getting the boys out of their quarters in the out-buildings. Cameo Risden came in. Aunt Polly wanted to ask him questions. He very gravely and courteously cut her short, advising her to be in readiness so that the start to the border be not delayed.

So it happened that surely not more than fifteen minutes later a sort of caravan was ready to strike out into the starlit night. A light spring wagon stood at the front door; a team of six young horses, disporting themselves like so many run-away colts taking a deep breath between bursts of running away, was being held down to the ground by the man on the seat and other men at the bits. Still other men held other horses, saddled. And Madden was everywhere at once. Bags were tumbled in; Gipsy and her aunt were helped up to their places. Madden shouted: “All ready?” The man sagging backward against the tug of the reins kicked off his brake and shouted back: "*Vamonos*!" And in a flash the six young horses were off at a breakneck run, the wagon whipped along after them as though of no more weight than a monstrous feather.

Aunt Polly was in ecstasy, so sure was the misguided soul that this was all but a bit of Wild West staged for their edification. Gipsy Wynne was in a daze. *Was* all this real? Was it just a huge, silly joke? And what had come over Aunt Polly?

She looked back. She saw man after man surge up into his saddle. The stars glinted on bridle bit and chain, on metallic trappings here and there—on rifles! Every man was armed. Who the men were she did not know at first; later she discovered that her aunt and herself were being escorted by Rogue Madden himself, for he raced by them, and she recognized him as he swept ahead, leading the way; and there was Cameo Risden; Johnny Bandini, too. The other riders, they could have told her, were Curly, Do-Boy Edwards, Anastasio Escobar, and the cherubic yet crafty Joe Quince.

"He's fooling us!" was the gay announcement jolted out of Aunt Polly. "We're not headed toward the border at all. We're going due south, Gipsy darling. If I were a betting woman—and I think I am going to be; honestly I do, my dear—I'd say that that young villain is kidnapping us! We're going to find ourselves in short order in the headquarters of the bandit chief!"

"If we don't get tipped over and spilled out," murmured Gipsy, clinging with both hands to the iron rail at the back of the seat, as the wagon took a sharp turn on two wheels.

"Isn't he a wonderful driver?" cried Aunt Polly. "And what riders those men are! They can do anything!"

The men who constituted their escort acted strangely, Gipsy thought. Three or four of them deserted the others and rode off into the north, disappearing beyond a little hill, reappearing later yet keeping at a considerable distance to the north. It was for all the world like a real escort with outriders watchful for the enemy.

"It's as good as a play!" said Aunt Polly. "Hold on tight, Gip. We're just getting to going strong now."

Such talk from Miss Polly Comfort of Boston!

Like a play? Was it just that?—Toroblanco? Toroblanco's trousers!—Make sense of this madness and you do more than Gipsy Wynne could do. She could only sense that there was something serious afoot. Desperately serious. Yet everything was like a farce; but it could be some absurd farce of an amateur who might crown his folly with a tragic ending.

What Madden did was lead the way a full mile south to strike into an old wagon road that wound through the hills, making a ragged semi-circle about that part of the country across which Toroblanco would come, did he come at all. Give him a head start of half a dozen miles and Toroblanco's party, if they found him at all, could hope to do so only by scattering their force, sending men in many directions. Let a handful of the vagabond crew overhaul him, he could laugh at them. He mustered a good seven rifles and was not greatly troubled by an attack of less than three times seven of Toroblanco's men.

"Wagon and all, if they give us half a show, we'll make it to the other ranch in eight hours," he estimated confidently.

"My!" said Aunt Polly, shaken but complacent, maddeningly complacent, her niece thought. "If I had my way I'd always drive like this! You get all the thrill of something dangerous, and you know it's as safe as being in church. It must be, you know, or he wouldn't be doing it. Six horses to one light wagon! Isn't it fun, Gipsy?"

"Ye-ye-yes!" was jolted out of Gipsy as the wagon shot down into the bed of a dry and rocky barranca.

The outriders drew in closer as they sped through a craggy pass; Gipsy made out the handsome Cameo Risden among them. Madden was far out of sight ahead. They crossed a long slope; every time a wheel hit a rock there was nothing easier to the slowest imagination than to picture the wagon upside down, its human freight bruised and bleeding and scattered over a stretch of fifty yards of steep hillside. But the wagon did not tip over, and the horses did keep to their flying feet and presently a level plain opened up before them. Again the riders spread out, rising briefly in silhouette against the starry sky, sinking down, vanishing as though they had sunk straight into the ground.

When the moon rose they were skimming what seemed a limitless flat prairie. Aunt Polly clutched Gipsy's arm. What a moon! The Moon of the South. Moon of Romance. Larger, more glorious than any Boston moon ever dreamed of being. A softly refulgent globe moving up by visible inches, as though in hesitant jerks, beyond a far-off hill. On the hill stood a single pine tree, black against the monster round of the moon. Sage and dry thorny cactus were silvered and softened; the sandy road gleamed like a pathway into the heart of romance.

". . . and the rifles make it all so real!"

The outriders, widening their protective arcs, had disappeared again. The driver of the six-horse team had long ago turned out to be a Mexican with hardly a word of English and, thought Gipsy, who had attempted her Spanish on him, a man of low intelligence. He could only show glistening glimpses of his white teeth, and shrug and make little restricted gestures with the two hands so busy with the reins.

"We are going north now, I think," said Gipsy.

"Mercy, child, I don't know," sighed Aunt Polly. "There were times back there in the hills when I'm sure we just went in circles. *Where* do you think he is taking us?"

"There were times back there," said Gipsy, and almost with a sniff as she mimicked her aunt's voice, "when I felt pretty sure that it was the horses that were taking us wherever it came into their silly heads to go."

Far off to the left a black dot rose up from the argent floor of the earth. It seemed at first merely to swell in size without actually drawing nearer; then of a sudden, resolved into horse and rider, it bore down upon them and turned out to be Johnny Bandini.

He called out something in Spanish. The driver answered. Not far ahead stood a lone tree by the wheel track which was serving them as road. The driver began pulling in his team; the horses slowed down gradually; they came to a fidgety stop in the black shadow which resulted from moon and tree's co-operation.

"Rogue thinks we're pretty much in the clear now," said Bandini, riding close to the wagon, on Gipsy's side. "He thought you might like to just sit still a couple of minutes. It won't hurt the horses any, either."

Gipsy caught at the words, "in the clear," and

demanded an explanation. The moon was higher now, more compelling; Johnny Bandini was young; Gipsy Wynne's head was uncovered, her face turned toward him.

So Johnny Bandini told her all about it. He figured all danger past, so what harm? Then, too, he was brimming to overflowing with the whole escapade. Either he forgot Aunt Polly's nerves, or had not found any occasion to be impressed by them.

They spent only three or four minutes under the tree, but Johnny Bandini spoke to the point, and the time was ample. Gipsy gasped; was there any sanity left in the world? Aunt Polly kept nodding her head at almost every word, a happy, serene smile on her face. Here was talk of Toroblanco again when she was so sure that Toroblanco, whose name Johnny had told her translated itself into White Bull, was a myth.

"As soon as you boys let me be still long enough to write a letter," she vowed, "I'm going to write to my brother Sam."

"As if he could help us now!" breathed Gipsy.

"Help?" Aunt Polly laughed. "You silly child!—Can we go on now, Johnny? Will you tell the man to let the horses run some more? Can they go any faster? I mean, of course, without doing them any harm?"

Young Bandini stared mightily, regarding her with mounting admiration.

"Faster! I wish I could have clocked this run!" he said regretfully. "That's all!"

He reined back from the wagon, flourished his hat, called to the driver and they were off.

Hours passed. Even the plain which had seemed so vastly broad came to an end. Among hills once more they proceeded, jouncing, rocking, swaying. A downhill slope invited to a fresh burst of speed, and they took sharp turns with gravel crunching under spinning wheels. From this broken country the running horses whipped them along down into other level lands dotted with drowsing cattle.

"My!" said Aunt Polly, shifting about to try to get comfortable—optimistic soul. She yawned unhiddenly, both hands being busied holding on, and added musingly: "Perhaps he told us the truth for once. Maybe we really are going to his other ranch across the border, a full fifty miles."

Everything began to affect Gipsy Wynne like a dream. All sorts of objects and thoughts and conditions drifted together and blended: Night, moonlight, stars; shimmering brush and stretches of white winding road; the stillness about her, the lively clop of horses' hoofs, the rattle of wheels and the infrequent calls of the driver. They were no longer going so fast; the men with their rifles were not so far away. She saw two of them riding ahead; four others dropped in behind, following closely. The seventh man she couldn't find.

The driver had noted her movement. He gathered his reins into one hand, pointing with the other, flinging out his arm triumphantly.

"*Al momento*!" he promised her. "*Mira*!"

She looked. Yonder, perhaps a mile or two away, flooded with the white moonlight, sprawled a big, rambling, adobe-walled house with adobe walls surrounding it. Seen from the slight rise which they were topping, the house and its yard and outbuildings were spread out like a picture.

After an instant of downright puzzlement Gipsy Wynne's mind cleared to the hot flame of anger. Oh, this was intolerable! That man—that Roger Madden! She set her teeth bitingly; her hands clenched into hard little fists. Was there no humanity in him? To make Aunt Polly endure all this, hours and hours and still hours of purposeless hardship—merely to bring them back to the place from which they had started!—She remembered a story of a mad king who got his courtiers out to hunt phantom stags by moonlight. Was Rogue Madden not only rogue but madman?

"What is it, Gipsy?" asked Aunt Polly sleepily.

"We're at the end of our ride, Aunty." She spoke in a queer, flat and toneless voice, the voice of repression. But she added rather tartly: "We're back where we started."

Aunt Polly sat up and rubbed her eyes and stared.

"Why, so we are!" she agreed. "H'm. That's funny. Now I wonder what he is up to?"

"You're ending a lot of sentences lately with prepositions, my dear," said Gipsy, an edge to her voice and some crispness in her tone now, so did she blaze inwardly.

"So I am," smiled Aunt Polly. She sighed comfortably. "Boston is such a long way off from here, isn't it?" Then she actually chuckled. "This is just the place for Boston people to come *to!*"

"For a nervous woman—" began Gipsy spiritedly.

"Shucks," said Aunt Polly, "that's all over with. I'm cured."

Madden was standing at the gate in the adobe wall, awaiting them.

"We made it in record time," he announced breezily. "Stand the ride all right?"

He put out his arms invitingly. Gipsy, cramped though she was in every muscle, ignored him and climbed down over the wheel.

"If this is your conception of being funny," she said in that hard, repressed voice. And then, flaring out, hot and bitter: *"Oh! I hate you!"*

Aunt Polly slipped gratefully and with a long sigh into the inviting arms. And Madden caught her up and held her close to him and, with never a dissent on her part, carried her through the gate and into the patio.

"Poor little Aunt Polly," he said softly. "I've

given you the very devil of a night, haven't I? Well, there's hot coffee and tea, too, and chocolate ready. And you're going to be in bed in two shakes, and have the best and longest sleep of your life."

"No cocktails?" whispered Aunt Polly, and both laughed.

Gipsy, following them disdainfully, caught her aunt's arm.

"You'd better come with me, Aunt," she said, her tone more smothered than ever. "You'll go right to bed. I'll bring you something hot."

"But I want to know what this is all about! There's some reason for it, somewhere."

"There's neither rhyme nor reason, I fear," Gipsy told her, and her eyes, bright with accusation and condemnation, made open war with Madden's.

Aunt Polly allowed herself to be led away. A Mexican woman hurried to them, inviting them to their rooms. Not Maria; some other woman they had never seen. They went through the dining-room and living-room; in the light of many candles everything looked at once the same and different. It was as though, during their absence, subtle changes had been made everywhere; they thought the furniture had been shifted about, new pieces brought in; even the flower pots in the windows held different plants. Gipsy, growing bewildered, began noting details more closely.

Rugs changed; books yonder in a niche where before there had been an earthern *olla.* In their own bedrooms where at first glance they thought everything quite the same—everything was changed! These were not the same furnishings at all.

The girl, leaving Aunt Polly sitting on the edge of a bed, ran into the bathroom, making swift examination. It was not the same bathroom at all. The other had had tub only; this one stall shower and tub! To have installed a shower bath, even had there been some stupid reason, would have required much longer than this one insane night!—Where was Maria? Where had that other woman come from?

. . . Far from Boston. Ending thoughts with prepositions. Was it after all, she who was *crazy?*

She heard Rogue Madden laughing . . .

CHAPTER X

It was some hours before Aunt Polly Comfort and Miss Gipsy Wynne knew rightfully where they were. They meant to rest in their rooms; the house was strangely quiet; they slept soundly and the sun was high before they awakened and went in quest of breakfast and information. The woman who was not Maria, an ample middle-aged Mexican named Eloisa, spoke an execrable English with strange fluency, and was eager to answer all questions.

Where was every one? Señor Madden and his friends? But she did not know that! They had come, as the ladies knew, with a rush; the way they always came. They had had coffee and eaten a bite or two; they had gone again and, of course, in the customary rush. One of them she thought had not gone with the others; that was Don Anastasio Escobar, but she did not know where he was now.

Gipsy, looking out of the breakfast-room windows, saw that though house, patio, yard and outbuildings seemed the same, this was another ranch. The contour of the blue hills against the sky, the grouping of oaks, the cottonwoods along a dry wash, were different. She asked eagerly to know what place this was.

Eloisa was quite as eager to give full information. This was the rancho of Señor Madden. He had several; two great beeg ones. The other was the place they had come from; that was fifty miles south, and therefore in Mexico. This one was on the American side of the line. The Mexican rancho had a long time ago been the country home of a great man of Mexico, a soldier and a politician, no less, Ramon Olivares himself. The elder Señor Madden had bought from him and had so very greatly admired the noble mansion there that he had caused this one to be made just like it.

But the girl, assured that she now stood on the north side of the international boundary line, which was to say the side dedicated to law and order, had other quick questions to ask that were not in the least concerned with architecture duplicated. How far was the nearest town? The nearest neighbour, telephone, customs officers?

Oh, there was no town near. The rancho itself ran on for miles; it was the biggest one in the world, Eloisa thought. "Telephono?" She shook her head; they did not have those theengs here. Señor Madden called them dam' nui-sants—

But the nearest town? That would be Nacional, said Eloisa, and a long ride on horseback. She had been there. It was Mexican; once you stepped across the line it was very gay, but dirty; Indians, more than you could count, in red and green blankets; saloons all along, and places to dance and gamble and watch cock fights. Oh, Americans went there; sure they did! Just to get drunk, though; they were no good. It was not a place for a lady to go, the Virgin forbid. Maybe she would never come back; her friends would never know what happened to her. Eloisa shook her head warningly.

"I wonder where all the boys have gone?" wondered Aunt Polly.

"Perhaps," her niece suggested serenely, "down to that charming Nacional. To get drunk. Being Americans."

"Nonsense," scoffed Aunt Polly. "I've no doubt there's a-plenty here for 'em to get drunk on, if that were in their minds. Good liquor, too, instead of the sort of thing that's sold along the border."

"You speak as one who is a connoisseur!"

"There was that cocktail, you know," Aunt Polly reminded her complacently.

Gipsy was looking at her aunt with a peculiarly penetrating gaze in those bright grey eyes of hers—more gravely than the subject of their talk seemed to warrant. But then, Gipsy had that kind of feminine mind, amazingly agile and mysteriously competent, which permitted of carrying on this kind of talk with every appearance of being absorbed in it while her thoughts were far away. She was wondering. Not about "the boys," as Aunt Polly insisted on calling them; not about what they might be doing or drinking; but about her own and her aunt's predicament, and a way out of it. They were prisoners. Just in what degree did Aunt Polly realize that? And what about Aunt Polly's nerves? Of late they seemed made of reinforced concrete; yet how far could one depend on them? How blind, in short, was this Aunt Polly, and how much did she see?

Gipsy said with a pretty assumption of carelessness, yet with that alert look in her eye:

"How about making a run for it while they're away?"

Aunt Polly looked mildly surprised.

"Aren't you having the time of your life? I am."

Gipsy balanced a fork nicely over a forefinger.

"You realize we're the same as prisoners here, don't you?"

"To be sure!" cried Aunt Polly enthusiastically.

"H'm. We were robbed, weren't we?"

"Of course, my dear. Wasn't it thrilling, really?"

"And you know who robbed us, don't you?"

"Rogue Madden. Who else?"

"And what of our losses? The things he took?"

"Hid," laughed Aunt Polly. "He knows where."

"But he says he, too, was robbed!"

"Pooh!" laughed her aunt. "Pooh, my dear."

The fork which Gipsy had made into a sort of teeter-totter went up and down. The girl lifted her eyes swiftly to the smiling face across the table and lowered them as swiftly. She remarked musingly:

"What of the trouble with the terrible Toroblanco? The near-fight, before we came? The meeting last night, before we left the other ranch? The affair of the pantaloons, as one might call it?"

"The terrible Toroblanco," said Miss Comfort, while annexing the little fat jar of marmalade, "is just about as real as the genie that worked for Aladdin, or the Fairy Peri Banou. I won't say that if it hadn't been for the things which my brother Samuel told me, I wouldn't have been taken in. I don't know. I might. 'Tisn't likely, though."

Gipsy tried a fresh tack.

"You know that this fresh young man, Roger Madden, claims that he is my legally constituted guardian? That he has every right and power to dictate to me what I shall do, what leave undone?"

Miss Comfort's eyes brightened with what might almost be termed a predatory gleam.

"He's the handsomest thing, Gip! They're fine people, too, the Maddens. You know all about his father; his mother was a Californian señorita, daughter of a very famous old Castilian line. He—"

Her niece cut her short with a look. It was like a big sign painted in bold black letters: "No Matchmaking." Miss Comfort sighed comfortably, marmaladed her toast, and observed:

"It would seem, my dear, that he really is your guardian. I know very little about law, of course. But the guardianship papers were all legal and in order, weren't they?"

"Of course. But—"

"Well, then, that should settle it. For at the time they were drawn up there was only one Roger Clark Madden of the Madden Ranch in the world; and he is the one. It's really most romantic, isn't it? Think—"

Gipsy dropped her fork and gasped in horror.

"You actually mean—you mean you believe—You don't mean, Aunt Polly," and for the instant she looked uncertain of all things and fearful of most, "that there could possibly be any truth in what he says!—my guardian! That man—taking the place of my father!"

She broke out laughing, but there was a ring of nervousness in her sudden mirth. She jumped up and went to a window, looking out into the garden. There were bars over the window here as elsewhere; she lifted a hand to one of the iron rods, shaking it impatiently. Suddenly she was oppressed; she felt like one in a dungeon. Even her aunt was deserting her. Of course, that was only and simply because Miss Polly Comfort did not understand; the dear old soul simply would not believe the truth. A fortunate thing for Miss Comfort herself; Gipsy saw that clearly enough.

Had her aunt known that she was living actual life in the raw, instead of sitting in a box looking on at a bit of cheap acting, no doubt she would, like the Watchful Sneezoff of Thackeraynian fame, have "started, staggered, groaned and died." But still Gipsy, staring through the bars, failed to see how this consideration helped her case.

She saw a movement in the garden. A man was lolling on an old green bench, smoking a cigarette. She looked more closely. It was the Mexican gentleman, Anastasio Escobar. He alone had spoken sympathetically to her; he had offered his friendship and the fruit thereof. She excused herself to her aunt hastily, promised to await her in the garden and went seeking Don Anastasio.

"Where are the others?" she asked him at once, when he heard her coming and arose, hat off, making her his elaborate bow.

When she had seated herself on the bench, making a place for him beside her, and he had been permitted to make himself another cigarette to replace the one he had so promptly abandoned at her approach, he told her. The others, all of them excepting the Mexican driver, had lost not over fifteen minutes in slinging their saddles on fresh horses and returning over the way they had come. Straight back to the other ranch, fifty miles away. For Señor Madden really had expected trouble with Toroblanco; an attack on his ranch and perhaps no end of depredation, burning and general vandalism. He had left Long Corbin, his foreman, there with a handful of men to fight Toroblanco off if he came. But of course he had gone back, and with him the others.

"And you?" she asked of Don Anastasio.

"He wanted someone here to safeguard you and your aunt," he answered gravely. "To me fell that honour, Miss Wynne. I hope it will not prove to be all honour and no service. If there is anything I can do?"

She watched him curiously all the while. What absolutely black eyes he had. She thought of the word, "inscrutable." A man could be thinking anything, with eyes like that. He was more the type of villain (or at least the stage type, and she knew no other first hand) than the villainous Rogue Madden was. Yet here she found herself about to turn to this saturnine and—yes—downright satanic-looking stranger for protection against the laughing, clear-eyed one.

"If I wanted to go—my aunt and I—before they got back—Would you help us?" she asked uncertainly, hesitant until the very end, then making the last four words gallop.

"I would have you understand," he returned quietly, yet with a flash of the eyes, some spirit leaping inside the man, "that I would help you in anything, at any time."

Surely that should have satisfied her. She had the answer she wanted. Yet, with it, she had more than she had asked; that flash in his eyes, the glint of a leaping spirit.

She asked again of the others, Madden and Cameo and Johnny Bandini and the rest; when would they be likely to return here? It would not be for some days, she suggested? What she was doing within herself, though she did not know it, was temporize. With Madden fifty miles away, there was no need of haste in making her departure; in placing herself in the hands of the friendly Escobar.

"Everything will depend on what they find at the other ranch," he told her. "If there is real trouble there, who knows?" He shrugged. "Toroblanco has twenty men at his back and can get twenty more; if men were killed, Toroblanco would not be so much as reprimanded by his government. He will have excuse enough. On the other hand, if Toroblanco has held his hand, and allows the opportunity to go by, Madden will undoubtedly ride straight back here. A few minutes to look around, to have a cup of coffee and change to a fresh horse, then back to see how it goes with you."

"But that would be a hundred and fifty miles ridden almost without rest!" she exclaimed.

He nodded. "That is nothing for Rogue Madden. Nothing for the men who ride with him. They are hard, Miss Wynne. He would make a ride like that on a bet, then dance all night."

Was he telling her the truth? She grew suspicious of everyone and everything. It seemed incredible that these men should dash back and forth across fifty miles as though running in on a neighbour across the street. That flash in Escobar's eyes! Was he urging her to flee now, putting herself into his hands? For that would be exactly what she did if she rode away with him.

It was a day like a diamond. The sunshot air was clear and fresh and clean; heat waves shimmered over the fields but it was only pleasantly warm here in the shade; ruby-throated humming birds darted into view, hung buzzing over the flower beds, zipped out of sight. A rare sweet peace pervaded the atmosphere; from afar came faintly the languid, musically-sad notes of doves. There was sheer, lazy, delightful, dreamful ease in sitting by the fountain in the patio, watching the water fall and ripple, breaking with diamond lights.

If only it could be like this day after day and straight along into eternity, thought Gipsy Wynne wistfully. She sighed and experienced the sensation of breathing deep the peace and hush about her. Yet a moment later it was she herself who broke the spell. She jumped up, saying eagerly:

"I feel restless! Let's *do* something."

In an ancient top buggy drawn by a gentle mare she and Aunt Polly, accompanied by Escobar on horseback, fared forth into the sunshine. Gipsy drove; Aunt Polly sat upright and interested at her side; Escobar murmured his delight at acting *cicerone.*

A grass-grown wagon road led them eastward through vast green fields of alfalfa and after that through other fields not so green, yet rich and fertile, given over to wheat which rippled like brown water and was dotted by small vivid islands that were oaks. Before them rose abrupt hills at the base of which, some three miles from the ranch house, they encountered a fence which not only called a halt to further progress in that direction but drew their attention to itself for the sort of thing it was. Strung on iron posts eight feet high, strands of barbed wire were so close set that not even a small child could have wriggled through. There was a truly formidable gate, closed and fastened with heavy chains and two padlocks. Aunt Polly, who had begun to sag, sat bolt upright again.

"It's like a barricade!" she marvelled. "And what a mysterious, dark-looking ravine on the other side! What do you suppose—"

"Look!" exclaimed Gipsy. "There's some-one—I saw someone—They're gone! Aunty, they hid when they saw us!"

"Someone isn't they," Aunt Polly reminded her, yet looked eagerly in all directions. "Why should they hide, child? What did they look like?"

"I got only a glimpse. They looked like—like Wong Fu!"

Wong Fu was an old servant of the Wynnes' and, though undoubtedly a placid soul, a more villainous-looking specimen never lorded it over an American kitchen.

"How could they look like Wong Fu?" demanded Aunt Polly almost tartly, for she resented having Gipsy spy anything which had escaped her. "Twins or what?"

"Chinamen, I think, Aunty," said Gipsy. She slapped the reins on the mare's back and they started northward; glancing back at the intriguing fence, she asked of Escobar: "Does it mark the end of Mr. Madden's land?"

He smiled enigmatically, and she was sure that she saw that queer flicker of light in his eyes again.

"No," he said at last. "Madden owns beyond that fence, too."

"But who were those men? And why did they hide?" she asked curiously.

"You have wonderful eyes! Are you sure you saw someone? I did not."

"And why the fence? And the locks?"

He only shook his head and returned briefly: "I don't know."

Their road led them on through little roly-poly hills smoother than those rifted ones they had left at one side, dimpled hills with oaks and shade and grass. Soon they lost sight of the barbed wire strung on iron posts and never another fence was seen; the land rippled away into free wide distances.

A clump of tall eucalyptus trees caught Gipsy's eye; a moment later she saw a grove of pepper trees and, through their more vivid green, the glimpse of a white wall. Her heart leapt at the discovery which she was on the verge of making: several pretty white cottages flashed their red-tiled roofs through the screen of pepper trees.

"Why it's a town!" she exclaimed, and thought triumphantly: "Aha, Mr. Rogue Madden! Other people, telephones, peace officers and an end to your nonsense!"

Escobar's words extinguished her flare of triumph.

"Hardly a town; just a few old people, pensioners, you might say, living on the Madden bounty. All this belongs to the ranch."

So her heart sank as quickly as it had leapt. Still her interest was piqued; she had never seen prettier, gayer little houses than these, spick-and-span and rather like a child's cut-out play town.

On a sunny porch a woman sat rocking. She was strangely at odds with the brightness and picturesqueness of the place, a pallid, washed-out sort of creature with colourless hair straggling in wisps about a querulous face. Gipsy had never looked on any human being so down at heels, down at the mouth and altogether cheerless. A man drooped wearily at her side; dressed in shiny black save for shoes of a grey dust colour, with long-tailed coat and no collar, he might have been some old-time minister fallen into bad times. A sadder, more bleakly ineffectual couple it would be hard to imagine.

"The Bowens," said Escobar. "The most worthless pair, I think, in North America. They ought to be turned out to starve."

"But they do keep their place beautifully!"

Escobar laughed. "Not they. They're far too sad to take any interest in life. Madden has a man here to keep things from tumbling down and going to pieces."

"You mean these people do nothing at all?"

"They eat; they sleep. The rest of the time they just put in being sad!"

"How about the folks in that other pretty cottage?" asked Aunt Polly, as they passed on. One glance at that twain of Marlborough Bowen and his helpmate Agatha was enough for her.

"They're as bad as the Bowens, I think. Ashton Ferribee and his wife. They're older than the Bowens; sixty, I guess. They used to work for Roger Madden's father; he's kept them here."

"Sad, too?" asked Aunt Polly, grown very brisk.

"Yes; they revel in some sad sort of religion, all their own. They expect each day to be the last;

they've been waiting for the world to come to an end a long time."

"Don't work, either?"

"No. The end of the world might come at any time, you know. They wouldn't want to miss any of it."

"What charming neighbours!" cried Gipsy, laughing for the first time to-day. "They must be bosom companions."

"I understand," Escobar told them, "that they hate nothing on earth as they hate one another."

"I should think so," sniffed Aunt Polly. "Drive on, Gip."

As they passed the second little house a man came hurrying to the door. Perhaps he had heard the slapping of reins and rattling of dry spokes in wobbly wheels, and thought it the crack of doom. At any rate he hastened, as though not to miss something of importance, a very tall, spare man in dingy overalls, with straggling white whiskers and gaunt, hollow eyes. He shaded his eyes with his hand, gave a grunt and retreated into his house.

"Rogue Madden must be a mighty good man," surmised Aunt Polly. "I'd have those vagabonds on their way in just exactly one shake of a lamb's tail."

Her niece didn't answer. She seemed thoughtful during the homeward drive. They passed herds and flocks; there were the prize bull, the new strain in goats whose coats were destined to become fine rugs, the pure-bred horses, all drawing not the least interest from her.

"I wonder whether the boys are back?" said Aunt Polly.

"You wouldn't be wondering if you had really believed that they had gone to the other ranch!"

"And pray, why not, Miss?"

"Only a hundred miles?" laughed Gipsy. "What are you thinking of?"

"Why that would be nothing for our boys! It was before four when they brought us here this morning; it's four o'clock in the afternoon now—"

"To be sure! Lightning could make the trip in a second or two, I believe; an aeroplane would make it in less than an hour; why shouldn't these 'boys' of yours run down on horseback, fight a battle, drink a cup of coffee and be back here ready to play?"

"Battle, pooh! There hasn't been any battle out here since Custer was a boy."

They left Escobar in the patio and entered the house. Rogue Madden met them at the door, looking gay and fresh in clean white flannels.

"And how do you like the Rancho of Joyous Guard?" he challenged them.

Aunt Polly beamed, while Gipsy regarded him narrowly. Whatever thoughts and riddles had been with her on the ride home she brought along into this first meeting with him.

"But," said Aunt Polly, "I thought the other ranch was to be called the Rancho of Joyous Guard?"

"Both," he grinned impudently. "Whichever my ward honours with her presence is sure to find her guardian at hand too."

"We love it, every bit of it," said Aunt Polly warmly. "We saw such a lot, too. A great high fence; a big sign saying 'Keep Out, for Fear of Your Lives.' Mysterious Chinese figures creeping about—"

He laughed. "So you saw all that? Fine!"

"And the pretty little houses," said Gipsy, "where the Bowens and the Ashton Ferribees live."

She spoke thoughtfully, looking steadily into his twinkling eyes. She even added after the fashion of one determined to be fair:

"We did think it very kind of you to take care of such poor old souls—"

"They're my colony of Gloomsters!" he told her chucklingly. "I feed and house 'em for the good they do my soul. I'm not much given to having the blues, you know; but when I do get 'em—Wow! I'd die if they hung on; I simply can't stand 'em. And whenever the blues do get a man, give him a dose of my Gloomsters, and it's all sunshine again! Honestly. All you've got to do is take your sorrows with you and ride over to my Colony. Those folk are so far down at the mouth that just brushing against 'em—"

"Oh!" said Gipsy. "So you just keep those poor people there to make fun of them!"

"Is making fun *of* them and getting fun *out* of them the same thing?" He grinned at her.

"Yes." She stepped by him.

"Hold on, Ward. I've got something for you. Look."

Curiosity turned her head toward him. A little gasp broke from her. Shining in the palm of his hand was a pretty old-fashioned brooch which old Jim Wynne had given his little daughter on a glad birthday long and long ago. Her eyes began to sparkle.

"Then—then you're going to return—"

"This. I found it."

"Found it?" All her scorn came blazing back.

"Yes. At the other ranch. Funny thing—I found it on the floor in the living room!" He looked perplexed. "How in the world it got there, I don't know!"

Why did he pile lie on top of lie! She would not believe, no matter what Aunt Polly might, that he had ridden a hundred miles since she had left him in the small hours of the morning. She would not believe that he had *found* her little brooch anywhere.

Her lips, tightly compressed, refused to shape any rejoinder. But her eyes, as she hurried out of the room, never so eloquent, said for her:

"Liar!"

CHAPTER XI

"So you didn't go back to the other rancho after all?" asked Don Anastasio.

"Of course we did," said Madden. "You heard me tell Miss Wynne."

"And the others? Cameo and Bandini?"

"They wanted a nap. I left them headed toward bed."

"And Toroblanco? No trouble with him?" Escobar looked very earnest, almost anxious. "He did nothing?"

"No. Nothing worth speaking of, at least. Sent me a letter! He's crazy, Anastasio!"

"No, not crazy. Not Carlos Toroblanco.—A letter, you say?"

Madden felt in his pockets.

"In my other clothes, or I've lost it. Very polite in a nice icy formal way. He said he was going to buy my ranch down there, and offered me ten thousand dollars for it!"

At a dollar an acre, without stock or improvements, that ranch would have been worth ten times the price offered. That was why Madden said with a grunt, "He's crazy."

"And he did not attack? He had men enough—"

"He explained that. Oh, he made it quite clear: Would a man wreck the place he meant to have for his own? He held his hand, he said, rather than bring devastation to what he already looked on as his own property!"

Escobar regarded him thoughtfully.

"It's enough to set you thinking—"

Madden snapped his fingers.

"How much thinking would you do about it if a man offered you a dime for a pet saddle-horse?"

"If that man were Toroblanco—" Escobar lifted his brows and shoulders in more the French than Mexican style, and all the while kept watching the other as though seeking something serious below the sunny surface.

But there appeared to be nothing beneath the surface. With a snap of the fingers Madden had disposed of Toroblanco. He turned to another matter, and now it was his turn to look with frank curiosity at his friend.

"The ladies tell me you took them on a tour? They saw something, eh, at the fence across the cañon?—How'd you happen to take them that way, Anastasio?"

Escobar stared at him frowningly.

"How was I to know that they would see anyone? Well, they thought they saw a Chinaman! Perhaps they did; perhaps they dreamed it."

Madden laughed and turned away. But Escobar caught him by the arm.

"I want to talk to you about that place beyond the fence, *amigo*," he said gravely.

And they were still talking about it, their voices lowered into a confidential key, when a door opened and the stooped figure of an old man came in. Madden dropped his discussion with Escobar at the middle of a word, and hurried to meet the newcomer.

"I'm sorry, Father!" he exclaimed contritely. "I'd actually forgotten. You have made out all right?"

He spoke in Spanish. One surmised at a glance that this newcomer was without English. And though he had only now bathed and changed to a suit of Madden's flannels, and therefore was not to be judged by his clothes, one knew him for what he was, a priest. His was a rarely sweet face, thin and careworn, yet with brave indomitable eyes shining out of it. Here was one who had suffered, God and his own soul alone knew how deeply, and whose frail body had come close to breaking; yet oddly enough there emanated from him a serenity like the light from a star.

This was Father Juan. Madden made haste to make him and Escobar acquainted and in a few words explained: Father Juan, in the wave of religious persecution just now sweeping across Mexico, had stood in his sequestered parish like a lone rock; false charges had been wrought against him and humiliation heaped on his white hairs; he had been imprisoned, spat upon. To save his life, everything else lost, Father Juan had taken to flight. It had been Madden's lot and the old man's good fortune that their paths crossed at a moment when the priest was about to succumb to exposure, hardship and starvation.

"I smuggled him across the border—eh, Father?—and here he is now looking like a new man," Madden declared gayly.

"You have been like a loving son to me," said Father Juan softly, a fine, firm voice bespeaking a finer and even firmer spirit. He smiled; it was a remarkable smile which softened the harsh lines of the emaciated face; it seemed, more than that, to lie across the shaded room like sunlight. "God sent you to me, I think, when my need was sorest. God be with you always, my son."

Madden inclined his head gravely, then looked up smiling.

"Of course, he can't go back to Mexico," he explained to Escobar. "There was rioting further south last week, two padres and a young nun shot. And Father Juan, at least for the present, has no taste for society. I must find a nice quiet retreat for him. And not too far away, Father," he said, and put a gentle hand on the old man's shoulder. "I'd like to see something of you."

By now Escobar understood that Father Juan had no English. It was in that tongue that he suggested carelessly:

"Another addition to your Colony of Mourners, eh, Rogue?"

Madden frowned.

"Good Lord, no! He's no gloomster, this dear old chap!"

Escobar strolled away. Madden conducted his newest guest to the library where they had a sip of wine and cigars together. Gipsy, passing through the garden, caught a glimpse of them, deep in conversation. She had seen the old man's attentive face; that face remained in her memory like a picture of one of the old masters.—A strange companion for Rogue Madden, was what she thought.

Later she saw the two going to the stables. She watched them riding off toward the north, followed by one of the Mexican ranch hands.

She did not see Madden again that day. Already it was late afternoon; he had not returned when Eloisa came to announce that supper was ready. Gipsy, her aunt and Anastasio dined together. In a word or two he explained Madden's absence; without giving details he merely told them that his friend had ridden off somewhere with an old priest. Gipsy sought to come at the missing details; Anastasio added only that the old fellow was a fugitive from persecution and that Madden had brought him home with him from his latest jaunt across the border.

Aunt Polly smothered yawns.

"My goodness!" she was forced to observe when her niece's pretty grey eyes settled solicitously on her, "it's grown mighty quiet all of a sudden. If something doesn't happen pretty soon—"

She smothered another yawn.

Escobar strove ineffectually to draw Gipsy into talk for two. He had launched upon a eulogy of the beauties of the evening in the patio when she shook her head; Aunt Polly must be got to bed—and Gipsy found herself playing her part in a duet of yawns.

"To-morrow will be another day; you'll see," prophesied Aunt Polly optimistically. "The boys are tired; that's all. They'll be rested by morning."

But she proved the poorest of prophets. From the still flowering of a lemon-yellow dawn throughout long golden hours down into the tinsel brightness of another dusk the hours slid only too smoothly by in unbroken quiet. Cameo and Johnny Bandini did not return that day; Madden was very little in evidence and, during the times when they saw him, seemed strangely silent and thoughtful. Anastasio Escobar was the most devoted of squires, yet must have felt that he did not suffice.

And this was but the precursor of other days of gentle monotony. Miss Comfort greeted each new day with bright eagerness, sure that something entertaining was going to happen. But from certainty she passed into impatience and then into a restlessness which grew intensified with the slow progress of the loitering hours.

Gipsy, taught by Jim Wynne to love horses, went on a few short rides with Don Anastasio. A dozen times it was upon her lips to bid him strike into a gallop with her across the miles and miles which thwarted her, racing for help. A dozen times she looked at him intently, trying to guess at his thoughts. Invariably she cut the ride short. She did not know whether or not she was afraid of him; why should she be? But she did know that she did not trust him. When she thought of riding out into the unknown with him, she came close to shuddering.

"I am the nervous wreck, not Aunt Polly! I'm imagining things."

Madden, having for a day or two effaced himself, turned up again not in the least like the proverbial old penny, but rather like a brand-new glittering and freshly-minted gold piece. He caught Gipsy idling under a grapevine arbour, promptly headed her off when she took the first quick step toward the house, and invited pleasantly:

"Let's go for a ride. The horses are saddled; I've got the prettiest little horse for you that you ever saw. If you like her, I'm going to make you a present of her."

Swift retort, bitter and emphatic, might have been the natural thing—say, either an hour before or an hour later. Just now she didn't feel in the least like bitter retorts. Besides, what good would one do? He'd no doubt be expecting it; it would turn aside from his easy good nature like rain drops off a turtle's back.

"I'd love to!" she said. And smiled.

Whether she surprised him or herself most will never be known. She did see that he had not expected this: her smile became a light-hearted laugh. She did not have to reassure herself that she had never been in the least fear of any physical violence from him.

"Good girl!—Obedient little Ward!" he chuckled.

She could not fight him with scornful glances and contemptuous words. She had discovered that. Well, there were other weapons in the eternal arsenal! She grew demure. That was something for him to think about. Let him make what he could of it.

Altogether they had a pleasant afternoon of it, their first pleasant hours together. He led her through many pretty places in the hills; they drank at a spring where the water trickled from a bank and overflowed a watering trough; they saw a band of quail and doves innumerable. Their way led, as they turned back, by his "Colony of Gloomsters," and he promised her a new experience if she would tarry for a moment and meet the "Marlibones." (Marlibones was a term to embrace both Agatha and her husband, Marlborough Bowen.)

They tarried not over five minutes in the bright little cottage; bright without, dismal and dreary and dirty within. Agatha and her husband, twin souls of bleakness, needed far less than five minutes for an outpouring of an incredible amount of woe. They were the sort of people who always knew that misfortune was just around the corner; they could think of nothing on earth but themselves and in terms of disaster. They never looked forward to health, but to sickness; never to life, but to death. Years ago they had bought their own coffins and kept them in a back room; Madden worked things about so that Gipsy was given a glimpse of them. And that was how the visit terminated so abruptly; she simply fled.

"What horrible people!"

—Never a word of kindness out of them; not so much as a thought directed beyond their own limited little dreary world; they squatted in the heart of a sunlit land and made a black shadow. Gratitude? A feeling of thankfulness to the hand that had put every necessity and so many a small luxury at their bony elbows? Certainly not.

"Wait until you meet the Ashton Ferribees!"

"I won't!"

But she did. The gaunt, hollow-eyed, white-whiskered old humbug calling himself Ashton Ferribee, greeted them sepulchrally. His wife, fat and greasy, and with quick furtive eyes, came hastening. Five minutes here, too, was ample. In the first minute conversation turned inevitably toward the swift-coming wrath of God, the end of the world. Ferribee chanted a half dozen of the most dire of scriptural passages; he could never see the promise in the firmament but always in his ears was the dull roar of the rising floods. His wife re-echoed everything. Gipsy Wynne was not in the least formal in taking her departure.

"There is one other of my colonists I'd like you to meet," said Madden. "A Miss Cocroft, a maiden lady who dwells suspiciously in this happy place. She is sure that the world has been inherited by villains; she knows she is being maintained here for some wicked ulterior purpose; if she were dying of thirst and a man stooped to give her a drink, she'd know he meant to pick her pocket—"

"No!" said Gipsy. "I've had enough, thanks."

"Well, then, this way," and they rode through a tiny pass in the hills where big sycamores and cottonwoods made the air cool and delightful, and emerged presently into a pleasant spot on a slope where still another cottage was. Of another sort was this one, very old and very picturesque with its time-battered adobe walls, its well and bucket, its vines and fig trees and miniature flower garden. The flower garden was a tangle of weeds, with only here and there a bright blossom or a tall victorious stalk; yet obviously someone during the last few days had been taking up the battle of the flowers, and the vainglorious weeds were already doomed to defeat. That "someone" rose from his knees behind a screen of tangled honeysuckle and stepped toward them at the sound of hoofs. It was Father Juan, smiling. Gipsy Wynne said later: "I fell in love with him at first sight."

"Life has been hard with him," whispered Madden, "and has sweetened him; just as it has been soft on my colonials, and soured 'em!—Does it always work like that?"

Nor was their stay here scarcely longer than at the other places, certainly not over ten minutes altogether. Only Spanish was spoken and Gipsy had to guess at some of the words; she fell to watching the faces of the two men. In the finely spiritual face of the old man was a shining gladness, a bright gratitude. He thanked God for his mercies, he thanked Rogue Madden as God's instrument!

Rogue Madden—God's instrument! Gipsy felt a little confused.

"He lives here all alone?" she asked at the end of the visit.

"Quite. It is his wish. He has been here only a couple of days, you know. And one of my Mexicans comes up every morning to do the chores."

"I am coming up every day, too," said Gypsy. "I'll talk Spanish with him. It's just what I need—and that dear old man doesn't require his solitude in such terrible big doses."

They rode homeward through the twilight. The dusk, like an anodyne, lay upon their spirits soothingly. Silent, they drifted. Now and then Gipsy sighed. How close to one's elbow Happiness stood at times!

"Why," she broke out passionately, startling him with her suddenness, "oh, why don't you play fair, Roger Madden? All this is so wonderful—life is so wonderful—if only you would—"

She bit her lip and fell silent again. He looked at her curiously, bending closer.

"Why don't I turn a new leaf?" he prompted when he saw that she had finished. "Make amends, start anew—and be a good boy?"

"Yes!"

"You don't believe me when I tell you the truth—"

"Be sure you do tell me the truth! Swear it is the truth—What is it?"

"I did hold you folks up—just for fun. I figured it was quite another party; I wanted to show 'em Wild West! I got away with it, just as I planned, and headed for home to hear your wild tales when you came. On my way home, another man duplicated my little trick. I was robbed. That's all."

He had never spoken quite so earnestly to her.

Their horses were so close together that her stirrup brushed his boot; despite the dusk they could see each other's eyes. Hers were intensely grave; it was always hard to be sure of his. But his voice did ring true—

At least she did ask:

"Who robbed you?"

"Toroblanco, I thought. That is why I went out and shook him down. I'm not so sure now."

"But my brooch?"

"I can't explain that! It's possible, of course, when I forked over my loot to the gentleman with the shotgun that the brooch remained in my pocket or even caught on my clothes and that I dropped it, myself, in the house. Only I don't believe it."

"What do you mean to do about it?"

"Hang it, Ward, that's what's got me guessing, too! I'm still suspicious of Toroblanco. If I hear of him, or anyone else, spending a lot of money along the border, or otherwise indicating he has fallen heir to a lot of money, I'll make him a call."

"But if you never do find out who took it? If you can never get it back?"

"Oh, don't start thinking that kind of thoughts!" he cried out in mock alarm. "I'll have to establish you at my colony, if you do!"

They were silent again when they returned to the house. Lamps and candles were burning and supper ready, as Eloisa announced on hearing them come in. A perplexed Gipsy Wynne stood drawing off her gloves; she wanted to believe what Madden had told her. She knew that he was watching her, waiting for her to speak—and so she was in no haste to lift her eyes from her gloves.

Eloisa, lingering in the room, was also waiting and at last, before Gipsy had made up a nicely balanced mind, the woman came to the end of her self-control and blurted out her news. It was about Aunt Polly: Oh, but Eloisa was worried about that lady! Mees Comfor' had been *strange!* Like an excited person all afternoon, jumping at any little noise and grabbing at anything at hand, a table or chair or Eloisa's substantial arm. She had not eaten—she had gone to bed already—at the door Eloisa had heard her making a sad little noise—

Gipsy looked alarmed and hurried away. Aunt Polly lay in the dark of her room.

"Oh, I'm quite all right, Gipsy!" she snapped, and Gipsy knew definitely now that she was quite all wrong. "If I'm a little bit nervous, who wouldn't be?—It's so quiet these last few days—so somehow *hushed* and *still!*—Better get me my medicine, my dear. I could s-c-r-e-a-m!"

Gipsy flew for the drug. She knew all the symptoms.

CHAPTER XII

What a wonderful thing it would be if even the most "far-sighted" of us could see as far as ten seconds into the future! Aunt Polly Comfort need not have experienced the slightest uneasiness about any long-drawn-out continuance of the depressing monotony which irked her. If she could have peered through a few thicknesses of adobe walls at that very moment when she confessed that she could simply "s-c-r-e-a-m!" and seen who was lifting a hand to rap for admittance, and if she could have seen in another direction some few scant hundreds of yards where certain racing figures sped through the dark, she would have scrambled out of bed forthwith, assured of a break in the doldrums. Had she been told something of that certain grey-haired, grey-imperialed gentleman who was about to enter the living-room at this moment; had someone informed her that he was known very widely across the Southwest as U.S.A. Smiley, or as Smiley Himself; had that someone read her his titles, official and popular, and told her what manner of man he was; then had it been announced that this gentleman, Smiley Himself, was taking a "vacation," and had she had the vaguest comprehension of what a vacation taken by U.S.A. Smiley might connote, she might have thought herself in the position of the sailor who whistled for a breeze and raised a hurricane.

Rogue Madden and Anastasio Escobar were going in to supper when the lively rat-a-tat-tat sounded on the door.

"Come in!" sang out Madden, and Smiley entered.

Madden stared; up shot his brows. He looked at once uncertain and a trifle apprehensive. Escobar muttered something under his breath.

"Well, well, it's Uncle Sam!" cried Madden then, and his voice was unaffectedly jovial in his greeting. The start had passed; he was glad to see the newcomer.

Uncle Sam—that was another name for this Smiley. He did look like the conventional caricatures of "Uncle Sam"; he was tall and lanky, weathered brown; sinewy; there were his white hair and little white beard; there were his deep-set, eagle eyes. Madden swore of him that he had so long been Uncle Sam's right-hand bower that he waxed gaunt and cadaverous and twin-like with him in his image.

"Hello, Rogue," said Smiley in friendly greeting from the door. "Just taking a bit of a vacation and—"

"Oh, Lord!" groaned Madden in mock-tragic tones. "Smiley-on-Vacation! Then there's to be the very devil to pay!"

Smiley was a United States marshal. Smiley-on-Vacation was Smiley unofficial; Smiley without the U.S.A.; Smiley untrammelled. The Unofficial Smiley did things which no government official on earth could hope to get away with. He exceeded all authority; "he stepped along on his own," knowing that his act could have no sanction from the government he served. If he wanted to make an illegal arrest, and there were times when nothing else satisfied him, it was Smiley-on-Vacation who did the job. If he chose to step beyond the boundaries of his province, as he often did; if, for example, he made up his mind to fare across the border and down into Mexico, where he had no business whatever, strictly and legally speaking, it was Smiley-on-Vacation who went.

"But there's someone with you," exclaimed Madden, glimpsing another figure just outside the door. "Bring him along in. We're just going to eat."

"Not with me," explained Smiley. "Don't know the gent. Some fellow who arrived just as I did. He has a letter, he says. For a Don Anastasio Escobar." The eagle eyes went, swift and sharp, to Escobar's face.

"Ah, yes, of course," said Escobar, and stepped forward hastily. He added, smiling, waving his hand: "A—a lady, you understand. *Dispensame ustedes, señores*."

He took the proffered paper; the messenger had

evidently no expectation of carrying back a reply and melted into the night.

Escobar read his letter almost at a glance. He smiled and shrugged; one gained the impression that it was a pretty little *billet-doux*, hardly important enough to a light lover. He crumpled it in his hand and moved toward the fireplace as though to burn it; the fire had burned down to a couple of black, scarcely smoking sticks. He put a hand in his pocket as though for a match. Smiley was watching him smilingly. Escobar again shrugged; he gave out another impression now, that of having attached too much importance to a mere nothing; he folded the paper carelessly and thrust it into his breast pocket.

"Uncle Sam," said Madden, "you and Escobar don't know each other. That's no business. Anastasio, my friend, shake hands with my friend, U.S.A. Smiley."

But it appeared that Escobar had scarcely time for hand-shaking. Something had touched him to the quick. He made his hasty apology. Would they excuse him a moment? He must run out after that *mozo*; there was a message to be sent back to the lady. He hurried out; they heard him running along the tiles of the corridor. A door slammed.

Madden grinned after him, then turned to Smiley.

"You old trouble-shooter!" he said genially, and

slapped a little cloud of dust out of the other's coat. "Take off your spurs, man; hang up your hat and curl up your moustaches. You're going to stay awhile.—And, to get the bad news off the books first, what brings you? What have I been doing—that you've heard about?"

"Who's your friend, Escobar?" asked Smiley, sitting down to remove the shining little spurs from his high black boots.

Madden started to tell him, and got just exactly as far as "He—" when another matter insisted sharply on their attention. It was a rifle shot; it sounded far off and was followed by another, then by a score of shots, thick and fast. The two men stared at each other; before either moved still another sound reached them. It was the rush of hoofs as a horse at a dead run came on from the south.

Madden regarded Smiley in sharp suspicion. "Some of your doings?"

"No. Don't know a thing about it. Maybe it's your friend's 'lady,' coming to shoot him up for neglecting her—"

Madden ran to a south door and jerked it open. The rider saw the orange glow of the open door and rushed straight toward it. He came down out of the saddle almost on the threshold, and was making his explanations as he dismounted. It was Johnny Bandini.

"It's Toroblanco with I don't know how many

men; he's raiding you. Cameo and I got wise. Cameo's out there. Says he'll hold 'em off ten minutes to give you a chance to dig in."

He was breathless with it. There was a further rattle of shots. Madden stared at him in amazement.

"Toroblanco on this side of the border? Raiding me on U.S. soil?"

"Toroblanco!" exclaimed Smiley musingly, and looked pleased withal.

"Good boy, Cameo!" cried Madden. "Good boy, Bandini.—Come in, man! Get the doors and shutters barred.—Shake out your hardware, Smiley-on-Vacation!—Be back in a minute—"

He broke from them, ran across the room and out at the other side. Johnny Bandini had not seen until now who this other man was.

"Smiley Himself!" he gasped. Then added expectantly: "Then you knew what was going to happen? You're ready for 'em!"

"I didn't know a thing, my son," said Smiley. "But I guess we're ready for this boy Toroblanco any time. And he's following his big nose right over here on my stamping-ground? Now that's fine!—Suppose we barricade, the way Rogue said. He'll be doing his stunt now; getting his men in or planning to protect the stables or something."

"What'll I do with my horse? Those devils will shoot him—"

“Why, bring him in,” chuckled Smiley. He was closing doors already. “There’s lots of room.”

Bandini promptly acted on the suggestion. The horse was afraid to enter, and needed coaxing; further, his legs trembled when he got a hazardous foothold on a smooth floor. But Bandini won, and the high-headed saddle horse, starting and quivering, was at last in the room.

“Cameo, you said?” asked Smiley. “Cameo Risden?”

“Yes. We were riding together, coming up here. We happened to spot the gang; they had camped, waiting for dark. We saw who they were; Cameo knew what they wanted as soon as he saw Toroblanco. He made me ride ahead; he’s down there where there’s a gully in the hills, and a lot of cottonwoods.—Damn it,” he cried excitedly, “if they get old Cameo—”

“If they get Cameo Risden,” grunted U.S.A. Smiley, “it’ll be the first time anybody ever did get him, remember that, kid.”

But already Bandini’s thoughts had fled far afield.

“Where are Aunt Polly and Miss Wynne?” he asked anxiously. “If it comes on to a fight—”

“Who the devil are Aunt Polly and Miss Wynne? I thought this was Rogue Madden’s place!”

“They must be in some other part of the house—”

"Cameo got a rifle?"

The firing was faster, hotter than ever. Bandini nodded.

"Yes. That's his now; the one sounding loudest; he's nearest us—"

"He'll come riding, any minute, hell-for-leather, with the mob at his heels," mused Smiley. "Here—keep this door open; the one you came in at. It's your job, kid, to get it shut the minute he's in; the bullets will come trailing him like a swarm of hornets."

Noises grew louder. They heard Madden shouting; he was out by the stable. Other voices joined his.

"I wish we'd brought Curly along," moaned Bandini, "and Long Corbin and Joe Quince and—"

"*And* a regiment of cavalry," snorted Smiley. "While you're wishing, young fellow, why not go the whole hog? Don't cost any more."

"I wouldn't care, if it wasn't for the ladies—"

"Who are these dames?" grunted Smiley. "And—Good boy, Madden! He's set fire to the straw pile out by the barn. If these wild Injuns get promiscuous 'round the stables we'll pop 'em over in the firelight like nailing shingles."

"He's coming back, Rogue is. He's got four or five men, anyhow—"

"Sh! Listen! It's Cameo coming. Stand by the door, kid. Slam it when he comes in."

Madden, with three men at his heels, came running in from the patio. From the south hoofs rushed on toward the house. The sounds of firing burst out again, accompanied by a rumbling thunder as of many horses running, a thunder growing steadily louder.

"I see him!" cried Bandini, and ran to stand in the wide-open door. "Come on, Cameo!—*Cameo—*"

But Cameo Risden, having held the fort as long as he estimated that was the proper thing to do, now needed no coaxing to come along. On a big dark bay horse that looked ink-black in the outer night, stooped low over his saddle-horn and riding, as Smiley had prophesied, "hell-for-leather," he rode into the yard. Nor did he pause to dismount until the door was safely closed behind him—which is to say, only after his horse had shot through, sliding stiff-leggedly across the tiled floor and leaving long deep grooves to last as long as the floor itself might last.

"Fine business, Cameo, old boy!"

It was Madden shouting joyously. But both he and the gambler were immediately ignored for a new sound and another presence only now revealed in a doorway. There stood Aunt Polly, her eyes dancing, her fit of nerves gone, as she clapped her hands delightedly. She had heard the shouts and shots and slamming doors; she had scrambled into a dressing-gown, and had been just in time to see a man ride a horse into the house! Now with two horses, Bandini's and Cameo's, in a room with armed men, with guns firing outside and voices thunderous in menace, shrill in imprecation, and out in the yard a great fire blazing so merrily-bright, Aunt Polly fairly thrilled.

At Aunt Polly's side was Gipsy, her face white, her eyes frightened. What a contrast they made, Gipsy so tense and anxious, Aunt Polly beaming so innocently!

The strangest look imaginable came over the face of U.S.A. Smiley. Smiley Himself had not the least inkling of any explanation; he saw a little wisp of fragile womanhood clapping her hands as one does when carried away by enthusiastic approval at the theatre; clapping her hands and laughing while, as far as Smiley could see, there was "the very devil afoot."

Rogue Madden burst into that utterly mad laugh of his. He saw Smiley looking at Aunt Polly, read Aunt Polly's thought, and as bullets tore splinters in the massive door, his own amazing sense of humour threatened to send him into convulsions.—In a moment they would be driving off Toroblanco's pack of curs, their tails between their legs. Now the moment was laughter's own.

"They're crazy! Simply *crazy,* these two!" cried Gipsy Wynne.

At such a moment Rogue Madden simply couldn't believe in death riding on a bullet. Life was the thing, and it bulked big and joyous and invulnerable. He saw Smiley and Aunt Polly looking at each other; he performed a rollicking introduction, while even Cameo Risden stared at him. And at the end, to please Aunt Polly, he cried out:

"None other than United States Marshal Smiley! A great man; they don't make 'em any greater. An old war-horse, hero of a hundred gun-fights, scourge of the lawless, terror of the wicked from end to end of the border—Smiley Himself!"

Aunt Polly smiled wisely. As though that sort of talk would take her in! The tall, pleasant-looking man with the white hair and little imperial, was just a dear, rather shy, likeable old baby of a man. She had set Cameo down as a banker; this Mr. Smiley would turn out to be a librarian; something like that.

Firing outside ceased abruptly. Men in the house regarded one another thoughtfully. Even Madden, after his one outburst, became thoroughly businesslike.

"They'll surround the house," he said gravely. "They'll want to make out what my fire out there is for. They'd set the barns, if they got a half chance—Say! Where's Anastasio?"

"He chased after that messenger boy," Smiley reminded him. "The one who brought the love note. Guess we've locked him outside."

"He's caught between the house and those devils! Stand ready, a man at every door. If he calls, yank the door open for him and get it shut in a hurry again."

He ran to Aunt Polly and Gipsy, commanding them into a place of some safety; into a corner, thrusting them down into a couple of big, low chairs behind the barricade of a davenport. Gipsy tried to speak but could not. Aunt Polly patted his hand, whispering up to him:

"Rogue Madden, it's the most lifelike thing I ever saw!"

A ragged volley of firing drowned her final words. At the far end of the room a half-shutter had been left ajar; a bullet tore through, scattering bright clinking fragments of glass. Aunt Polly's smile became uncertain. She looked startled.

"Rogue!" she whispered, "one of the men is using real bullets! You don't think there is any danger, do you?"

While Madden groped for an answer and before anyone could close the shutter, a second bullet brought a second shower of glass splinters, and went on its way, imbedding itself with a vicious thud in the adobe wall near the fireplace. Aunt

Polly shrank down in her chair and was visibly shocked.

"My! That *is* dangerous, Rogue Madden!—Aren't you boys overdoing it?"

In a stifled voice Madden could only mutter:

"Some bird out there didn't change to blanks—"

"And he won't know, and will—"

"Oh, he'll know all right.—You see, as soon as he fired those two shots, he realized that they had lead on the front end of 'em."

Aunt Polly shook her head.

"He might not know—"

Madden looked at Gipsy. She was pale and her lips were compressed; a shiver shook her as though it had grown cold in here.

"That man ought to be told!" insisted Aunt Polly. "You boys get so reckless sometimes. If one of you should get hurt—"

Madden went close to a shuttered window and shouted at the top of his voice:

"Hey, you birds out there! One of you is using real bullets. Better be careful. You might hurt somebody!"

Aunt Polly nodded approvingly. To Gipsy, in a side whisper, she said:

"The two horses, in here! That is the most realistic touch of all!—*Now,* what do you suppose they are plotting?"

Gipsy could only moan inarticulately. At

every moment she expected to see some man in the room topple over, shot through the heart. The men had grouped about Madden; he was whispering hurriedly, giving his orders. Those who had rifles, and most had, scattered and left the room by the three doors which opened into other parts of the house. Johnny Bandini and a young ranch hand who looked like a Swede, remained with the two women. Each of them had a revolver in his hand.

"It's—it's all r-right," stammered Bandini, tremendously excited yet equally eager and, except for a nervous tremor now and then, almost as cool-looking as he would have liked to appear. "We'll have 'em on the run in two shakes. With men like Rogue—and Cameo—and Smiley Himself!—Whew! Guess old Toroblanco picked the wrong night! He'd never have tried it on, only he thought to catch Rogue pretty much alone."

"Can't we peek at what they're doing—" whispered Aunt Polly.

"Rogue said we were to tie you up, if you started to budge from your chair," said Bandini earnestly.

"Oh, you heavy villains!—Tell me, Johnny, who *is* that Mr. Smiley?"

"Rogue told you. United States marshal, and the hardest man to go up against that any tough crowd along the border ever tackled. He's—"

"He's most likely a darling old book-worm. There's a man in our public library—"

"Smiley Himself—a book-worm! Oh, Lord!" cried Bandini.

Stumbling along through dark rooms, headed toward a small shadowy door at the west end of the house, Madden demanded of Cameo:

"How many men do you think Toroblanco has with him?"

"I'd say not over a dozen or so. He didn't look for your being ready for him. We ought to make monkeys of them, Rogue."

"Sure. Slow now. There's a low wall yonder; see it? Now! Run for it!"

The two stooped and ran. The fire at the straw pile was blazing high by now, lighting up the outbuildings, barns and corrals. Dim, distant blurs were Toroblanco's men. Madden and Cameo stood straight and began firing.

Smiley joined them.

"They're keeping off behind the barns, Rogue. If you've got any stock in them—"

But Rogue Madden was off at a run. He had at least a dozen head of the very finest in horseflesh in his stables; horses that were infinitely more than just horseflesh to him. It could not possibly fail to suggest itself to such as Toroblanco to fire the barns.

By the time Madden had covered two-thirds

of the open space between house and stables bullets were raising little puffs of dust about his feet. He felt a bit of gravel flick him on the hand and for a moment thought that they had hit him; he raced on, not daring to stop and return their fire. From behind him came the sharp, quick reports of Cameo's and Smiley's rifles; he'd have to let them do his shooting for him. Conscious of bullets swarming all about him he thanked his stars that there were better shots on earth than the raggedy ruffians who thus far were so consistently missing him, and also that night-shooting ever presented difficulties. It was with a deep breath of relief that he plunged into the fragment of darkness of the stable.

He heard horses stirring nervously in their stalls; at the sound of every shot they tried to break free. He ran straight on to the ladder-steps leading up into the loft, went up it with a rush and floundered and groped his way to the high window under the rear gable. From an out-thrust beam depended the block and tackle used for drawing bales of hay into the loft; he grasped the rope to steady himself and looked out and down.

What he saw informed him that if he had not come too late at least he had arrived barely in the nick of time. There were several dark figures below, busied close to the wall; the flares of two matches lighted simultaneously left him in no doubt as to their purpose: One man was setting fire to a hastily improvised torch of a wisp of dry hay; another was igniting a spill of paper which gleamed snowy white; a third was scattering armfuls of hay along the wall.

As Madden's roar of rage sent the dim figures scurrying, the fire which they had set began to run through the scattered hay. Madden whipped his rifle forward and let them have it; he had the grim satisfaction of hearing one of the running men let out a wild yell, and saw the figure stumble and fall and then go running crookedly off into the darkness. He let the man go, being more concerned just then with what lay below; already the flames were licking at the stable. He caught the dangling rope again, slipped out through the window and slid to the ground. Though now he presented a target which even Toroblanco's riflemen ought not to miss he leaped upon the fire, trampling and scattering it with his boots, kicking it away from the stable. He heard many voices yelling, was sharply conscious of a scattering of shots and of bullets whining about him. With the fire almost out, the last wisp of burning hay kicked away, he was all for getting under cover again and had made his first running step when a bullet stung him. He kept on running, turned the corner of the barn and threw himself down behind a watering-trough for barricade, eager and anxious to return as hot lead as they sent him—praying for just one good glimpse somewhere of Toroblanco himself.

In a sudden lull he sought his wound; a bullet had grazed him only, scarcely more than burning a two-inch shallow furrow along his left forearm. He grunted as he touched the place gingerly, then concerned himself again with the raiders. As he lifted his head he heard the shrill blast of Toroblanco's whistle; and though the sound came from a safe distance and even the direction was hard to gauge, he somewhat relieved his feelings by pouring several shots toward the spot where he imagined Toroblanco sitting on his white horse and directing the attack. After the whistle was still, voices shouted again, for such as straggled at Toroblanco's heels could do nothing, either set on or retreat, without a storm of whoops and jeers. As the sound of voices died away there was a scurry of hoofs, sounding in many directions, but gradually pouring themselves into one rush of sound which swiftly grew fainter with every thud. Toroblanco's band was going as it had come, like a storm wind heading south.

Madden pulled off his coat, found his slight wound bleeding freely and bound it up as best he could with a handkerchief—all for Aunt Polly's sake! Later iodine and a clean bandage, but he had no desire to return to the house bearing visible evidence that one of the boys who had forgotten to change to blank cartridges had done the very thing she feared.

From thinking of Aunt Polly it was no great step to Gipsy Wynne; he recalled just how she had looked at Smiley when she had been told that he was a United States marshal! There had been no trouble in reading her thought: The first thing Miss Gipsy Wynne would do would be put herself under that official's protection and demand to be conducted elsewhere—and Rogue Madden didn't want her to go! He would never see her again and all her life long she would hold him to be a thief, brawler, highwayman and villain in general.

As Cameo and Smiley came running, Rogue Madden said earnestly:

"Look here, Smiley; this Aunt Polly of ours—"

"Never saw such a woman in my life!" cried Smiley enthusiastically. "She never turned a hair!"

Madden hearkened a moment to the rumble of running horses, already grown faint in the distance.

"I wish we could ride it out with those night hawks," he said regretfully. "No use, I suppose, with the head start they've already got—"

"Let 'em go this trip," said Smiley. "Their time is coming. What about your Aunt Polly?"

Madden explained that gentle soul's serene conviction that everything was a huge joke, informing an amazed Smiley that she was in reality a nervous wreck, and that if she should come to realize what she had actually lived through—Well, she'd simply curl up and die.

At first Smiley, knowing Rogue Madden's proclivities as well as he did, was chary of giving credence.

"You're stringing me, Rogue!"

But as Rogue grew even more earnest and when Cameo Risden spoke up and sustained him, Smiley scratched his head and said, "Well, I'm damned!" and then laughed.

Madden pondered; again his thoughts embraced Gipsy Wynne and her unspoken determination to ride out of his life under the aegis offered by a government official. He'd see about that! He spoke up swiftly, dwelling on Aunt Polly, thinking of Gipsy.

"Look here, Smiley: Aunt Polly wouldn't believe for a minute that you were a U.S. marshal; she's so dead sure that everything I tell her is something to build melodrama on. We've got to handle that little woman with gloves, see? The first inkling of the truth would bowl her over. So let her think that she was right as usual and that I was trying to fool her about you. Let her think you're a—oh, anything humdrum and harmless and everyday and peaceful—a retired druggist or a bee farmer or a botanist or—"

"Oh, all right, all right.—By the way, Rogue, what has happened to your little pal, Anastasio Escobar?"

Madden started. He had forgotten Anastasio! A

quick fear pricked him that Anastasio had been caught between the two fires.

But when they gave up looking and calling and went back to the house they found Escobar there; he had crept around to a side door and Johnny Bandini had let him in.

"Catch up with your messenger?" asked Smiley.

"No," said Escobar with a shrug. "He must have taken to his heels when the shooting started."

Rogue Madden had paid them scant attention; he was watching Gipsy and noting how eagerly she was watching Smiley. Aunt Polly laughingly joined the group. She beamed upon the replica of Uncle Sam.

"So you're a United States marshal?" she bantered.

Smiley played his part.

"Oh, this Rogue of ours must always have his little joke," he laughed back at her. "Now, if I told you that I am a rum-runner operating the swellest saloon, dance hall and gambling den on the border, what would you think then?"

"Oh!" said Gipsy under her breath.

And Rogue Madden, despite a twinge in his arm, was inclined to be surer than ever that his life-long contention was grounded on the very bedrock of truth: "This world of ours was the best of all possible worlds."

CHAPTER XIII

"You and this Toroblanco party seem to have met up before, Rogue. I wish you'd tell me all you can about him."

Smiley, having asked the question, considered the growing ash of an after-breakfast cigar. Rogue Madden considered Smiley.

"Interested particularly in Toroblanco?"

"I'm on vacation, you know," said Smiley. "At such times I can allow myself to be interested in anything."

"Oh, to be sure! You and your vacations!—I'm almost sorry for poor old Toroblanco. He's a rum old duffer, and all that; but I haven't made life all nice and happy for him, and here you go asking questions about him.—By the way, Uncle Sam, do you know that when you first showed up I was dead sure you were after me for something."

"Maybe I am. What should it be for?" ended Smiley sharply.

Madden laughed at him for his ingenuousness.

"How should I know? A man does things now and then which the minions of the law think he shouldn't; then he forgets all about them, getting wound up to do something else he shouldn't. But the minions, old boy, don't forget, do they?"

"No," said Smiley curiously, "they don't

forget. Now suppose you spin me the yarn; tell me absolutely everything you know about Toroblanco."

So Madden told the tale. Smiley stopped him here and there along the pathway of his recital, putting shrewd questions which brought enlargements upon various points. Matters which Madden might have ignored were suggested to him by Smiley's astute promptings. Thus, even Toroblanco's offer to buy the south ranch at a ridiculously low figure was mentioned.

Smiley appeared more interested than ever; even the marvel of an inordinately long ash could not hold his attention.

"A letter from Toroblanco, eh? Haven't happened to save that letter, have you?"

"I don't think so; don't know. Hanged if I remember what I did with it. Important to you? Well, it's just barely possible I stuffed it into my pocket."

"Go look for it, Rogue. If you'll find it and bring it to me, I'll promise to go bail for you first time you're in jail."

Madden went to his room, rummaged and came back with the crumpled, pencil-written letter. Smiley accepted it with an expression of expectancy. He read it so carefully that he seemed in fact to study every single word, letter by letter. At last he put it down on the table and took another scrap of paper from his pocket. This one was folded neatly and he unfolded it with the gentlest of fingers. It bore all visible evidence of having had quite other and ruder treatment before now; it was torn and ragged and was trimmed in black charred edges.

"The old sleuth is hot after clues," grinned Madden. "Grabbed somebody's papers out of the fire, eh?"

Smiley, quite leisurely about the whole business, at last folded the two papers and put them safely away in an inner pocket.

"Let's go take a ride, Rogue," he said curtly, standing up.

"Which way? How soon will we be back?"

"Who am I to prophesy? In two or three hours maybe, and maybe never. A man can't tell, can he, whether he's good for another sixty years or sixty seconds? I sometimes think that helps making it all worthwhile.—Anyway, it won't do any harm to stick a gun in your pocket."

"On our way, Uncle Sam! Only, if you can scare up any excitement on any dinky little ride that will bring us back in two or three hours—well, you're an ace high little finder, that's all."

He was surprised by a steady look of inquiry which he received. What a curious look in old U.S.A. Smiley's eyes! And suddenly, when Smiley put two hands on his shoulders, gripping him tight, and stared at him so intently, Madden was more surprised than ever.

"Hello! What's up, Uncle Sam?"

"I wonder!" Smiley muttered. "I wonder.—Look here, Rogue, you idiot; answer me something. Just exactly how deep in this dirty game have you gone? Are you in the slime up to your neck, or just your bootheels?"

"If I only had the faintest suspicion of what you mean," grinned Madden.

But Smiley was of no mood for grinning and cut him short, grown severe and harsh of voice.

"Chop that stuff out, Rogue! You know what I'm here for!"

He dropped his hands and Madden, as though relieved of their weight, shrugged his freed shoulders. He kept on smiling, but there was a noticeable narrowing of his eyes.

"What game?" he asked evasively. "I've generally got two or three games running along together, you know. Just which one?"

"How about the hill ranch adjoining you on the east?" snapped Smiley. "The one with the high fence around it?"

"So that's it, is it?"

"Tell me about it."

"What shall I tell?" Madden's eyes narrowed again; all assumption of jesting was abandoned as he grew watchful and guarded.

"It belongs to you, doesn't it?"

"Well"—he began to weigh each word—"what about it, Uncle Sam?"

"Will you answer a question or two, or not?" Smiley was sharper than ever and a glint of anger brightened his eyes. The two men stared at each other soberly a moment before Madden said drawlingly:

"Why don't you add the usual fair-warning gag: 'Anything that you say will be used against you'?"

"Rogue, you're an infernal rascal and a dam'-fool idiot, and I swear I don't know whether to jam you in the pen or the bug-house. That's a fact."

"And so you invite me on a little ride! To find out?"

"Come ahead," snorted Smiley. "Only don't tell anybody where we're going. Is that a promise, Rogue?"

Madden began rolling his cigarette. He spilled his tobacco slowly into the brown paper, caught the yellow strings of the muslin bag between his teeth, drawing it tight very deliberately. He rolled the wheat straw into a pretty little cylinder, and licked the free edge; he tucked in one end of his completed cigarette as tenderly as ever mother tucked in babe for its slumber. Only after he had projected a big opalescent ring of smoke and had watched it spread and vanish in a shaft of morning sunlight, did he speak.

"It's a promise," he said, and went for hat and revolver.

They went out and Madden called to a stable boy to saddle the horses. Smiley strolled through the corral and to the back of the barn; as he turned a corner Madden saw him studying the ground. He was interested in the spot where last night there had been the attempt to set the fire.

"Sleuthing some more," chuckled Madden. But he grew grave-faced again on the instant. "He's a white old Injun," he mused. "Wonder how bad things might happen to be?"

The stable boy wanted a word with him and he nodded and went to hear the tale that was to be told him. His brows lifted as he listened. He went on into the stable; for some interested minutes he stood examining a certain sorrel, yellow-maned and tailed. It was a clean-limbed high-headed horse; a horse for a horse-fancier to look at approvingly. Incidentally, it was an animal which did not belong to the Madden ranch.

Madden remained grave. What the boy had to tell him, added to what was already tumbling over in his busy brain, augmented his gravity. And then all of a sudden, simply because even through the dark skies of his preoccupation there shot a mad inspiration like a streak of lightning, his eyes cleared.

"Where's Smiley's horse?" he asked, hardly above a whisper.

The boy, wondering at him, pointed to a far, dim stall. Madden hurried to it, regarded

Smiley's mount critically, then called out loudly:

"Rode your horse pretty hard yesterday, didn't you, Smiley?"

"Hard enough," came Smiley's voice, dull with lack of interest since his thoughts were elsewhere. "Why?"

"I'll lend you another for our ride."

"Maybe I'll not be coming right back. I may not blow in on you for two-three days; can't be sure," said Smiley, and moved along, step by step, busied with his thoughts and investigations. His look was such as might have been that of a man who told himself that he might at any moment pick up a diamond—and quite as possibly might not.

"Which way do you think you might be going?" asked Madden, hoping that it would be toward the northwest, knowing that all directions were possible, and ever ready to hope for what he wanted, no matter how "long" a shot it might be. And how those long shots did have a way of galloping home for Rogue Madden! A look of devilish glee sprang up into his eyes when Smiley replied carelessly:

"Up toward the Zack Burtonshaw place, likely. They're newcomers; don't know 'em personally, and would like to. Why so keen an interest, son?"

"I'm going to lend you another horse, that's all. You can leave your hard-ridden, wind-broke, spavined plug here until you come back."

It was all one to Smiley; or rather he thought that it was. So, mounted on the sorrel trimmed in golden yellow, he rode off with Rogue Madden, all unsuspicious of anything in the least out of the way.

When they came to the high fence and its gate like a barricade with the three big padlocks, Madden sat reflectively sideways in his saddle and asked his question:

"Just what do you think you're looking for over there, Uncle Sam?"

Smiley countered with a curt:

"Do you own the place or don't you?"

As before Madden hesitated. His answer, slow in coming, was scarcely any answer at all:

"What if I said that in a way I do—and in a way I don't?"

Smiley's hard eyes brightened.

"Aha! Well, that's good news, Rogue. I think I know what you mean, and why you pull back so hard in the traces. You bought the place, of course? The deed stands in your name?"

"Let me not contradict any county courthouse records."

Smiley snorted and after the snort spoke somewhat waspishly:

"But you bought for someone else! Another man came to you and gave you a cock-and-bull story that nobody but an idiot would fall for, and you fell for it! He handed you the money to do the buying with—I'll make you a nice little bet, Rogue Madden! Ten to one, the odds will be!"

Madden never looked less like caring to place a bet. His voice roughened as he demanded as sharply as Smiley had spoken:

"What are you driving at?"

"He gave you the money, a nice lump sum to buy a lot of good-for-nothing land back there—and for his own reasons he didn't hand you a check. Neither his own nor any other man's. He went out and got the cash and forked it over to you. And how's that for a guess, my boy?"

"Maybe you're right and maybe you're wrong." Madden shrugged with a fine assumption of indifference. "You're still the great little guesser, hey, Smiley?"

"Final question," Smiley rasped out. "Who is this jasper that has made a sucker of you? Spill me the gent's name, Rogue."

"You can go chase yourself," Madden told him promptly.

Smiley laughed unpleasantly.

"Which, in the most inelegant of parlance, means to inform me that he's a friend of yours? Of course. I knew that at the jump. You'd do any dam'-fool thing for a friend, wouldn't you? And you've got more 'friends,' as you call 'em, than any man I know. You are just about as bright at times, my son, as a cotton-tail that runs out to play with a lot of coyotes."

"I'm going back." Madden gathered up his reins. "You can go ahead alone; there's nothing I can do about that, but I'm not in the party, thanks."

But Smiley was of another mind and spoke to the point.

"No, you don't! If I have to, I'll throw a gun on you and run you in! Put you under arrest, that's what I'll do. Until all this mess that you've helped stir up blows over, maybe the best place for you would be inside a good jail, anyhow. It's about the only place I could put you and feel reasonably sure you'd be out of mischief for a spell."

Madden stared at him curiously.

"You'd run me in? That's a wild blazer, Smiley. You've no charge—"

"Accessory, my boy, if nothing worse. Accessory before, during and after the fact! How's that strike you?"

"And the fact itself?"

"Come ahead. Let's go see."

They rode along the fence for a mile, left their horses in a steep-banked gully and came to a spot where evidently Smiley had been before.

"It's a million-dollar enterprise," said Smiley, not without grim approval. "This fence itself cost something, didn't it? Comes as near being man-proof as any I ever saw.—Guess you know why I don't cut the wires, don't you, Sweet Innocence?" he chuckled.

"Hanged if I do. You don't seem to mind trespassing!"

"Nary. But I don't like monkeying with other men's wires. I don't put it beyond this friend of yours to have his own little electric light plant stuck away back there in the hills. Cut a wire and flash a signal that visitors are coming?"

"Don't miss much, do you, Smiley?"

"Here's where we go in," said Smiley. "This way is used, I've the hunch, more than the noble gateway."

He slid down into a gully, dragged at a couple of boulders placed in its bed under the barbed wire, scooped out handfuls of sand and gravel and wriggled through. Madden, though obviously of no stomach for the venture, was constrained to follow him. Ahead of them was a brushy hollow with a deep ravine beyond, into which led a dim trail.

"Pretty game for you to be messed up in," said Smiley disgustedly. Madden made no reply.

Their trail wound this way and that to avoid the spiked blades of cactus, and in a secret and furtive way all its own, to seek out the tallest patches of brush, whether sage, mesquite, or chaparral. What individuality a trail may have; what tales it whispers! It may be the purposeful maze trod out by deer; the straight pathway, man-made, from cabin to spring; the tinier runways of the little fellows dashing wildly from security through the open and back to security. Here, underfoot, was a highway of concealment, with something sinister about it, even when the sun flooded it.

"Tell me," said Smiley sternly, as he came to a sudden halt and pointed down a slope, "did you know about *that?*"

Madden's gasp of astonishment answered better than words. No, Madden had not known.

They had come to a vantage point, slinking along the final few steps as furtively as any that had trod the way before them. From a boulder-strewn ridge, themselves hidden behind boulders, they looked down a steep slope and into a tiny, harsh, hot valley. Down there was a cluster of several buildings grouped about a well, thinly veiled in the grey shade of a half-dozen dusty cottonwoods. The buildings, scarcely worthy the name, were ugly affairs set up in the swiftest, easiest way, crazy frameworks under dirty canvas, one long, low shanty, the others small and square.

In a group under the cottonwoods were half a dozen saddled horses, all but one of them with a rider up. That one was a beautiful white stallion, a pawing, teeth-bared, snapping devil, its frothy activities at the moment held in check by two horsemen, one at each side. The sun flashed on this animal's ornamental trappings of silvered bit, silvered headstall and rich Mexican saddle. Its master was even now approaching. He came out from one of the little square houses, walking with a wide swagger, his broad sombrero cocked at the ultimate tilt of arrogance. As far as one could see him he was to be recognized as the chest-inflated Colonel Don Carlos Toroblanco. Smiley, watching his companion out of the corner of his eye, saw Madden's start of surprise.

"And you didn't even know who your own pardners were!" jeered Smiley.

Rogue Madden stared incredulously.

"You're crazy! That's Toroblanco!"

"I know it. Tell me something I don't know: just what, for example, a man would find inside those shacks."

A perplexed Rogue Madden made no answer. Smiley regarded him shrewdly.

"It's your land, Rogue. The deed is recorded in your name. And you don't care to talk about it?"

"What have I to say?" grunted Madden, and stirred uneasily. "You know as much about it all as I do. More, maybe."

"A great deal more, maybe. I wonder?—You're hardly the man, are you, Rogue," he said with swift alteration of tone, a bitter sharpness in his words, "to make a pardner of the man that killed your own dad?"

Madden gripped him by the arm.

"My God, man! Toroblanco? You know?"

"Toroblanco—or another. What's the difference? He's one of this outfit. One of your friends!"

"It's Toroblanco! I'll get that—"

"Toroblanco—or another. I know. I could tell you. I will tell you—when the time comes. If it ever does come."

"Damn you, Smiley, you'll tell me now!" cried Madden hotly.

"Don't get gay with your Uncle Smiley," he was told curtly. "If you want any favours out of me you'd better come across with a few yourself. We're going to stick around a bit; we'll squat in a nice shady place and have a chat."

"You're of a mind to let that devil ride off?" demanded Madden, amazed. "You could pull him for raiding on U.S. territory last night. You could—"

"Oh, shut up!" snapped Smiley impatiently. "Don't go telling me what I could do. What do you suppose I'm on vacation for? Watch 'em. There they go, Toroblanco on the big white horse, as good as a clown at the circus, leading 'em off northwest into the big cañon. H'm."

Madden watched the small cavalcade ride away into a shadowy ravine where presently they were hidden by a brushy shoulder of the hills. He drew a deep breath, then turned smouldering eyes upon the white-haired man at his side.

"I'm riding back to the house," he said, and was

curiously eager. "And I can't tell you a thing."

Smiley, never looking so innocent, sighed and asked in the most resigned of tones:

"Some day, maybe? When do you figure you might be able to open up, Rogue? In exchange for what little news I might have?"

"I don't know—maybe to-day—"

"Aha!" flashed out Smiley, triumphant. "And now I know!"

"Well, I'm on my way."

"Not back to the house, though. Come along with me to the horses. We'll get 'em watered and hid; we'll take a flask and a couple pounds jerky off my saddle; we'll spend a day in the hills.—And by midnight, if not earlier, you'll be grabbing hold of me to tell me all you know."

But Rogue Madden, still with that eager look in his eyes, said sharply:

"I've got to go back home, I tell you."

Smiley laughed softly.

"No use, my son. He did the big sneak long before sun-up. You might find a little note from him, explaining something or other. But he's up and away!"

"He?" said Madden. "Who? What are you driving at, Smiley?"

"Driving straight ahead, by glory! Who's *he?* Why, your little playmate; the gent that gets love letters by fast messenger, just as your other pardners swarm in for a raid across the border!

Your precious Anastasio Escobar, that's who!"

"What's Anastasio got to do with anything here?" demanded Madden with a little grunt.

"What's a cat got to do with cream? But maybe before the day slides by I can show you two-three things. Anyway, when it gets good and dark."

There were other things than flask and dried beef tied to Smiley's saddle strings. He carried them with him when he led the way up another ridge and into a patch of shade. Here a man could stretch out at his leisure upon the thick dry grass; from here he could keep an eye on the camp in the little valley.

Smiley opened up a small packet. It was flat, the size of a book. The string removed, he revealed four sizeable bits of cardboard which placed together nicely on a flat stone, edge to edge, became a checkerboard.

"Sit in, Rogue; I'll beat you four games out of five. Say, it's a great day, hey, boy? I've been looking forward to a day like this. I'll bet you we can play a hundred games before we even have to budge."

Madden bristled and demanded explosively:

"You mean to squat and play checkers at a time like this?"

"Aw, shucks, Rogue," expostulated U.S.A. Smiley with a smile which was rarely winning, when one considered what a crooked little smile it was, “can’t you make allowances for a man taking a vacation?”

Smiley Himself on vacation was Smiley untrammelled, Smiley like a mountain lion, crouching for his spring.

Madden subsided. They played checkers.

CHAPTER XIV

The day was one of mystification for Rogue Madden. Before he sat down to the interminable checker games he tried doggedly and all in vain to reconcile what he had seen with what he had already known. All that he succeeded in doing was to build up fresh puzzles for himself. A score of times the merciless Smiley had to force his attention to the obvious move.

What a devil's own medley resulted from the things which he had known and the thing he began to glimpse! He pondered his own father's death down in Sonora, his back to a wall, his fearless and scornful eyes upon a squad of the scum of the earth, and asked himself: "Toroblanco?—or another?" He had had Toroblanco in his own hands, had him twice at his mercy! Was it Toroblanco?

He saw distant figures down in the miniature valley during that endless day, many of them, twenty or forty or perhaps fifty. Chinese, and others. Now and again Smiley studied them through his binoculars; when Madden put out an impatient hand, Smiley only shook his head. Madden would see what he would see when he saw it. They were waiting for night.

Men departed into the hills; at times returned

mounted; at times rode back into the hills along the trail up which Toroblanco had vanished. Smiley watched them with placid interest, twisted at his small white beard and returned his bright gaze to the checkerboard. Madden resumed his fruitless speculation, striving to make some meaningful patchwork of dissociated fragments. It was the task of fitting puzzle blocks together, the pattern itself missing. The questions which did burst from him, Smiley simply and pointedly ignored.

"Getting dark," said Smiley, just before time for the world to come to an end. "Let's step, Rogue."

Madden leaped up, all eagerness. Smiley led the way, going guardedly as they moved down the slopes and drew nearer the cluster of canvas-covered buildings.

"You asked once why I supposed this place wasn't better guarded," he said, offering a first explanation. "Because I fixed things that way. A man blew in here before day, if I'm not mistaken, telling the boss of this outfit that one Smiley was off on the wrong scent and would be a good hundred miles from here by now."

"Fox," grunted Madden. "Also you're a great boy to answer a question when I've forgotten all about it and am interested in something else."

"This way," commanded his guide in a whisper.

It was dark down in the hollow with nowhere

so much as a gleam of light. If there were candles or lamps within the canvas enclosures, not even the glow showed on the grey walls. Shaded lights behind blanketed walls spelled furtiveness and secrecy.

Smiley moved along unhesitatingly. They came close enough to one long, low shelter to hear voices inside in a murmurous babble. Smiley went on. He approached one of the small square huts and stopped, listening; he went straight on again and stopped at its door. Catching his companion's arm, urging him toward haste and quiet, he jerked the door open. The two stepped into a dim, candle-lighted interior and Smiley closed the flimsy door with a backward thrust of his heel.

"Hello, Bennie," he said softly.

Bennie looked up as they came in, ferret-eyed. Madden knew who he was: Bennie the Rabbit. He just missed being an albino, a thin, anaemic man with a wisp of yellow hair in his eyes. His was a face often seen in Nacional; where the dregs of earth settle there are always the dregs of those dregs, such as Bennie the Rabbit.

His red-lidded eyes darted by Smiley to probe at Smiley's companion.

"Who's this bird?" he asked fretfully. "I thought you was comin' all alone."

He spoke in a thin, reedy voice. He had been sitting listlessly on the edge of a bunk of tumbled, befouled blankets, but got up now and went for cigarettes to a box serving as a table.

Smiley, adept at ignoring questions, passed over Bennie's now.

"Word came that I was off to the east?" he asked instead.

Bennie nodded and glowered morosely.

"Yeah. That dirty bum—"

"We'll have no names, if you please," he was interrupted sharply, and again Bennie stared inquisitively at Madden.

"Oh, I don't give a damn. Say, I'm broke again, Cap."

Smiley might have been ready for this. His hand was in his pocket and brought out a couple of banknotes which he dropped on the box. Bennie flashed his eyes greedily over them.

"You're a good guy!" He stuffed them into his pocket, gave a queer hitch to his narrow shoulders and grew eager. Already the money was burning holes in his pocket. "Ready when you are, Cap. Raidin' to-night?"

"Not to-night, Bennie. Just taking a little look around. You've got things fixed?"

"Trust me." Bennie leered at him. "And you picked a reg'lar night, I'll say! They's a bunch comin' from Zack—"

"Good," cut in Smiley. "Suppose we get busy."

Bennie stooped and blew out his candle. The door opened; his thin figure appeared in the dim rectangle, vanishing promptly. Smiley and Madden followed at his heels.

He led the way back among the huts and to the larger building. He scuttled by a door; they hastened after him. At that moment the door opened. Even doors here were furtive, opening softly, closed so swiftly and silently that one was scarcely certain they had moved. Someone had slipped out of the door, and demanded harshly, though in an undertone:

"Who's that?"

Bennie answered in his characteristic voice, half whining and half snarling:

"It's me. Bennie. What's it to you, Blodgett?"

Blodgett cursed softly and went on his way. Bennie, too, went about his own affairs. At the rear of the big canvas shanty he stopped.

"Here you are," he whispered into Smiley's ear. "Look; you work it this way—"

Near the corner a seam in the canvas had been opened into a slit six inches long. If interested in what went on within, you pulled the separated edges slightly apart and placed your eye at the spy-hole. Having finished, you had but to release the canvas and it fell into place sufficiently closely to keep its secret from any but a thoroughly searching investigation.

"The walls is hung with blankets inside," ran on Bennie in his dry whisper. "I burned a couple of holes to match. Now I'm gunna fade."

"Beat it," said Smiley. He caught Madden's arm, pulling him close. "Want the first peep, son?"

"I'm nobody's damned gum-shoe," said Madden under his breath. "You and your Paul Pry business—"

"Ssshh, you idiot!" Smiley applied his own eye to the opening, then put his lips close to Madden's ear to inquire: "Think you know what's inside, don't you?"

"Yes—and it's none of my business."

"A herd of Chinks? Just smuggled over the border? Eh? Well, look!"

A "herd" of smuggled Chinese, of course. What else? He could hear them talking, couldn't he? Could hear other voices, those of border Mexicans, too. Of course. Just then the door opened and closed again. Smiley had returned to his vantage point, but quitted it almost immediately and clutched Madden again.

"You will look, my boy! Here comes the Resident Boss! And it's not the man you think, at all. And I'll tell you this: It's somebody you don't know, but the minute you see—Well, you'll know who it is; and maybe you'll begin to see what a goat you've been."

As Madden stooped to the slit in the canvas wall a sudden voice startled him, for it was a woman's voice, and who would look for a woman here? It was a lilting, pure-toned, musically pleasant voice—and the tone was the only thing pure about it.

What Madden saw, ignoring the other occupants of the room, was a border celebrity. Though it was the first time he had ever seen her he knew who she was on the instant. She was still young and her features, the actual physical features themselves, were rarely and arrestingly beautiful. Yet the impression one had of her was anything but beautiful.

She cried out her obscene greetings to the roomful of Chinamen and half-breeds, and stood still, her hands on her hips. She was as striking and colourful as a richly-hued snake, a small, slight, graceful figure theatrically garbed in a trim, black velvet jacket, a short black velvet skirt, gleaming high patent leather boots, with a small turban of black velvet on her head, sparkling with rhinestones. About her waist, hidden under the loose jacket excepting in front, was a broad yellow belt or sash, and one knew, if ever he had heard of Black Velvet Jess—and from more than one police blotter her name had gone into more than one newspaper—that the jacket also hid an automatic pistol which she knew how to use.

"Come away," whispered Madden queerly. "Tell me what the devil is afoot here."

"You've answered it: it's just that. The devil is afoot here making him a fine hell-brew."

There were a score of men in the long room. Bennie the Rabbit came in even now. Chinamen, most of them, men who spoke little of any tongue other than their own, but seemed earnestly bent on picking up English. With these was a sprinkling of border types including four or five Americans; not a face among these latter that was not rank with its besetting vice. From the moment Madden had seen Bennie, he guessed what that vice was; from the instant he realized that Black Velvet Jess was here, he knew.

There were cards in the room, and bottles; nothing more natural. But there were other things: bunks along the walls, an atmosphere thick with a sweet stickiness.

Madden moved away, perplexed, disturbed. A moment later Smiley joined him, muttering thoughtfully:

"It's a big game, Rogue. You don't glimpse the half of it. Those coolies are paying five hundred bucks apiece to get scattered over the States. Two-fifty down, to be landed across the border at this detention camp; the other two-fifty at the end of the trail. Figure a business of five hundred Chinks a year; tidy huh?"

"I knew about the Chinks—"

Smiley grunted.

"So you knew that much, did you?"

"Well, I guessed, then. Just the same as knew." He shrugged indifferently. It had been none of his affair. Smuggling went on all the while; it was the concern of the fellows who went in for that sort of thing, theirs and the government's.

"Come ahead, Rogue. There's something else."

They groped their way across the floor of the little valley for a couple of hundred yards where they stopped under an oak. Here, presently, they were joined by Bennie, demanding whiningly:

"Get an eyeful?"

"Lead the way, Bennie. To the other dump."

Bennie led along a trail that wound deep into a ravine. They followed him, but with fifty paces intervening. That was Smiley's precaution. Once on the way Bennie met someone coming down-trail; he stopped the man in parley; Smiley and Madden slipped out of the trail and waited for the man to go on by.

"Here's the place," said Bennie, when they came up with him.

It was another canvas shelter, aloof, hidden; round like a circus tent. Through a hole prepared for them they looked into a big bare room. There were a small bar at one side, a couple of rude tables, half a dozen chairs. A pine floor glimmered under candle shavings used in lieu of wax.

"They're coming along pretty quick, I tell you," said Bennie, anxious to be off. "About a dozen this time, I think. Black Velvet Jess will be takin' care of 'em." He indulged in his dry, whispering laugh. "Don't know who they are, Cap, or where they come from. They use cars on the main road as far as Burtonshaw's, you know; ponies into the hills. Just a bunch of kids. Great sport for a moonlight night, heh?"

"Fade out, Bennie," commanded Smiley.

"Kids?" muttered Madden. "What's the hop-head mean?"

"Quite a big game, quite a big game," sighed Smiley, not without admiration. "Ever see a trail of ants get into the kitchen, Rogue? Sugar or sweets at the end of it. Trail of Chinks? Dope. That's where the pretty part of the game comes in. If it was only smuggling those darned heathens—"

"It's opium they're smuggling!"

"Well, there's money in it. Didn't I say this was a million-dollar outfit? Take that theatrical jane back there; she never shot nickels in her life, boy.—Look how nicely everything runs: They smuggle the Chinks here; hold 'em; teach 'em, by gravy! It's a regular school. They learn enough English to get 'em by; they learn to speak their pieces, too, naming American towns, American bosses they've worked for. And they bring the hop. That's about half of it. The other half? There's that crowd of fool kids coming in to-night for a party! How many of 'em will cops all over the Southwest be running in next year for every crime you can think of from larceny to murder? Oh, it's a school all right, where they teach a lot more than English as she is spoke!"

"A school for addicts?" exclaimed Madden, and a little ripple of disgust ran through him. "Good God, Smiley—"

"You named it." And Smiley chose to laugh softly. "Run by you and your friends! Something to be proud of. A finishing school with degrees given by such as Bennie the Rabbit and Velvet Jess. Management, Rogue Madden, Toroblanco, *et als*."

"I did not know that Toroblanco had anything to do with it! I tell you, man—"

"You took his money, didn't you?" snapped Smiley. "The money that bought this land?"

"No! Not Toroblanco's money—"

There was a note of mockery in Smiley's voice as he demanded:

"Sure, Rogue? Another man handed it to you, of course. Gave a pretty good explanation how he got it. Rather big sum for him, wasn't it? But you believed him?"

Instead of doing anything to relieve Madden of his perplexities, Smiley was only augmenting them.

"Look here, Smiley. I happen to know that—Well, the man for whom I did buy this place is no friend of Toroblanco's at all. Quite the reverse."

"Since when?" sneered Smiley.

"Since—Why, since a certain night not very

long ago!—What are you doing about all this? Raiding to-night, after all?"

"The two of us? Against all this mob?"

"We'd come pretty close to cleaning up on the whole crowd of 'em—the way I happen to feel right now!"

"From what I know of you," grunted Smiley, his tone more kindly than his words themselves, "I'd advise that whenever you get a hunch to do a thing, you turn square 'round and do the opposite!—*Ssshh!*"

Quiet voices and scarcely audible footsteps sounded on the trail, not far off, approaching from the long, low building. As voices and steps came closer Smiley drew Madden after him, backward, into deeper dark. The voices were those of Bennie, who had gone back toward the hollow, and of Black Velvet Jess.

"What's the big idea? What's eatin' you, Velvet?" that half whine, half snarl of Bennie's demanded.

"I'm worried, Bennie," answered her voice, almost cloyingly sweet. "Worried about you! You've been acting sort of funny. I have noticed and Blodgett says so, too. I have been wondering—"

"Blodgett?" sneered Bennie. "Dam' fool, Blodgett. He's full o' hop—"

"Where'd you get all your money, Bennie?"

"Whaja mean? What money?" The sudden

shrilling of his voice was like a vocal spasm of terror.

Bennie's scream broke short off as a confusion of sounds came from the dark trail: trampling as Bennie, a moment too slow, tried to leap away, a blow and a sibilant breath accompanying the physical effort, a gurgling moan, further trampling of feet and a heavy fall. Madden would have sprung forward but Smiley's two hands gripped him and dragged him back.

Stillness settled again over the dim trail. One of the darkest of the shadows stirred and resolved itself into a woman in black velvet, stooping over something on the ground. What Madden could not see his electrified thoughts pictured horribly. Velvet Jess carried a knife as well as automatic pistol under that little soft jacket of hers; she used one as skillfully as the other. A knife had served now. She stooped, wiped the blade clean and drifted soundlessly away through the darkness, returning to the hollow.

"You'd stand back and let her get away with murder?" gasped Madden.

"Yes! We had no chance to stop her; it came too quick. She's smart, that woman. I warned Bennie to look out for her. Well, her time's coming, so you needn't—"

A shrill cry cut through his words like a bugle note. It was Black Velvet Jess screaming out in a clear-noted voice which carried far across the hills:

"The bulls! Up by the dance hall! They just knifed Bennie the Rabbit!—Tumble out, you boys! We got to get 'em. There are only two or three. Come a-running!"

"Damn cat!" muttered Smiley disgustedly. "She can see in the dark! Quick now, Rogue, or we're done for."

He sprang away, running round the dance "hall." Madden leaped after him. But, while Smiley ran on, Madden stopped a moment. He struck a match and set the avid little flame to a ragged fringe of canvas. Those "kids" would go without their party to-night.

The fire caught hungrily and went soaring aloft in bright hot plumes, spreading a ruddy light among the shadows of the ravine. Smiley called Madden a fool, yet waited for him. Together the two plunged into a thicket, and after them came a lively spattering of rifle and pistol balls.

CHAPTER XV

There were hours during the days which followed when the Little Blue Devils had it pretty much their own way at this Rancho of Joyous Guard. That brood of gloom plied their trade with a will; they fanned sulphurous fires with their own hot breaths; with sharp cloven hoofs they trod their lugubrious trails. Spiketail and sharp little horn were busy and Rogue Madden cursed his own folly and himself for a fool.

To the rhetorical question, "Ain't Nature grand?" there is but the one answer: "Sure she is!" She has more laws than the United States themselves; at times she appears no whit more proficient in having them enforced; but always, in the end, she can sit back smugly and see the punishments meted out and the refractory brought sharply to heel. Hers that infinite patience which counts a million years as no more than a split second on Johnny Bandini's stop watch. "Whatever goes up must come down," says this Grande Dame. "My laws of gravitation make it so." And whether it be the pyramids, the oldest *sempervirens* or the newest Empire building, we may be sure that in time it will come down. And she adds platitudinously, yet none the less forcefully, "The higher they climb, the harder they fall," which is a way of saying, "The more they defy me now, the harder they'll be spanked for it later on." Or, as they voice it in the laboratories, "Action and reaction are equal and opposite." Or, finally and at last pertinently, "When a rollicking, gay-hearted rascal like Rogue Madden does have the blues, he has 'em *bad.*"

He began with naming himself a fool, and growled: "That makes it unanimous!" A fool not to have his eyes opened long ago, or rather, the greater fool in that they had been open, yet he had refused to use them to see with. From his expedition with U.S.A. Smiley he returned home raging—and seeking Anastasio Escobar. But Escobar had betaken himself elsewhere; there remained not even a pencilled note to say where or why.

Long ago Escobar had come to him with a tale which, from a friend, was to be swallowed whole. Rogue Madden, where he gave his ever-ready friendship, gave that which should invariably accompany it, loyalty to the uttermost. Escobar had handed him the money, cash, as the astute Smiley had opined. He had said: "I have debts at the moment; financial worries. Given time, I'll be all right. But if I am known to possess property, my creditors will pounce upon it. Buy this land for me, my friend; let it remain recorded in your name. Later, when the clouds blow over, I'll assume ownership."

What did Anastasio want with the land? Madden did not sit up into the small hours bothering himself about that. There was where his loyalty stood solidly on the basis of friendship. It was no affair of his. He guessed, of course; in his heart he knew a part of the game. Escobar came and went, visiting him frequently, now at one ranch, now at the other. At the southern ranch Madden had known at times that his outbuildings were used over night by Escobar; he had heard Chinese gibberings and had glimpsed Chinese faces. Smuggling, of course, but it was Anastasio's business, Anastasio's and that of Mexico and the United States. Certainly not Rogue Madden's. Was it any concern of his if Cameo Risden as a professional gambler satisfied himself with his own queer codes, lining his pockets with other men's money, come at through various means? Cameo was a friend. Did it concern him how Johnny Bandini disported himself at the border race tracks? If, as recently, Bandini and the border authorities were at odds, Rogue Madden merely welcomed a friend to tarry and find sanctuary under his roof as long as it suited that friend. Nearly every man who constituted a unit in that gay entourage of his was in some degree a law-breaker. That never troubled him in the least, provided they were merry devils. He was no Cain, but he did subscribe to the doctrine that he was not his brother's policeman.

He and Smiley had had a narrow time of it after Velvet Jess screamed and men poured out like a swarm of angry bees, and bullets began to whistle. But the dark was friendly, the brush thick in the ravine, and their legs long and dependable. They took to headlong flight as naturally as deer when the hounds open. A couple of hours later they came back circuitously to their horses. And such was Madden's tardily stirred concern that he forgot all about it being the sorrel horse with the yellow trimmings which he had forced on Smiley.

"No," said Smiley to his invitation to come back to the ranch house overnight. "Vacation only comes just so often, you know, old kid, and I've got a lot to cram into this one. I'll bend around through the night on a little ride-and-go-see, and will drop in on you later during the week or next week, maybe. So-long."

"But we've scattered your Chinks and the rest of the lay-out," Madden reminded him. "That nest'll be empty by daylight."

"Oh, never mind. I'll pull in those birds any time now. And those are all small fry, all except Black Velvet Jess. And it's the tall guys I'm after. So long."

Could Rogue Madden have yanked a sleeping Anastasio out of bed, there would have been an accounting that night. Opium in whatever form was a loathsome thing with no place in Madden's scheme of life. He had an imagination; it had been stirred by what they came upon in the dark hollow. Smiley, out of a full stock of knowledge, had told him things which made healthy flesh crawl. Smuggling Chinese was one thing; Madden could consider a thing like that a huge joke. It was good, clean fun. But the land locked away behind the high fence constituted something vastly more serious than a mere detention pen for undesirable aliens. It was a school of vice in which Bennie the Rabbit and Velvet Jess had been the instructors. It is said that one addict makes a dozen; Bennie and Jess made addicts by the hundred. They operated cunningly between supply and demand: They helped increase the supply; they helped increase the demand. They befouled with the slime of the white fiend the very marrow of a lot of adventurous, hare-brained young fools.

Did Don Anastasio Escobar know? Madden meant to ask him, and to look straight into his eyes while he had an answer. But Anastasio had betaken himself elsewhere. Why? What the hot haste?

Another consideration arose from the presence of Toroblanco at the detention camp. What did he there, swaggering?

Smiley had dropped so many unexplained fragments. "In partnership with the man who shot your own dad!" Was that Toroblanco? Smiley knew, and would not tell. There was that scrap of paper with the charred edges; Smiley had been so eager, so triumphant when he compared it with Toroblanco's writing. And that amazing offer from Toroblanco to buy his big ranch for a comic song! What lay under such folly? Even Cameo Risden had sensed something sinister, when Madden had been content to say, "The man is crazy," and forget it.

The evening's adventure had been far from pleasant to Rogue Madden; he slept little that night and arose the next morning to accuse himself, as Smiley had put it, of having been an accessory before, during and after the fact. And the "fact" itself, as he now could see it, was no gentlemanly thing. He was in for a moody morning.

The Grande Dame aforementioned, having bided her time in her characteristic patience, took her own malicious glee now in being in a position of "I told you so" satisfaction. "The higher they climb, the harder they fall." "Action and reaction are equal and opposite." "The gay dog, when he does have the blues, has 'em of the deepest indigo." Gipsy Wynne, for some reason of her own or for no reason at all, was as crisp this morning as new-starched linen. She had a way of looking at a man, Madden discovered for the first time, which had the effect of setting him off by himself at some enormous distance, and on a level infinitely far below the plane indicated by the soles of her shoes. She could have done pretty nearly anything with him in this mood of his; had she created the tiny opening he would have burst through it like a clown through a paper hoop, all tumbling eagerness to confess his sins, shortcomings and general idiocies. But with a glance and a flick of her curly eyelashes she banished him to another planet.

Across that yawning chasm he regarded her bleakly. There never was a girl like her: he saw that now quite clearly, when he should have seen it the night he took it on himself to hold her up at the point of a gun and rob her! He had locked her in her room! He had tricked her into remaining, when he had allowed the Yorkes and Tommy Burton to go. He had commanded her obedience! He had sworn that he was going to teach her to call him "Papa!" Oh, Lord!

Well, he had kept her, a sort of prisoner, at first just for fun, later because he dared not have her go running around, telling what she knew and ultimately because he wanted her near him. What if he opened his hand and let her go now? What did a released bird do when offered liberty? It experienced a moment of bewilderment, finding it hard to realize that it was free. Then with a swift dart, a rising into the free air, a gleam of sunshine on fleet wings, your bird was gone. You stared foolishly after it, thinking, "It will come back to me." But you knew better. It was gone for good.

He and Gipsy Wynne should have been friends from the outset; son and daughter of old friends, it was the natural thing. But he had set to work so swiftly and energetically to dig a gulf between them. To let her go now was to see her vanish on the far side of his chasm. To hold her was to widen the abyss.

He saw her laughing and talking with Johnny Bandini, who, it suddenly dawned on him, was not worthy of sharing the same earth with her. Savage impulses awakened in him; he wanted to kick Johnny Bandini over the moon. He'd like to have that impudent young scallywag doing his silly tricks far out in interstellar spaces.

"Time was when I was a happy man," groaned Madden.

Time was when it was a fancy with him that each new day was another little blue box opened by Aurora playing at Pandora's game. Only Aurora had been the better of the two at the business, spilling out a thousand bright-winged, laughing creatures to one with a sting. But now the gift boxes were no longer that dazzling celestial blue; a darker, dingier, muggier shade altogether. Better if they had been kept under lock and key.

He was briefly, though ashamedly, grateful when Cameo Risden took Johnny Bandini away with him. Where they went Madden did not press them to tell; to Nacional for a game, perhaps. The two had of late grown to be great friends. Fine. Joy be with them—in Nacional or elsewhere.

He turned toward Gipsy. But she looked the other way. Frankly she admitted that she regretted the departure of Cameo and Bandini; she missed them, Johnny Bandini particularly; he was a perfect dear. Madden asked her to ride with him; she elected to ride alone. She wanted to visit the old priest. For Father Juan must be lonely and so was she. And she would practise Spanish with him.

Madden turned toward Aunt Polly. She was the busiest person ever imagined. She had a hundred letters to write; she wrote volumes, it would seem, to her brother Sam alone.

"Go play with Gip," she ordered, and seemed utterly blind to Gipsy's aloofness. "I'm busy."

He went instead to visit Father Juan. Gipsy had paid her call in the morning; he made his in the afternoon. The old man was serene; used to the bludgeonings of adversity, he had learned quiet thankfulness for present peace. He worked in his little garden, making it orderly, creating of its tangles a pleasant place to loiter and muse. He had a bench under an olive tree where he read from the two precious volumes which he had saved and brought with him into this exile. The birds grew tame in his garden; he said that they talked with him. He watered his roses and they took on new vigour.

He and Rogue Madden smoked together,

indulged in long silences—and talked about Gipsy Wynne. Father Juan was teaching her Spanish. He remarked how quick and bright and friendly she was, and Madden fell to frowning. She was, said Father Juan, like his birds that came to preen in his garden and to scatter their soft-noted songs through the cooler parts of his days—and Madden sighed.

Rogue Madden had once maintained, not altogether in jest, that when a man's spirits were so low that nothing else would revivify them, a visit with his Gloomsters was sure to fan the vital spark back to life. From Father Juan's little cottage, he rode straight to his Colony of Mourners. Agatha and Marlborough Bowen were on their front porch as usual, Agatha rocking dispiritedly, Marlborough sagging against the post which sustained the bright roof overhead, both steeped in customary doleful dejection. Madden dismounted, tied his horse at the fence and came to the steps, sitting where he could see both of them.

"Well, how's everything to-day?" he asked. He knew what he was about, putting a question like that. It was equivalent to jerking the props out from under a pall of gloom, bringing it down on his head. He invited it.

It came. Marlborough made the responses, Agatha echoed him right along in a crooning monotone of misery. Everything was very bad indeed. Marlborough went into detail. He harped on but one string and ever had. Yet that string was as dependable as ever, as good as a new one; better, seasoned with age. It was growing dusk; these two "Marlibones" made the hour their own, dolorous and dreary. Palpable exudations seemed to ooze forth from them and to pervade the sunless end of the day. Marlborough, had he been a melancholy poet instead of merely a sad humbug, could have written a poem worth ten of "The City of Dreadful Night." His dismal croakings went on and on; Agatha's crooning echoes were a perfect aid in a sheer triumph of the lugubrious. After five minutes of this Rogue Madden knew full well that he should have leaped to his feet and gone charging away, shouting with laughter. What the deuce had come over him? There was nothing funny in the Marlibones at all now. That bad taste in his mouth was still there. He ought to laugh, and he sighed instead. He wandered away to call on the Ashton Ferribees.

"How's the world using you folks?" he asked recklessly, jerking out another set of props.

Down on his head came the insecurely sustained burden. Speak here of the world, speak of the end of the world. The dawning of the day of wrath was almost upon them. The Ferribees wrung their bony hands; they plunged the deeper dusk into black midnight. And Madden wondered why the mischief he couldn't laugh at them.

He rode away. To have played his system out to the bitter end he should have dropped in on Miss Cocroft and heard from her lips the tale of wickedness growing on every hand like green bay trees, but he hadn't the heart.

"I ought to go home and drink ninety-nine bottles of brandy. But it wouldn't cheer a man like me and probably would send me tearing around, cutting everybody's throat."

He had a few words with Aunt Polly. She was as cheery as any cricket; he vowed she was getting fat! But she was preoccupied strangely; she said, "Gipsy's in the library," and went humming about her own affairs.

"Mind if I come in?" he said from the library door.

Gipsy looked up in what seemed a deep abstraction.

"Why, of course—I have found something so interesting here!—"

To ignore him would have been pointed, so she did not ignore him. She even smiled faintly, that mechanical sort of smile which only assures the one on whom it flickers like cold winter sunshine, that she who smiles is thinking of something else. Gipsy was being what Aunt Polly called a minx. She withdrew into her book; the covers of it were big formidable gates through which she passed like a princess in a fairy tale entering the iron castle, leaving the ogre outside.

Madden slumped down into a big chair at the far end of the room. Gipsy's face was brightly illuminated by her reading lamp, Madden's in scowling shadows. The book in her hands was a great, big unwieldy volume which looked dry-as-dust and no doubt was. Yet Gipsy, not in the least overdoing her expression of interest, seemed absorbed.

On the long library table there was the usual litter of books and magazines. Madden took up a volume at random; it chanced to be a history of California. He had been reading interestedly in the annals of that romantic state when last living alone here; Bancroft and Hittel occupied a major part of the table, left undisturbed all this while. As he had made his selection at random, so did he let the pages flutter as they listed. He was thinking not at all of Californian history; what had he to do now with the spacious days of the Spanish dons?

Gipsy, in her role of minx, knew perfectly what was going on. She had a much better conception, for example, of what was passing through Rogue Madden's mind than of what lay on the printed page before her deceitful eyes. Here was a very impertinent, presumptuous and masterful young man reduced, and at least partially through her efforts, to the very ground floor of humility. No one, excepting of course her Aunt Polly, could have guessed that Gipsy was not absorbed in her reading. Yet she missed nothing of her companion's lack-lustre expression or of his drooping listlessness. She could almost have found it in her heart to be sorry for him! Almost, mind you.

She even knew when his vacant eye remained a long time on a single page, that it was not that his interest was snared; only that he had not the ambition to turn another page. Thus she knew, too, when of a sudden a group of words sprang out at him; when, despite himself and herself and his defeat and her victory, his mind was all without any warning riveted; when he began to read with a queer, intent eagerness. Gipsy frowned. In a flash tables were turned. She stirred restlessly. It looked as though, if she weren't quick about it, it was going to be too late for her to be sorry for a young man abashed and humiliated!

Rogue Madden came to his feet with a bound, tossing his big volume up to strike the ceiling, catching it "as catch can," sending it with a disrespectful flip to the table. There was no need for her to look to see what book it was; she had known all along. But she couldn't imagine what in the world he could have read in a history of California to affect him like this. His eyes were dancing; from the look in them you would have sworn that here was a man who had never in a merry life known what the Blue Devils were. For the first time in days she heard that care-free, devil-may-care laugh she knew so well.

Gipsy stood by her guns. Which is to say, she lifted her brows and went on pretending to read.

He caught up his hat and sped away. A quick halt and turn in the doorway tricked her. Their eyes met, hers with wonder in them and a hint of honest disappointment before she could lower them.

"It's a long worm that has no turning!" he announced breezily if enigmatically, and tarried only long enough to mock her with a deep bow. Then he was off and away; she heard him laughing down the long corridor.

Of a sudden Gipsy, who had been so serene and content, felt lonely. She went questing Aunt Polly, who was quite non-sympathetic.

"Go and play with Rogue Madden," was her advice. "I'm busy."

Rogue Madden, too, was busy. Happy also, one would have said. Action and reaction again. He came up like a rubber ball. He began his mornings noisily. He sang cheerily and tunelessly in his bath; he breakfasted alone and early; he hurried off to the stable and his horse. Where he rode, what kept him away so long, Gipsy with all her astuteness had not the vaguest idea. Aunt Polly, the more perspicacious of the two at this crisis, vowed he was up to mischief again. Each day Gipsy, taking her lesson in Spanish, spent her hour with one who could have explained much. But Father Juan, humouring Madden and mildly pleased with their game, was pledged to secrecy.

Gipsy even went again and again to that particular volume of California history, hoping to hit upon a clue. She knew about what part of the book he had been reading when his idea exploded; she sought it with that patience she could command, and that was not great. She started guiltily and put the book down at every step.

Madden had read how a rascally American had whiled away his time by teaching a guileless old Spanish priest to speak English! And here he found an occasion made for his hand.

"It will help pass the time for you, Father," he said innocently. "Think, too, what a surprise it is going to be to Miss Wynne!"

Father Juan was delighted and agreed it would be fun to surprise his pupil in Spanish. Some day soon, so wholeheartedly did he give himself to his labours, he would burst upon her astonished ears with a whole fusillade of her own tongue.

Madden, who should have been ashamed, and who did often enough have the grace to be ashamed long after he had accomplished an outstanding bit of nonsense, set to work with a will to teach his pupil a considerable vocabulary of the wrong words. He took his text from the pages he had read. The two planned together on the first speeches which Father Juan was to make to Gipsy Wynne.

"It's a dirty trick I'm playing on you, old boy," grinned Madden, saying the words in English and meeting Father Juan's candid eyes with equal candour. "But you're a good old sport, and after it's all over you'll laugh at it yourself!"

Father Juan asked him to interpret, to remember that not yet could he understand when one used such big words and spoke so rapidly. Madden interpreted—liberally.

Father Juan learned that the English words Little Goose meant Charming Young Lady. He learned many other quaint and curious things.

The bright particular afternoon came tripping along promptly. Rogue Madden was no man to wait. Father Juan glowed. Madden hid behind a rose hedge. Gipsy Wynne strove to bring her mind to her task.

She saw Father Juan beaming at her. She knew that he was about to say something important. And it was still so difficult for her to grasp the meanings of Spanish words.

"Hot dog, Leetle Gooze!" said Father Juan.

He had looked for surprise. He saw amazement stamp itself on her expressive face. Father Juan chuckled softly.

"Why—why, you talk English!" exclaimed Gipsy, not knowing what else to say.

He laughed out in his delight. He made a little gesture.

"You haf fonny nose, Leetle Gooze!" he told her gallantly. He was very distinct in his enunciation, striving with each new word.

"Father Juan!"

Nothing was to be made of such an expression as froze upon her face, unless one had the right clue. Father Juan made amazed gratification of it. He quite failed to see the horror. For he thought that he had said, "You honour me by coming to see me, Charming Miss."

Father Juan arranged his new words, made sure of having them in order, and spoke on with his most ingenuous smile:

"A girl ees jus' seely monkey, no? You, Leetle Gooze, jus' seely monkey! You make me laff, Fonny Face!"

Gipsy gasped and looked wildly about her. Father Juan swelled with pride. This surprise event was turning out to be whatever a benevolent old priest would have termed, in his own phraseology, a "knock out."

He extended his arms dramatically; happiness radiated from him. Gipsy backed a couple of paces away from him.

The atrocious old wretch! Pretending all this long time that he couldn't speak a word of English, then bursting through all barriers of ordinary conventional decency like this!

Gipsy was hard beset for once in her life to find her tongue. In the old man's guilelessness, in his winning smile, in his clear eyes she read the exact reverse of all that shone so serenely there. An old reprobate, she suddenly saw him; a humbug and a—a cheat. Above all, an insulting old fool!

With that she found her tongue and blazed out at him. She did not for an instant consider it as a possibility that he did not understand all that she said. Luckily for him, he caught never a single word. But he did see from her face that something had gone wrong.

Gipsy whirled and fled. But even as she ran to her horse she listened to sounds behind her. Father Juan was talking excitedly, in Spanish now. Who was with him? The garden had been empty. She looked back wonderingly and made a significant discovery: There, only half hidden by the rose hedge, was Rogue Madden, contending with smothered laughter, like a man in some terrible convulsion.

And at last there burst out that irrepressible, utterly-maddening laughter of his! She bit her lips and hurried on to her horse. This, then, was some more of his doing. She did not understand yet just what it was, but one thing she did know. She put it forcefully into words; not for the first time, but never so hotly as now:

"Oh, the beast! I hate him."

CHAPTER XVI

Aunt Polly Comfort, as later on was clear enough to both Madden and Gipsy when they had time from their own affairs to give to a consideration of her, had walked in mystery. Had not both of the two young people been so deep in their own preoccupations, they must have seen all along how she went about enwrapped in the veriest trappings of secrecy and furtiveness. Aunt Polly, imbued with what she fondly thought to be the "spirit of the West," was at every moment of the day deliciously atingle with expectation. "Something was going to happen." Always something was about to happen. She thought that really she had never known any individual as easy to deceive as these Westerners appeared to think that all Easterners must be. Was all her sophistication to go for naught? Couldn't she *feel* something in the air? These quiet days, what were they but an interim of preparation?

Added to her zest was a high degree of curiosity together with a newborn desire to be a part of whatever was going on. The element of surprise was not necessary to her enjoyment; besides, there could be no complete surprise now that she knew so positively that they were preparing a new bit of entertainment. And she even fancied that as soon as she was in a position to glimpse an explanation of what was afoot she might find an opportunity to take a hand herself. What a lark if she could somehow manage an added surprise all her own and play the delightful game of surprise the surprise party!

Anything was fair in a game of this sort. Listen at the keyholes if you could. But there were no keyholes at this hacienda of Joyous Guard; old-fashioned latches and bolts and bars only. And also there were no opportunities at eavesdropping to yield her any results.

But during these last few days she had had the satisfaction of coming several times on men talking quietly, and of seeing how they grew silent when aware of her presence. She had seen that tall old gentleman whom they called U.S.A. Smiley and Rogue Madden together, talking so earnestly. A U.S. marshal! Ridiculous; it made her laugh. Then his second lame explanation; proprietor of dance and gambling halls! What colossal fibbers men did grow to be out here.

These two rode away early one morning. They breakfasted alone and were simple enough to fancy that the household slept! Aunt Polly was wide awake, up and about. She watched the way they went. She went out to the stable and told a stable boy that she wanted a ride in the early morning. The old buggy was brought out, the gentle mare harnessed and away drove Aunt Polly in the wake of the plotters.

She was far in the rear; the two riders had galloped and she had progressed at the slowest imaginable trot. But from a little knoll she caught a glimpse of them just as they rode down into a distant hollow and learned that they had gone straight to the high and mysterious fence. They were away all day and until late in the night; she heard Madden return.

What was it that was hidden behind that fence? What on earth could it be? There was not another fence like it on the ranch. She had never forgotten how Gipsy had been positive that she had seen someone hiding beyond it; someone who looked like Wong Fu, their childlike old cook at home. Other figures, too, Gipsy had thought; Chinamen, two or three of them.

Cloaked in her amazing innocence, Aunt Polly would as soon have thought of being afraid of a pet rabbit as of Wong Fu or any that resembled him. She bided her time, chose her opportunity and went forth upon an expedition of investigation. She marked how Rogue Madden and Gipsy deported themselves; she smiled knowingly and was richly content. She did not doubt for a minute that they had fallen in love the instant that they had looked into each other's eyes. Now Madden grew sombre because Gipsy teased; and Gipsy teased on because Madden grew sombre; and neither had eyes for Aunt Polly.

And so it happened that while Father Juan was astounding one of these young people and convulsing the other, Aunt Polly was hastening with horse and buggy back to that tantalizing and most intriguing high fence. Having already reconnoitred, she lost no time in making her entrance. The rocks which Smiley had rolled away in the gully had not been replaced. Aunt Polly crawled through, dusted her skirt with her grey-gloved hands, and went forward along the zigzag trail, beaming and eager.

The very spirit of that trail, secret and stealthy, became Aunt Polly's guiding spirit. She crept along silently; she hid in clumps of mesquite; she listened to the hush about her and went on cautiously. For it was her part to see and not be seen; to find the way to have her own joke on the joker.

She had on stout walking shoes; the sun was not a bit too hot; every step of the way she enjoyed herself. From the top of the hill just ahead she was going to see something; she was sure of that. Just what? Piquancy lay in the uncertainty. But at any rate she recalled the poetic lines about Cortez on his peak of Darien.

"A town!" exclaimed Aunt Polly. "Right here!—I might have known!"

But when she looked again she realized that

it was no town after all, but only a strange little group of huts looking lost and quite deserted among the hills. No smoke ascended from any stove pipe nor was there a sign of anyone going about. Just a few little houses looking to be fast asleep in the warm sunshine. But pretty, she thought, with their walls painted a greyish white which took on a silver tone.

"The town itself must be the next hill. And this, I suppose, is a sort of suburban outskirts."

She waited and watched until she grew impatient, yet no door opened, no dog barked, no horse appeared and no single individual put in an expected appearance. So Aunt Polly found the trail which led on down into the hollow, and continued her investigations.

"Goodness! It feels lonesome out here!" she admitted to herself.

But she went on untroubled and quite blithe. She made out that the greyish white walls were only canvas. She discovered the one long building and, passing by a couple of the smaller ones, approached it wonderingly. It did seem entirely deserted. The door was open; she stood looking into the bleak interior.

"What untidy things men are," was her natural comment.

Here and there an abandoned quilt trailed from a bunk; boxes which had served as chairs were scattered all over the place; strewn across a rude table top and on the floor were cards, broken glass, butts of cigarettes, match ends by the score.

"They've *been* here," murmured Aunt Polly. "Plotting their mischief."

Her first impulse, quite instinctive, was to set the place to rights for them. But a moment's reflection made her see that she would really have an almost impossible task; besides there was no broom. It would have been fun to have everything in order; they would wonder, when they came back. Or would they even notice? Men and boys, boy-men like these, were such unnoticing animals.

While she stood there dallying with her thoughts she thought that she heard voices. She grew rigid, turned her head slowly and even held her mouth open to hear better. Voices without a doubt! But where?

Why, in one of the further cunning little houses! She drew away from the larger building and went tiptoeing through the sunshine, guardedly approaching the hut from which the sounds came. As the voices grew louder a smile played about her lips; she gave herself whole-heartedly and in bright anticipation to her eavesdropping. Step by step she drew steadily nearer until at last she could hear perfectly—

And then a shadow crept over her face and darkened all that anticipatory shining brightness in her eyes. The two men in one of the huts were speaking Spanish, and when Aunt Polly had said, *Buenas dias*, and *Gracias*, she had exhausted her Spanish vocabulary.

Now that was quite too bad, she thought, and the shadow on her face concentrated in the little deepening furrow between her brows. But though this was a blow to her hopes, no single blow need ever connote defeat to the determined. At least she would make out who it was plotting here behind that enchanting fence.

Heavy, sullen, downright ugly tones rolled on like pigmy thunder housed up in distant caverns. One man was doing most of the talking; he seemed earnest and rather savage about it, too. Aunt Polly was astute enough to realize that it was just as well that she, being a gentle lady, did not fully understand.

"Shocking," she thought, yet was not unduly concerned since she did *not* understand. "I imagine they don't mind being rough, off by themselves like this."

Where one voice ended the other picked the thought up. She started. Well, here was discovery. The second speaker was that darkly handsome, really devilish-in-a-striking-way Don Anastasio Escobar. And the man with whom he was speaking he addressed as Toroblanco!

"Well," thought Aunt Polly, "there *is* such a man as Toroblanco, then! I began to think him a myth. Oh, I wish I could understand Spanish!—

Why didn't I bring Gip along? She's so clever at languages."

Anastasio Escobar had but little to say, yet that little was said forcefully. Toroblanco broke in with his sullen mutterings. Aunt Polly, despite her snug cloak of certainty that everything was a bit of fun and frolic and despite the warm afternoon sun, shivered. It sounded like hate and anger and all unthinkable evil when that man spoke as he did. She was for a second tempted to creep away and hurry back home.

Anastasio Escobar laughed. It was not a pretty laugh as laughs go, yet a laugh it was unmistakably. Aunt Polly breathed again; of a sudden she wanted to laugh out loud herself. How sweet and clean and peaceful the dear old world was! A pretty little Mexican dove lighted on a dead limb not twenty yards from her; she saw the light pour over it, making the little feet look like coral; she heard the dove begin to call in its low, crooning, tenderly sweet voice. Her smile came back.

Altogether she was going to be entirely satisfied with her expedition if only she could have at least one peek at the redoubtable Toroblanco! It could be managed, she was sure. A rear canvas wall showed her a small tear; she began tiptoeing again.

She applied her eye to the hole in the canvas. One of the men was Anastasio Escobar, right enough. And the other whom he had called Toroblanco was swarthy and arrogant and—handsome, too? Perhaps, she thought with reservation. For he was scowling now, and his black eyes burned most unpleasantly, and there was more than a hint of cruelty on the lips shadowed by the thick black moustache. His hat was on his head, set far back and giving her a full view of his jet hair which was inclined to curl and which looked oily. A long cloak, excellently befitting a villain in an opera, concealed his extravagant uniform.

"He is just the type," she nodded sagely to herself, "that Rogue would choose for—"

Something touched her foot and she glanced down. She had stood so still that a little lizard in its wanderings had come close to her; she had felt the little fellow trickle over her shoe which no doubt he had mistaken for a stone on which he had thought to sun himself. Lizards, cobras, tarantulas and rattlesnakes were all the same to Aunt Polly. She began screaming at the first sight of the thing; she was still screaming and standing perfectly still when the lizard vanished among the rocks and Escobar and Toroblanco burst upon her.

"Miss Comfort!" exclaimed Escobar, and began looking in all directions as though for her companions.

"It was one of those snake-things that runs on legs," she shivered, pointing tremblingly.

Toroblanco, a hand under his cloak, apprehensive in look and gesture, scowled wonderingly first at her then at Escobar.

"You are all alone here?" demanded Escobar sharply.

She nodded. The colour began to come back into her blanched cheeks. Already she was accounting herself a ninny to have given everything away. Perhaps she had been on the very verge of a grand discovery.

Toroblanco began speaking hurriedly. His words were unintelligible to Aunt Polly at whom he kept staring all the while he was not glancing about, like Escobar, as though seeking the others of her party.

Escobar answered as swiftly. Aunt Polly, while thinking how rude men could be when startled, heard the names Rogue Madden and Miss Wynne. Evidently Anastasio was telling the other man who she was.

"Come inside," he commanded abruptly, not in the least the smoothly courteous gentleman she had always thought him. He even grasped her roughly by the arm.

The three went into the hut.

"I'll thank you to take your hand off my arm!" said Aunt Polly indignantly. "I think you forget yourself, Don Anastasio."

He looked puzzled, but he did withdraw his hand. Then suddenly his expression changed; he became the gentleman she knew, and bent nearly double in a belated bow.

"A thousand pardons, Miss Comfort!" His white teeth shone in a broad smile. "I did forget myself. You startled us, I must say! That scream of yours; it was like murder being done!" He began to laugh softly. "This gentleman with me, you should have seen him jump!"

Instantly mollified and a little proud of her achievement, Aunt Polly began smiling with him.

"This gentleman," she reminded him. "We have not met, you know?" Her smile grew positively gleeful; there was triumph in it and cunning. "He is the terrible Mr. Toroblanco, I think?"

Toroblanco withdrew his sentinel eyes long enough to marvel at her. "What a woman!" he muttered under his breath. Don Anastasio was for a moment a queer picture of uncertainty. But his mind worked swiftly and his smile came back; then he laughed again and made a wide gesture.

"You heard me speak the name Toroblanco? It was of Toroblanco that I spoke, not to him. This gentleman, whom I am ashamed that I did not present at once, is my most excellent friend, Señor Romero." He performed the introduction; Toroblanco bowed profoundly. Escobar added, "Señor Romero, too, is a farmer; a gentleman rancher. You have no doubt heard Mr. Madden speak of him? They are friends."

"Yes," said the new Señor Romero, with a little

involuntary twitch of the thick lips under the thick moustache. "Frien's, me an' heem."

"Of course," nodded Aunt Polly. "All you boys are friends of Rogue Madden's. I never knew a man with so many, or so many kinds!"

"Now that we've caught you," suggested Escobar as casually and as pleasantly as he could manage, "hadn't you better tell us what brought you out here?"

"If only I hadn't screamed!" she laughed back at him, conscious of a queer strain in his manner, yet finding her own ready explanations for it. "Those little, crawly things simply scare me into fits. Well, as you say, since I'm fairly caught, I might as well 'fess up."

She could not have asked two more earnest listeners. She explained how, when at times perhaps she had let them think her gullible, she really could not swallow everything! She had realized perfectly well that there was something going on under this false surface of placidity, and it was the simplest guess in the world that that mystifying fence had something to do with it.

Toroblanco muttered; luckily for Aunt Polly's sense of what she termed common decency she could not understand. Escobar agreed hastily with what she had said. To be sure. And so?

So she had meant to have a peek all her own below that deceitful surface of things. She had

had her chance when both Madden and her niece were away. And here she was!

"My friend, Señor Romero, though he speaks English as you have heard," said Escobar gravely, "does not understand everything when it is spoken hurriedly. Am I forgiven if I explain in Spanish?"

Here was the courteous Escobar whom she knew; she made up her mind it was only fair to forget that grip on her arm and his rudeness under stress of discovery. He began explaining to his friend. The two spoke quickly and at length. She heard her own name two or three times; that of Madden and Gipsy; at least once that of Smiley.

Toroblanco quitted the hut unceremoniously. What a swagger the man had! Escobar turned again to her.

"At first we feared you had spoiled the fun," he told her, and laughed as at fears past. "You have confessed; so now do we. It was, as you guessed, a prank of Rogue Madden's. My friend, Señor Romero, was to play the part of Toroblanco. He was to have men hidden here; several of his Mexican farm hands. There was to be a kidnapping! You and your niece were to be the captives and he would pretend to hold you for ransom!"

Aunt Polly laughed in his face.

"As though that sort of thing would have fooled us!"

He stared at her more curiously than he had ever done. Aunt Polly, as a victim of the fixed idea, was a novelty to him.

"So, as I said, we feared you had spoiled the fun. But it is not so! If you will help, we are going to have our fun yet. And the joke will be on Rogue Madden himself!"

Now *that* was exactly what she wanted.

Escobar explained fluently. She listened eagerly. When presently Toroblanco came striding back with a Mexican half-breed at his heels, Aunt Polly was committed heart and soul to his alluring scheme.

CHAPTER XVII

When Gipsy Wynne fled in all hot haste from her amazing encounter with Father Juan, Rogue Madden found himself forced to an explanation—and an apology. All laughter drained out of him when he came to look closely into the old fellow's eyes.

"Father," said Madden, suddenly humble, "can you forgive a fool for his folly?"

"I sometimes fear," said the old man absently, his face all puckers, his eyes going again after the fleeing figure on horseback, "that forgiving fools their folly is one of the high functions of true priesthood!—But tell me, my son, what was it?" He grew more and more anxious. "Her face looked so strange. She seemed frightened, even, and shocked. I failed somewhere among my new words? I made some terrible, unforgivable blunder?"

"I ought to be kicked," confessed Madden, half grinning and half rueful. "You'd be clear in your rights if you put the curse of the Mother Church on me."

He explained to an amazed and incredulous listener. Father Juan's eyes brightened angrily.

"Perhaps my sense of humour dulls with age," he said stiffly. "But, señor, I had not expected such treatment at your hands."

Quite obviously, Gipsy need not have feared Madden overtaking her. As a matter of fact she had reached the house and left it again long before Madden had brought the very best-humoured old Father Juan back into a mood of chuckles—and, incidentally, had vowed to build him a little church all his own, wherever he said, and to see that he had a congregation every Sunday morning, even if Rogue Madden himself had to go out in the brush and rope a lot of half wild Indians for the occasion.

What Gipsy did was to rush straightway in search of her aunt. By no means given to the habit of talking aloud to herself, she did indulge in many outspoken threats and in one or two really snapping bits of repartee. But, of course, Aunt Polly was nowhere to be found. Gipsy hunted high and low, in the house and through the gardens, and at last came back to her own room in high dudgeon. She did not know what to do; what she wanted was very, very clear. She would like to whisk herself and her aunt out of this despicable place with no more ado. For, she told herself bitterly, no matter where they went they would be in no sorrier plight than right here.

It was dark already. She lighted the candles in her room and then went to her grilled window, looking out with very bright eyes. Ugh! It was a perfect prison here. How had she ever tolerated it all this while? And Rogue Madden! She had been fooling herself, pretending that she thought that there was good in the man hidden under the surface, needing only a woman's hand to bring it into its own in the shining light of day! What nonsense. She had known better than that all along. He was a liar, a brawler, a crook, a gambler, a thief, everything that he should not be. She had only to shrug her shoulders at him, take her hat and walk straight out of his life.

"Ssh!" came a whispered command from the dark.

Gipsy sprang back from her window, startled. A hand appeared out of the blackness, a hand which came very close to being black itself and Gipsy, alarmed now, put her own hand on her door and was poised for flight. The fingers at the window held a scrap of paper looking very white by contrast; it was allowed to flutter to the floor. The whisperer, himself but vaguely glimpsed, added to her amazement:

"*Una carta.*—From your Tia Polee!—Eet ees ver-ee see-creet!—pssh!"

Who on earth was Tia Polee? She couldn't even guess, having forgotten that *tia* meant aunt. But the paper had fluttered far enough from the window for her to be sure that the hand could not grab her, so she caught it up and read the short message in Aunt Polly's own handwriting:

"GIPSY DARLING:

"I've made *such* a discovery! Come to me immediately; the messenger will bring you. Don't let that rascal of a Rogue Madden know; make him think we've both gone to bed. Just pick up a few things for overnight and *hurry!*

POLLY COMFORT."

Gipsy closed her door and came back to the window, trying to see the man's face. She began asking questions rapidly: What was it all about? Where was her aunt? How were they to go?

But the messenger had very little English and seemed to have about the same amount of intelligence. Gipsy knew the word *caballos*, and therefore gathered that the horses were ready.

It did not dawn on her to be afraid. The letter from Aunt Polly was ample preventive of that state of mind. And all of a sudden she was electrically eager to be gone. Here, sudden fulfillment of a wish just now expressed, was the way to be rid of Mr. Roger Madden! No matter where Aunt Polly was, she was clear of the house and of Madden's espionage. Gipsy would take care that they lost none of the advantage of this hour.

"We are going on horseback?" she whispered guardedly.

Whether or not he understood she was not sure.

But he answered, "*Sí, sí, sí*!" He, too, was eager.

Gipsy caught up a small bag, dumped its contents out, refilled it hastily with what she deemed necessary, and stood ready. The hand at her window made a wide gesture, indicating the direction to take, and vanished; thereafter she heard soft footfalls. She blew out her candles and went to the door. The house was very quiet. Down the long corridor she tiptoed. She went out into the patio, set her bag down, and turned back into the house, seeking Eloisa.

"My aunt and I will want no supper to-night, Eloisa," she said carelessly. "You will tell Mr. Madden when he comes in that we said good night? And you will let us have a big night's sleep, won't you, Eloisa? Maybe you will let us sleep late in the morning, too?"

Done with Eloisa, carrying out Aunt Polly's commands to the best of her ability and at the same time amusing herself in anticipation of Rogue Madden's state of mind when he learned they were gone, Gipsy returned toward her room. Once she was sure the coast was clear she darted outside, caught up her bag and hurried around the house. A low whistle advised her just where her guide awaited her. He took her bag, helped her to mount, and they rode off into the night.

And Rogue Madden hadn't come back yet! What luck! She laughed softly. The night was splendid with a fresh fragrant breeze from the fields of sage, with great big flaring stars, with a glorious sense of freedom. Yes, and of triumph. And of adventure. And, above all, of a glowing satisfaction. She wished she could see Madden's face in the morning. The house would be kept quiet, so that she and Aunt Polly could have their good long sleep. The sunny morning hours would drag on; Madden after a while would begin looking at his watch. He would do his share of wondering before noon came; he would learn that no breakfast had been sent in and would remark on how queer it was that his guests did not even come out for lunch—and about that time he would feel the first prickings of fear that there was something amiss. And then he would learn that both his birds had flown!

"I wish I had left a note for him," thought Gipsy. "Just a line or two to mystify him further—and to gloat!"

So busy were her thoughts that at first she did not even notice which way she was riding; her guide led on at a gallop, and time flew. But presently she began to cast ahead instead of behind, speculating on Aunt Polly's mysterious communication and on Aunt Polly's own whereabouts, and thought to ask her guide how far they had to go. He mumbled something which she thought might mean, "Not far," and she sighed resignedly and gave over asking questions.

Of a sudden they came to a halt. She made out

now that they had come to the high barbed-wire fence and had stopped at the padlocked gate. Only now the locks were open, the chains down, the gate itself slowly swinging open. She could see the star-shine on the wire. Since gates did not unlock and open themselves, there was someone here expecting them.

"Aunt Polly?" she called softly.

"Your Aunt Polly is a little farther on," said a voice. She started, recognizing it as Anastasio Escobar's. "If you will ride on, Miss Wynne? Straight through the gate. It is but a little way."

"Don Anastasio!" she exclaimed.

The first hint of alarm, only a hint and so vague that she was scarcely conscious of it, assailed her now. Anastasio Escobar's awaiting was at once unexpected and vaguely disquieting.

Puzzling over Escobar's presence, she passed through the gate. A hand caught her horse's reins; the gate clicked behind her. She heard the clink of chains and the snap of locks.

"Where is my aunt, Don Anastasio?" she asked. She meant to speak casually and indifferently. But all of a sudden her hint of alarm was grown into more than a hint.

"I am going to ride with you," he said quietly, and she saw his horse now and watched him mount. The man with her bag had finished with the gate and was again in his saddle; he held back, prepared to follow them. "It is but five minutes, ten at the most, from here. In the hills yonder."

What a fool she had been to come all alone, or worse than alone, with a stranger! Of course everything was all right; there was the certain and cosily commonplace assurance of her aunt's note. But she need not have rushed headlong like this. She should have taken a moment to think.—What nonsense! She was not alone now, was she? She was with Anastasio Escobar, a gentleman and a friend. He had from the beginning made clear that he did not endorse Rogue Madden's high-handed treatment of her; he had offered his services in any direction; he had always spoken most courteously and fairly.—And yet it remained that already she was thinking rather dismally of her precautions taken that Madden should not discover her absence until late to-morrow at earliest.

They rode slowly. Escobar reined his horse aside that Gipsy might go ahead along the dim trail that was too narrow for both abreast. He kept close at her heels. A perfectly mad impulse urged her to lay her quirt over her own horse's shoulders, to race away, eluding him in the darkness. But all sanity told her how perfectly mad the impulse was, how certain to end in failure if not to make her ridiculous. She kept to the trail and began to puzzle over Escobar's manner.

From the top of a hill she looked back. Only Escobar followed her now; the man with her bag had disappeared. Strangely, she had not been afraid when alone with that man, but alone with Escobar she was afraid.

She looked ahead. Down in the dark hollow she saw a light; it gleamed a moment and winked out.

"That is where Aunt Polly is?" she asked quickly.

He came up with her on the hilltop.

"That is where she was a few minutes ago; when she wrote that note to you. She has just gone on; she wants you to follow her."

On the slight bridge of his words imagination ran from dawning concern to positive terror. He was lying to her! He had her in his power and God alone knew what he meant to do with her. Aunt Polly was not here and might even be miles away. Something rose in her throat. She swallowed; it rose again. It was hard to speak coolly.

"I am going back," she said.

But she knew that she was not to be allowed to do what she chose if it clashed with his will. He was so close that he could lay his hand on her reins.

"Miss Wynne," he said, his tone one of great reluctance, "I am sorry, but—but I think it would be better if you rode on with me to overtake your aunt. You see, she expects you."

He had started out to say one thing and had switched to another. She sensed that he had come very close to unmasking; on the verge of dictating to her, he had decided to delay this change of front if possible. He would plead with her not to go back. But if she refused to do as he requested then, she was sure of it, would come the unmasking; then, the command and force, if she made that necessary.

She demurred meditatively, though her heart was beating furiously.

"She expects me? Oh, of course. But—" To keep him from noting a tremor that was coming into her voice she broke off and shrugged. "She is not far?"

"Not far," he assured her.

"There is someone down where that light shone out."

"Your aunt was there. She will have left word for you. Shall we—"

"Oh, by all means. Let us hurry."

He dropped her reins but kept close to her as they rode down into the little valley.

She made out the canvas huts only when she was close to them. A door opened at the sound of hoofbeats; a lantern held low showed her a man's legs in shaggy *chaparejos*; the toes of small boots peeped out at the bottoms; there was the winking glint of spurs. A few hurried words passed between this man and Escobar; they spoke in undertones and, it seemed to Gipsy, both at the same time. She could make nothing of what they said.

"It is as I told you," said Escobar, turning to her. "Your aunt has gone on, but expects you to follow her."

"Who is this man?" asked Gipsy, ready now to be suspicious of every shadow.

The one of whom she spoke understood, for he laughed. The laugh was insolent. He jerked up his lantern so that its light poured out over her face; his own was fleetingly revealed and the girl shrank back in her saddle. And there were those who held Toroblanco a handsome man. Gipsy saw only a heavy, dark countenance which leered and mocked her.

" 'Who is this man?' " he repeated, mimicking her, and laughed again. "That is funny, Anastasio, *no?*" He slapped his leg and her horse started to dance away from him; but he was as quick as a cat and caught the reins.

"If you will get down, Miss Wynne?" said Anastasio.

"No! Why should I? If we are to follow my aunt—"

He himself dismounted and put out his hand to her.

"We shall stop here a moment only. It is but a little thing that we ask of you. It is only that you write a short note to be sent back to Rogue

Madden. That done, we will hasten after your aunt."

"What should I write Rogue Madden?" she asked, defiant of tone but inwardly quaking.

The man with the lantern put his hand to his mouth; there was a long shrill whistle. Immediately she heard a rush of many hoofs, and vague forms loomed in the dark until she made out a full dozen riders. Their horses slid to a standstill; she fancied the riders were saluting the man who had called them.

"Will you come, please?" asked Don Anastasio as pleasantly as ever, yet with what she thought was a trace of impatience behind the smooth utterance. "It will be a minute only."

She dismounted hastily. The man with the lantern led the way into the hut; Escobar came at her heels. On a rude table were paper and pencil.

"What am I to write?" she asked.

"Something like this: 'Dear Mr. Madden: Not being the fools you thought us, my aunt and I have made our escape. You may expect to hear further of us, if not from us, when we have reached Los Angeles.' That and your signature will be all."

"You would force me—"

"It is fate, Miss Wynne, that forces all of us."

"And I thought you a gentleman!" she cried scornfully.

He bowed.

"A gentleman—of fortune."

She had taken up the pencil; now she flung it down and with head held high and eyes blazing, she said crisply:

"I'll do nothing you command me to do! If you think I am afraid, you are mistaken. I'm not to be bullied by you or anybody like you."

The man with the lantern laughed again. Though he spoke Spanish now she understood every deliberate word:

"What eyes! My God, what eyes she has!"

Escobar shrugged.

"I would not lay a hand on you for the world; you know that, I think." She knew nothing of the kind and was distinctly relieved to have him express himself; relieved, though she put no trust in him or faith in his words. He continued gravely: "I am thinking of your aunt. She has gone ahead. She still thinks everything a joke. If you follow on, it may be arranged so that no shock of discovery of the truth need be feared. If, on the other hand—" He had a way of leaving his meaning hanging loose at one end; he shrugged and so let her form her own mental pictures.

"I suppose," she said presently, "that what you mean is that you think you can hold me prisoner and demand a ransom? That is the sort of thing which men like you try every once in a while down here near the border, isn't it?"

"You will think of your aunt as well as of

yourself," he said curtly. "You will then decide what to do."

She put her face into her hands and tried to think. Well, if the worst came to the worst, it was only a matter of ransom. And there was Aunt Polly, already in their hands—taking everything as a joke! When she lifted her eyes it was to look steadily, searchingly at Escobar.

"If I could only be sure that you would take me straight to my aunt—"

"On my honour." She flicked him with the scorn of her look at that, but he remained unruffled, concluding: "Within the hour."

She sat down on a box, took up the pencil and wrote.

CHAPTER XVIII

"Well, my son," remarked U.S.A. Smiley, "if ever I saw a gent look down in the mouth, you're it. What's come over you? Old age set in, or what?"

"Hello, Smiley," said Madden. "Back again, huh?"

Smiley snorted.

"Of all the bright, shining and original remarks! What's gone wrong, Rogue?"

Rogue's grin was a failure, a mere cold gleam of winter sunshine.

"Guess it's old age, Uncle Sam. Been thinking of taking my bed roll and going to live with the Marlibones."

"H'm," said Smiley. Standing at a window opening upon the patio, he looked about the grounds and observed with a too-marked casualness: "Where are the womenfolk? Seems sort of quiet."

"Gone," Madden told him cheerily. So cheerily that Smiley cocked an understanding eye.

"Guess you've been falling in love, boy. That's all. No great shakes to that; won't hurt you."

"Falling out of love," laughed Madden, as one for whom life had no illusions.

"And going to live with the Marlibones!"

Smiley's laugh was a real one. "Why not with the Ashton Ferribees, instead?"

Madden caught the implication; the Ashton Ferribees with their confident contention that the world was about to come to an end—

"They're behind the times," he told Smiley, and with a far better grin now; "the world already came to an end—this morning. Hadn't noticed, had you?"

"What did you let 'em go for, if it gores you like that? I met up yesterday with Cameo; he told me how you were guardian to the girl, and she had to graze wherever you staked her out."

"They fooled me, Smiley; simply took advantage of a trusting nature. I—You see, I got me a fine hunch for teasing Gipsy Wynne, who'd been torturing me a whole week. And before I got through laughing, they were gone."

Smiley poured himself a drink, helped himself to a cigar, went back to his chair and stretched his long legs. He had but just arrived, from what direction he had not explained. It was late afternoon and he showed signs of having ridden far.

"Shucks, Rogue," he puffed out with the first cloud of smoke, "you ought to have more sense than playing jokes on womenfolk. One thing the Lord didn't make Eve out of was Adam's funny bone.—And by the by, young fellow, if I served you your rights I'd pull a nine-inch knife out of my boot and carve your heart out! Great idea of yours, wasn't it, sending me off Zack Burtonshaw way on that sorrel nag with the yellow tail!"

When he saw that even now he had barely caught Madden's interest, Smiley snorted a second time, and then fell to chuckling softly. Suddenly he slapped his knee and burst out laughing.

"Great idea of yours, you infernal jackass, to send a United States marshal riding around on a stolen horse! You knew I didn't know Burtonshaw and Burtonshaw didn't know me—and so you sent me up to call on him riding a horse you figured had been stolen from him! And you laughed yourself sick, thinking how we'd no doubt come to shooting each other up before anybody got a chance to explain anything!"

"No," said Madden. "I haven't laughed about anything since the War of 1812."

"Here's the way it all worked out," said Smiley. "You found the sorrel horse here after your Mex friends raided you. You knew it for a Burtonshaw horse and had your own reasons to be dead sure your friend Toroblanco had stolen it. So you put me aboard and sent me up to introduce myself! All right. I go ahead as innocent as a fool. I meet up with Burtonshaw and I have my own reasons for not telling him who I am. His eyes crawl all over the horse and he soon leads himself to making a mistake. You see, smarty, the horse wasn't stolen at all. Burtonshaw had loaned it to Toroblanco. And Burtonshaw was looking for a man to be sent up by Toroblanco. The two, as I guessed long ago, are like that." He interlaced his fingers. "So Burtonshaw goes right along leading himself by the nose into making a mess of things. He has just about as much sense, anyhow, as most of these birds who think they can put a raw deal across on their Uncle Samuel."

He stood up and shook himself.

"I got just exactly out of Zack Burtonshaw what I went up there to get out of him," he announced grimly. "Thanks to you and the sorrel, Rogue."

"Oh, that's all right," said Madden absently. "You're quite welcome, I'm sure."

Smiley, folding up again as he sank back into his chair, regarded him thoughtfully.

"You'll never be happy again until you get that girl back, Madden," he said. "I can see that plain. And I'll never get your mind on my business until I pry it loose from her. Let's have the tale. How did she make her getaway?"

Madden took a carefully folded piece of paper from his pocket and handed it over.

"That's all I know about it," he said.

Smiley read with interest:

> "DEAR MR. MADDEN:
>
> "My aunt and I, of course, have taken the first chance to leave. If you hear from

us at all, it will be when we have reached Los Angeles, and then through our lawyers.

GIPSY WYNNE."

Smiley, having read, read again. He turned the paper over and over in his hands, and at last asked:

"Didn't hand you this herself, so it's fair to ask who did? Left it in her room?"

"No. Eloisa picked it up on the floor in the living-room. Looks as though it had been slipped back under the door after she went out.—Here; give me that paper before you tear it all to pieces."

"Nice little souvenir, I'd say! All right; here's your *billet doux*.—Mad when she wrote that, huh?—Notice anything funny about it, Rogue?"

"Funny?" groaned Madden. "Oh, Lord!"

"Funny is what I said. What's that for stationery for a Gipsy Wynne? Pencil, too; hasn't she a nice little fountain pen with gold trimmings?"

"What's that got to do with anything?" snapped Madden.

"I liked the old lady," said Smiley. "She was a peach. Never turned a hair with all the fireworks popping. She quit on you cold, too? Never a word?"

"No, never a word. Yes, Aunt Polly was fine."

"Took all their traps? Like they meant to stay

away for good? Or just a tooth brush, so to speak?"

"How do I know? Think I've been prowling around their rooms?"

"There's your faithful Eloisa to report—"

"I told her to lock the rooms and leave things alone. I won't have her poking around if they did leave anything. And I guess they didn't carry their trunks."

Smiley dropped the subject. It was not closed in his own mind, merely dropped so far as Madden was concerned. He turned to other things.

"Want something nice and lively to do, Rogue, that is guaranteed to drive dull care away?" he asked with a sharpening of the voice which brought Madden's head up with a jerk.

"Yes! Anything. Just so we snap into it, Smiley. Something doing about that bunch of Chink and dope runners?"

"Aye, aye, me lad. Something very much doing. Strictly unofficial, you know; I'm still on vacation, don't forget. And I've got a burning desire to go where I've no business to go. A little trip across the border. What say?"

"I've said it! Toroblanco?—And tell me, Smiley: Is Toroblanco the man—"

"Who stood your dad up and shot him?" Smiley grew grim and hard. "Toroblanco, or another," he said finally, as he had said before. "That's as far as I go now; but when this little party of ours is all over, you'll know."

"When do we go?"

"I want a nap. Also a bath and a shave; then something to eat. Say a couple of hours. You can leave word with your men here you won't be back for two-three days. A week, maybe. Maybe never."

Madden nodded and went out to give his orders. Smiley watched him go, then hurried through the dining-room to the kitchen, seeking Eloisa. Having done with her, making her a shining present of a new silver dollar and engaging her at length in gossip, he went wandering through the various rooms before he retired to his own.

When some three hours later, looking fresh and carefree, he appeared before Madden, it was to say without preliminary:

"And you haven't any idea which way they went or how? Foot, horseback or flying machine?"

"There's not a horse missing from my stable; that's been bothering me. I did find out that Aunt Polly took the old top buggy and went off somewhere by herself in the afternoon. Nobody paid any attention; what's more, nobody saw her come back."

"But she did come back?" asked Smiley sharply.

"The horse and buggy did, so I guess she

piloted ’em home. The horse was running loose in the corral this morning, the buggy standing back of the barn.”

“It’s a long walk from here, no matter where you go,” Smiley reminded him. “Most likely they had friends on the outside? That what you’ve been thinking?”

“It might have been Johnny Bandini; you could tell from the way he looked at her that he’d lie down and let her walk on him, going Sir Walter one better. It might have been Escobar; he dug out of here in a hurry, and I haven’t seen him since. He told me once that I didn’t have any business playing jailer to her.” He shrugged. “What’s the difference? She’s gone—And you and I are on our way.”

Smiley looked very thoughtful. For a second Madden thought that he knew something and was going to give it voice.

“Oh, well,” was all that Smiley decided to say, “we’ll know what we know when we know it; and I’d bet you better than a pinch of mud that we’ll see the two dames again before the skies fall. Let’s drift.”

“The horses are ready. Riding light, or all loaded down with heavy artillery?”

“Light. I’ve generally got a pea-shooter on me, and I’m counting on you having all the young cannons a man might need down at your other big ranch. Am I right, Romeo?”

"So that's where we're headed? Yes, I've got pretty much of an arsenal down there. Pocket some cigars and here's hoping you live long enough to smoke 'em all."

They jogged south into the blazing sunset.

Later, when Smiley told all that he knew and much that he had surmised, he confessed to a blunder. He was, for once in his life, too cocksure, and had leaped to a wrong conclusion.

In fact, he thought that he knew as much of Toroblanco's plan as that individual himself knew. He had learned that the ruffling swaggerer was at outs with the very faction in Mexico which had given birth to his tallest hopes; it was just the case of another little bubble exploding, caught in a bubble-jam which is to be skimmed off now and then from the troubled surface of the ever-turbulent political pots of the south. He knew that there lay a tramp steamer in an out-of-the-way port, and that Toroblanco, with fat pockets, had his eye on it. But he ignored certain other essential facts.

Thus it came about that Smiley counted in full confidence on the brigand—for that was all that Toroblanco remained, shorn of his governmental authority—being to-night in Nacional; on being the next day at a favourite camp spot, the hill ranch of Vidal Chavez, half-brother to the butchered Butcher, and something over half a dozen miles from Madden's southern ranch. But, as it turned out, Toroblanco had given Nacional a wide berth altogether, and was making free with Madden's Mexican ranch while Smiley and Madden were crossing the border headed straight into something which smacked of a trap.

"Cameo and young Bandini are waiting for us," said Smiley. "Either at your place, or along the westerly fringe of the hills. I've kept in touch with Cameo, you know. He had pulled Bandini in on the party. Bright boy, that, by the way."

A nod in the dark isn't worth much, but Madden had sprinkled their scant talks with far more nods than words.

It was long after midnight when they came to the undulating lands where the little rocky hills spilled out into the levels. They stopped and regarded the broken country filled with the mystery of the night.

"Cameo was to ride up this way during the night, and take a little look-see," said Smiley. "I suppose he's looked things over, found everything the way we expected, and hooked it back to bed. Nice and quiet, and—"

"Shut up!" snapped Madden. "Listen!"

Smiley bit off a word and the two men strained eyes and ears against the void of the night. There was nothing to see but dark outlines sprawling under the stars; nothing to hear until faint and very far off a coyote's quick bark stabbed at the silence and was gone.

"Thought I heard—" began Madden.

Then both heard it. It was the distant pounding of hoofs, faint, dying away, then louder and appreciably nearer.

"Might be Cameo—" muttered Smiley. "Might be—Ssh! There's more than one horse—A dozen! What in the—Oh, Lord, they've gummed the works!"

There had been a rifle shot, then another, then a scattering volley. Flashes of fire flared out and vanished. The rush of hoofs grew louder, drumming out fast and strong. Down into a dip of land went the horsemen and sounds were muffled. Then the drumming came again, louder and nearer, as up over a crest of the hills rose two forms in silhouette against the star-studded sky.

"Cameo and Bandini riding hell-for-leather," cried out Smiley, "with stray bullets dusting their coat-tails."

He jerked out his old friend of many a hard-disputed moment, a big black forty-five, waving it over his head as he shouted at the top of his voice:

"Come ahead, Cameo! Come ahead, Bandini! We're with you!"

His voice sounded exactly like the voice of some enthusiastic race-track visitor, standing up in the grandstand and urging his favourite horse home. Cameo and Bandini heard, shouted something back, and swerved slightly to come charging down where Smiley and Madden awaited them. But they did not check their speed for an instant.

"Come on!" sang out Cameo Risden, and Madden and Smiley drove their spurs home and rode at his side. "There are close to twenty of the devils, and they've all got rifles. It's up to us to outrun 'em. All Bandini and I have is a couple of automatics. Rifles at the ranch house."

"Lead on, McDuff," growled Smiley.

Like four great greyhounds their four horses shot out across the open flats, taking the straightest and shortest way home. Their pursuers topped the hill; they yelled like the Indians which, in part, a good many of them were, and started shooting again the instant that they spied their fleeing quarry.

"Just for luck—being on vacation!" grunted Smiley, and turned in the saddle for one tempting long shot.

"That's no good and you ought to know it, Smiley," Cameo chided him. "Just let your horse sock a foot in a gopher hole—and where are you? Riding is our job right now."

"Right as usual, Cameo," admitted Smiley regretfully.

"I'll race you to the corrals!" cried out Johnny Bandini.

Madden laughed at him.

"Good sign, Rogue!" Smiley tossed the words at him. "I was scared I'd never hear you laugh again."

"Come ahead, Bandini," Madden shouted. "I'll take you up on that. What horse are you riding?"

"One of those devils is shooting mighty close," cut in Cameo.

"It's Silver Heels," Bandini answered Madden's question.

"With a good man up, Silver can run," was Madden's retort. "But I'll bet you ten bucks I beat you to the stables."

"You boys seem to think you're funny," Smiley remonstrated. "This is a life and death matter." And even Cameo laughed at that. "Spread out, boys," Smiley ran on. "They'll never hit a single running object, them running too; but if we all pile up together they might make a lucky shot."

Johnny Bandini, despite his breeziness under fire, was a full length ahead of the field.

"Pretty close to six miles to go, Bandini," Madden warned him. "Look out you don't let your pony give all he's got in the first lap. You'll never come in the money that way."

"We're not gaining as fast as I thought we would," said Cameo thoughtfully. "Those war-whoops have better horses than usual."

"New string from Zack Burtonshaw's," Smiley

shouted back at him. "Pretty fair stock, Burtonshaw's."

"Watch a Joyous Guard Rancho horse run away from them!" Madden bade them. "I'll bet any man—"

"Look out! Dodge that bullet!" Smiley yelled at the top of his voice, and cackled derisively as three men ducked their heads.

They rode all the while just exactly as hard as four fine horses could carry them; and a man's flesh did have a way of crawling at times, even though he played at devil-may-care, when a bullet went zipping past. There was a sharp-banked gully which Bandini sighted just in time to lift his horse up and over it; he yelled a warning and the three other horses cleared it safely. Beyond was a long level expanse, dotted with grey sage; they swept along across it at a steady, sand-flipping run. Now one man, now another, looked back.

"If a horse doesn't take a tumble, they'll never pull even with us," Smiley said complacently. "But I'd just as soon be set down in a flock of alligators as out here. Hope you go in for sure-footed horseflesh, Rogue."

"Sh!" muttered Madden. "What the devil's that?"

At first no one, saving Johnny Bandini alone, knew or could imagine. Then they burst out laughing. It was Johnny Bandini's harmonica; in the final gesture of irrepressible youth, he was blowing away with all his might at "Yankee Doodle."

And so while they ran for their lives, they laughed. And because there were no better riders hereabouts and certainly no horses behind them to compare with these flowers of Madden's stables, they rode thundering into the ranch yard a good half-mile ahead of all pursuit. At the end of the ride both Bandini and Madden asked their mounts to show what stuff they were made of; and Madden rode to victory by a couple of lengths.

They turned the horses into the stable and ran on to the house.

"There's no one here," Cameo prepared them by saying. "I'll explain later—"

"Hang your explainings; let's get in and grab a rifle or two and be ready."

"No one here, you say?" exclaimed Smiley. "But there's a light—"

The door opened as they raced along toward it. It was Anastasio Escobar who had opened it. The instant that he saw who they were he whipped back, the queerest imaginable expression on his face. Smiley was staring at him and it looked to a very discerning Smiley as though Escobar had thought to be opening the door to an expected party, and was dumbfounded that here was another sort of party altogether. But Smiley didn't stand gawking.

"Get the doors shut and fast!" he boomed out. "Every window shuttered. Rogue, bring in an armful of rifles."

Doors slammed; shutters whined on old iron hooks and were shut and barred. For a moment Escobar stood as if transfixed, then, under Smiley's bright eyes, he bestirred himself. Just then Rogue Madden came hastening back empty-handed from his quest of weapons.

"Something funny!" he said, his voice sounding sober and flat. He stood in the doorway, rolling a cigarette. "Someone's raided the gun-room. There's not a single rifle left."

CHAPTER XIX

They received the information in silence. Even thoughts ceased functioning for a dull moment: here was news that stunned. Smiley was the first to speak.

"Remember the Alamo!" he said, with a snort of pure disgust.

Madden regarded Escobar frowningly. Between him and this man whom he had so long called friend there were certain explanations due. Madden would have been glad to go straightway into those matters, but here suddenly arose another and paramount consideration. He asked bluntly:

"What do you know about the rifles, Escobar?"

"Nothing. I came only a few minutes ago. I found the place deserted and—"

Cameo interrupted, speaking slowly and thoughtfully:

"I know where the boys are. Don't you, Rogue?" And when Madden looked wonderingly at him and shook his head, Cameo made his own explanation. "Long Corbin gathered all hands and is now expecting you 'way out yonder the other side of the hills, five or six miles away. And I guess you didn't send him any word at all?"

Madden looked puzzled.

"No. Word about what?"

"One of your men, a Mex named Tony Robles, came in on a run just about dark. Said he had a message from you, that you wanted Corbin and all hands to meet you about midnight. I thought it was a part of Smiley's game. Anyway, that's where your men are; maybe they took the extra guns."

"But I sent no word by Tony Robles!"

"Guess Toroblanco did," said Smiley. He may have been speaking to Madden or to Cameo, but his eyes were all the while bent on Escobar. "Toroblanco could have bought him up or could have put the fear of death in him. Anyway, we've dug ourselves into as nice a little hole as any flock of jackasses ever did. What have we got for shooting irons? Four-five revolvers against a young army heavy with high-powered rifles! Prunes!"

"Our one chance is to get back on our horses and make another run for it," said Madden, and went quickly to the door opening upon the patio. "Dark as it is, we'll have better than an even break."

"You're crazy," said Smiley. "Stick your head out and listen to what you can hear! We've got a fat chance of forking horses now."

They listened. Already pursuit had caught up with them. Above the noise of hoofbeats voices were to be heard from various directions. A man far off to the east called and a man to the west answered; there were half a dozen rifle shots; bullets rattled against doors and window shutters. Madden closed and bolted his door and came back into the room.

"Wonder if they know we're short of rifles?"

And all this while Smiley's eyes were on Escobar.

"Sure you don't know a thing about the guns, Escobar?" he asked.

Escobar stiffened and shot back a look as good as the one Smiley gave him. He answered indignantly:

"I have told you. I know nothing."

"History repeats itself," said Madden. "And they say the third time's a charm! This makes three times Toroblanco has had us corked up indoors while his little men did target practice."

"It's apt to be the last time, too, isn't it, Rogue?" Cameo remarked.

"It's my hunch," Smiley said, "that those birds do know we're short on arms. But it's only a hunch, and I seem to be doddering here of late."

Of a sudden his face twitched with rage; they could hear the rasp and grind of his teeth. He exploded wrathfully:

"Just when I thought I had that Toroblanco just where I wanted him, he's laughed his damned head off at me!"

There were a few more scattering shots, all fired from a safe distance.

"There's no sense wasting powder and lead like that," spoke up Johnny Bandini sharply.

Cameo clapped him on the shoulder. Bandini was nervous and Cameo had never given any indication of having such things as nerves in his body.

"Those shots are just to whisper the glad news to us, Johnny. They're not attacking; they are only advising us that they are holding us penned up until their big chief and the rest of his litter show up."

"And I'll bet that not a man in our crowd has more than six or seven shots to his gun," said Smiley moodily. "Lord love us, what silly sheep we are and old Smiley Himself the bell wether of the flock! I could go blow out a blood vessel."

"What will Long Corbin do when we don't show up?" Madden demanded of Cameo. But the gambler gave him no hope there. Long Corbin had word to wait, and he would wait. Long enough, at least, to let things zip along to a conclusion here without him.

"Oh, I don't know," Madden persisted. "We can hold the fort quite a spell, you know.—And there's an old saying that has a lot of satisfaction in it: 'We can get as many of them as they get of us.' "

"Our little job, anyway, is to sit tight and wait—"

"While we're waiting," said Smiley crisply, eyeing Escobar with eyes which fairly glittered, "there's one little thing I'd like to get done." He jerked out his old black forty-five Colt. "Mr. Escobar, I'd like mighty well to take care of your gun for you. Just hand over any hardware that may be weighing you down."

"You don't understand," retorted Escobar. "I am no friend of Toroblanco or those men. Once already—"

"Oh, I know; I know. Once already you fooled part of the people with a grandstand play that you'd chip in with your friends against your own country itself! But you know how it goes about fooling all the people, don't you? And you never fooled Cameo Risden and you never fooled me. Fork over!"

Escobar's eyes flashed to a meeting with Madden's. He found nothing but inquiry and open suspicion there. He shrugged. Always, with no other answer offering itself, there was that shrug of Escobar's.

"You are making a mistake—"

Smiley glared at him.

"Not this time. I've made so many mistakes on this deal already that I've run out of 'em!—Remember that little love letter?" Smiley barked out at him. "The one you got just before

Toroblanco raided the other ranch? Well, I found it back of the stables next morning; what was left of it after you tried to set fire to the barn. It happened to be in Toroblanco's hand! Funny, huh? Funny it came just in time to give you a chance—*Look out!*"

"I'll hand you his gun, Smiley; I know where he carries it," said Cameo. And while Escobar stood rigid Cameo drew out his weapon and gave it to Smiley. Whereupon Smiley looked satisfied and pocketed both weapons.

"Having sifted out the pole-cats," he announced cheerfully, "there's four of us white men left. Only about forty of the rabble gathering out yonder. Why, that's fine!"

"So," said Madden heavily, "that's the sort of friend you've been, Anastasio?"

Even the muscles of Escobar's face were rigid. But a new look gathered in his eyes which so seldom gave any clue to his thoughts; they were sullen now and dogged. He knew as well as any man when words were useless and now kept silent. Madden shook his head and turned away; it hurt, it always hurt, when a friend disappointed you.

"And you don't know the half of it yet, Rogue," Smiley told him.

"And I don't want to know it," returned Madden curtly.

Outside a man, shouting at the top of his lungs,

began calling to them. They gave attentive ear, curious to know what he might have to say. And at least he appeared to answer one question for them.

"Oho, we got you in a nice trap!" he yelled at them, and even through adobe walls and the outer dark intervening they had no difficulty in picturing the mockery twisting at his face. His tone reeked insolence and vindictive triumph.

"I'm telling you something!" he went on. "You stay in that trap, see? Until the general comes. You don't even stick a nose out, or we shoot it off! We are twenty-four of us already; and twenty more are running this way! And every man of us has a good rifle and lots of ammunition.—And you have no rifles! Oho! Oh, ho, ho, ho!"

While he was speaking, Smiley was creeping to a window. He opened the shutter an inch and decided not to thrust his own nose out but to let the nose of an old-fashioned forty-five act as his proxy. But in the end, though intrigued and greatly tempted, he only sighed and closed the shutter and came back. He just couldn't afford the luxury; there was not a single ounce of lead to be wasted and the man who shouted at them was taking no chances.

But if the besieged had no lead to squander, such was not the case with their besiegers. Now and again, in a din made the more hideous with hoots and jeers, rifles cracked and bullets tore at the wall and door and shutter.

"We've got a chance to break through, I tell you!" said Madden impatiently. "I, for one, am all fed up on this. Let's get going."

"Fine chance, you simp, with our horses in their hands," Smiley fired back at him. "No, we play this hand out on the long chance; maybe we can hold 'em off until Long Corbin gets tired waiting out in the hills for men that never come. Corbin's no fool and may smell a rat. Those birds are doing no harm yet, they'll wait for the old bull, and let's hope he keeps 'em waiting all night!"

Johnny Bandini was fidgety. He couldn't quite conceal the fact, strive with himself as he might. Fear—that was what was the matter with him. In the very blazing heyday of lusty youth, it is so hard to say to oneself: "It will be all over with me before sun-up." But he was ashamed of being afraid, and he did get himself in hand. He looked at the others; they loved life as much as he did, didn't they? Or at least, almost as much! And they hadn't turned a hair.

Bandini moistened his lips.

"Time before," he cried out sharply, "we played cards!"

"Why, deal 'em up!" said Madden, and laughed.

Cameo brightened.

"Better than doing nothing but wait," he admitted.

Smiley looked them over approvingly. Then

he sighed and blew his nose. A sudden rare and unexpected spurt of sentiment stirred his old heart. So he swore a little and twisted up his moustache ends and was the first to fling himself into a chair.

"Being on vacation," he muttered humorously, "I don't mind if I skin the crowd of you.—Take a seat, Escobar!" he barked out sternly. "Money, thank God, is as clean from one man's pocket as another's, and I'd take joy in breaking you. Also, I want you where I can watch you."

Escobar made no reply. He appeared to consider the matter, then smiled and sat down in the chair Smiley indicated and at Smiley's side. Bandini, thrusting by Madden, slipped into the chair next to Escobar. Madden looked to the doors again; by now all outside doors of the house were barred, but those two leading on one side to the gun-room and on the other into the dining-room were left wide open, avenues down which pistol balls could be sped to meet any of Toroblanco's men who might break in through some other room. All lights were extinguished excepting the two lamps kept for the game. Bandini had found cards and not thinking of such small matters as cutting for deal, began passing out the five poker hands.

"Hear the fools shouting and yelling," growled Smiley disgustedly. "Maybe they want to scare somebody."

Johnny Bandini, all credit to him, made his

confession with a crooked little smile. His hands were jumpy at the cards and he knew that this sign of nervousness had been seen though no one spoke of it.

"I'm scared already," was what Bandini said.

Again Cameo patted him on the shoulder.

"Good kid!—We're all scared, Johnny! You're not the only one; don't forget that. But a man gets used to anything in time, you know, even to being scared."

"Now that's a fact!" exclaimed Smiley, nodding to right and left. "I've got goose-flesh all up and down me this very minute. Give me a chance and an open field, and I'd do the first hundred yards in nine seconds flat, and that would only be warming up for the next hundred! Dealer antes, kid; mustn't forget that, even if you are scared. No limit, I take it, gents?"

"I'm short of kale," Bandini admitted.

"Your credit's like an honest man's gold!" Madden told him warmly. "And listen, kid: you been working for me at real wages! Riding my horses around, you know! And didn't I tell you to name your own wages? Name it now and—"

"Don't be a piker, Rogue," Cameo told him. And explained when Madden looked to him for the answer: "Give the kid his money in the morning if we're alive! Don't go taking credit to yourself for a wide-open burst of generosity which won't amount to much if we're all cold in to-morrow's sunshine."

Madden laughed and Johnny Bandini giggled and the game went ahead. They played out the first hand and, curiously enough, it was Anastasio Escobar who won.

The deal should have passed to Smiley, but he waved it aside and whispered as he drew himself silently up out of his chair:

"You take it, Madden. Cameo, keep an eye on Escobar for me for a minute, will you?"

He quitted the table and went tiptoeing back to the window which once before he had opened. Very stealthy about it all, he again moved the shutter slightly and again he brought his forty-five up to the thin crack. It was in a shadowy corner of the room, yet he took all the chances there were as he peered out. But he was of no mind to hold himself long in such reckless jeopardy. He saw what he had heard, and his weapon roared out, sounding in the room as loud as a small cannon. A wild scream answered him from the patio. He came back to the table looking pleased.

"Afraid I spilled blood on your front porch, Rogue," he chuckled. "Heard the varmint creeping out there. What's bet?"

Fresh outcries, harsh with menace, burst upon them from the outer dark. But suddenly Bandini, who had reached to the floor for a fallen card and briefly rested his head on Escobar's shoulder, was electrified.

"I've got a new trick!" exclaimed Johnny Bandini, of a sudden surging to his feet. "It's worth a dozen of any you ever saw me pull! Just a minute, gents. I won't hold up your game long. Remember that the hand is quicker than the eye, so get your wits about you! Now, watch!" He rolled up his sleeves; he made a wide and meaningless gesture, yet they saw that a lively earnestness burned in his eyes. "Here's where one guy does another a good turn!—Thanks for the wages you're paying me, Rogue. And watch me flip you something in return!"

Cameo alone may have guessed what was coming. No man was less prepared for it than was the one most concerned, namely, Anastasio Escobar. Bandini, having sprung up from his chair at Escobar's side, made another of his swift movements; in truth the hand was far, far quicker than the eye. Quicker even than Escobar's start when, all too late, he must have understood. For Bandini's hand darted under Escobar's coat, came flashing back—and triumphantly held out something over the table. Escobar leaped up, cursing; Smiley waved him down with the ancient Colt. The others stared wonderingly. A glad cry burst from Rogue Madden.

The thing in Bandini's hand was a long flat black case; and on the instant Madden recognized it.

"Open it up! Spill the stuff on the table! See if it's all there!"

The contents of the black leather case were spilled among the cards. Two folded papers, in legal-looking typed covers with Abner Yorke's name on them; a pad of bank notes; a glittering cluster of coruscating feminine trinkets, brilliant gems catching fire.

"And you did that to me, too?" said Madden thickly. "Good God, Anastasio!"

"It's a lie!" cried Escobar wildly. "It's a cursed trick of this devil's-brat!"

"What's all that stuff?" asked Smiley blankly. "Who's been robbing Tiffany's dump?"

"You know, Rogue," said Cameo coolly, "I thought all along at first you were stringing us with that yarn about somebody holding you up with a shotgun, you know. But Bandini and I got talking about it, and then I thought of something. You'll remember: A year or so ago, it was. You were expecting a crowd from the East. Escobar and I were with you. All of a sudden you got the hunch to 'show 'em Wild West.' Remember now? And you told us what you were going to do? Then they didn't come and that was that. But when the Yorke outfit blew in you got the old hunch again from the telegram; and you hopped to it." His hard eyes drifted to Escobar. "Escobar must have remembered, too!"

"And dropped a brooch here, at the ranch

house," said Madden sternly. "So—so she would think—Escobar, if we should happen to come out of this alive, I think you'd better shift over to China to round out your time."

It was just at this moment that all sounds outside ceased so abruptly as to make them turn their eyes, filled with question, toward the unseen patio. Then, through that curious stillness pierced the shrill blast of a whistle. Toroblanco had arrived to take a hand.

"We'll have to play fast if we ever finish *this* game," said Cameo Risden.

"Sh! Forget the game!" said Smiley in a tense whisper. Oh, those incredibly sharp ears of Smiley! He had again heard something which the others missed, a sound, this time, in the house itself.

It was the merest thin whisper of sound that Smiley had heard. But now the others heard a quiet step in the gun-room. Each man had his weapon in his hand; each was set to fire at the first sight of the stealthy oncoming figures. A board creaked; two revolvers cocked—

"Good God!" cried Rogue Madden wildly, and struck up Cameo Risden's weapon.

In the doorway, almost ghostly in the dim light, stood Gipsy Wynne, white-faced and shaken. At her side was Aunt Polly, and the queerest smile they had ever seen trembled on Aunt Polly's lips.

CHAPTER XX

In his own peculiar way U.S.A. Smiley was a great man. Had he no other claim upon the public's admiration, he must still have received his rich share of plaudits for being one of those rare and wonderful individuals who had it in him to sit serene under the canvas roof of a three-ring circus and munch his peanuts in full confidence that he would not miss a single thing that went on, be it that the lion bit a man, or that a clown said or did something really funny, or that a trapeze "artist" actually missed and fell.

Here, now, in the living-room of this Rancho of Joyous Guard, Smiley found the band playing and the three rings whirling in full blast. But nothing escaped him, not even Anastasio Escobar's stealthy step toward a door. That step was checked by the slightest gesture on Smiley's part, the while Smiley was marvelling at the look on Rogue Madden's face.

You never saw a man so *glad!* That was what hit Rogue Madden first, and all of a heap. Gladness! She was here; she had not gone away at all; she had not vanished out of his life! What did he care or know just then of bullets or Toroblanco's whistle or any lack of guns? *He* didn't know that the two other rings were going at all.

The thing to do with a joyous fact was to accept it joyously. Madden took a quick step toward Gipsy, both hands extended. And, Smiley noted, she impulsively took as quick a step toward him! But she stopped first, abruptly and before they met. Her face was pale; her eyes shone inordinately bright, looking large and frightened.

Toroblanco's whistle shrilled again on their ears.

It loosened tongues. It also was a challenge to Rogue Madden's reasoning faculties, and a knife-point in any balloon of gladness.

Smiley stepped where Escobar stood and whispered in his ear. Escobar sat down. Gipsy could scarcely fail to observe the litter of jewels and bank notes on the card table; Aunt Polly exclaimed over it, talking so fast that many of her tripping words were lost, ending with a gale of laughter as she declared "they had caught the robber!"

It was no time for explanations, but the look on Escobar's face told much, a dozen words from Johnny Bandini told more, and Gipsy Wynne grasped the fact that Rogue Madden had not lied to her after all. So she, too, had her own little flash of gladness. It merely shone out and vanished in her eyes; it touched her lips but not into words; impulsive again, she put out her hand and Madden fairly pounced upon it. But by now he was all concern; that she and Aunt

Polly were here only made a desperate situation a thousandfold more desperate. What mischance had brought them into this affair?

"We were kidnapped!" cried out Aunt Polly, and once more that truly remarkable laughter of hers drew all eyes upon her. "Think of it! Kidnapped and held for ransom!" She grew dramatic, flinging out both arms, pointing at Escobar. "Behold the vil-yun!"

Escobar and Toroblanco together had brought Gipsy and her aunt here; the place was deserted when they arrived. That had been only a little while ago. Then Toroblanco had had to hurry away; he was to return soon. He had kept his word; his whistle told them so.

"Aunt Polly is a brick," whispered Gipsy. "She still thinks everything is a joke! *How can she?*"

"It was so *thrilling!*" said Aunt Polly. "We were locked up in a little room at the far end of the house. Iron bars, prison doors! The thud of hoofs! The shooting of guns! *My dears!*" There were bright spots in her cheeks; she dabbed at her eyes with her tiniest lavender-edged handkerchief. "But we broke out, didn't we, Gip? And we crept along down a dark corridor—and we burst so dramatically on the gentlemen at cards and—and loot!"

"If we only had guns!" burst out Johnny Bandini excitedly. "The rifles are all gone!"

Gipsy made haste with her bit of information.

"I heard them talking, Toroblanco and that man." That man, her fleeting glance told, was Escobar. "It was in Spanish, but I understood part of what they said. One of them, the first who got a chance, was to do away with the rifles.—I think it was Toroblanco—"

She was interrupted by a businesslike rapping at the front door. It was only a demand upon their attention; through the ensuing silence a voice addressed them from the patio. Because the speaker had to make himself heard through a heavy oak door and because, too, he had a bad cold, his utterance was none too distinct.

"What do you say?" shouted Smiley. "What do you want, *hombre*?"

The *hombre* blew his nose—they could hear that quite plainly, since Toroblanco might have used this man's trumpetings instead of his whistle and boasted of a bugle in camp—and repeated himself.

"His Excellency the Colonel Don Carlos Toroblanco, sends me here to tell you what you are to do. You will do what he says, or you will all be killed in ten minutes."

Madden remembered Aunt Polly and winked at her. After all she had experienced, did she still think everything so much play-acting? He came near groaning aloud; therefore he winked instead. And Aunt Polly, though there was still that queer look on her face, winked back at him. To be sure he overlooked the fact that she did not understand Spanish.

"What is the little thing we are to do for His Excellency?" Smiley shouted.

"There is a paper I have here; Señor Madden is to sign it. That is one thing. There are other things, too."

"Shall I run out now and get the paper?" asked Madden as though quite innocently considering doing so.

"I will bring it in," was the answer. "First you swear to let me go without harm. You swear that, open the door and I come in."

"It's a trick!" warned Bandini. "Look out!"

"No, it's on the level, I think," said Smiley. "But we take no chances; the old Bull has fooled me once already. We can do with less light; one lamp is enough. Get it in a corner and shade it."

He hurried to his window, in deep shadow now, and again opened the shutter a cautious inch. Presently he signalled; he had made clear that there was only one man in the patio.

Madden and Bandini went to the door, their weapons in their hands. Cameo stood behind Escobar so that he could cover both that gentleman and the door itself. Madden lifted down the bar and opened the door no wider than he judged ample for a man to slip through.

"All right, we promise not to hurt you," he said sharply. "In you come."

Without an instant's delay Toroblanco's messenger stepped into the room and the door was shut again and barred. Smiley fastened his shutter and rejoined the others.

The man who had just entered was what one would expect of Toroblanco's messenger, a half-breed and an evil enough customer if looks counted for anything. He was one of the raggedest of the ragged; an old blanket with a hole through it for his head served him as a cloak; an ancient torn black sombrero, which he had no thought of removing, covered his ragged black hair and cast his gaunt, savage face into shadow.

"These are the things to do," he said in surly satisfaction. "Señor Madden signs this paper." He proffered it. "You let the Señor Escobar come away with me. Then you send to His Excellency the Señor Madden himself, and the Señor Smiley. With these things done, His Excellency marches away with all his men."

"What's he want with you, Rogue?" demanded Smiley.

Madden waved the paper and laughed.

"Nothing much. He just wants a deed to this ranch. This is a bill of sale."

"And I suppose," put in Bandini, "that he wants you to come out so he can thank you for it?"

"Having your signature, Rogue," said Cameo, and began cutting a cigar-end with precision, "he'll slit your throat, and you know it. Not alone to assure himself there'll be no trouble about the title to your land later but as much as anything for the fun of it."

"What does he want Smiley for?"

Smiley spoke for himself and with a wry smile:

"He knows it's to be one of us, sooner or later. I reckon he'd rather have it sooner—and that it would be me!"

Madden was frowning at the paper in his hand. With a sudden start, as though a new thought had struck him, he demanded:

"We can talk this over, I suppose? How much time will the Bull Calf give us?"

"His Excellency," the half-breed muttered, "gives you ten minutes. Not longer."

"Why, then," cried Madden, and his eyes were shining strangely, "a lot can be thought of in ten minutes. Smiley!" His voice grew sharp and emphatic now. "Get everybody into the next room. Shut the door. Leave only Cameo here with me. I want a word with him alone."

Smiley looked at him suspiciously. He was opening his lips to demand what mad thing the mad Madden had in mind, but was cut short.

"Into the next room, and lively, for the love of Heaven!" Madden gripped him by the arm and shoved him toward the door. "Take this *bezugo* along. Escobar, too, and watch him! All of you go but Cameo."

Toroblanco's messenger began to protest, but

Smiley hustled him through the door. The others followed. The last to go was Gipsy. Madden caught both her hands and pressed them hard.

"God bless you," he whispered. "I've been a fool. If we ever come out of this, I'm reformed for life! Don't worry; it's going to be all right."

Gently he forced her to follow the others. Then he slammed the door after her and ran back to Cameo Risden. His eyes were on fire with his purpose; his words tripped over one another as he rushed into his explanation. At the end the gambler meditated.

"You can try it," he said thoughtfully. "You may get away with it and you may not. If you fail, none of us, not even you, will be any worse off. Good luck, Rogue."

A couple of minutes later Smiley put his head in at the door. Cameo alone stood guard.

"Where Rogue?"

"He's all right," said Cameo coolly. "Hold that greaser in there the full ten minutes, Smiley."

Smiley puckered up a worried face, but he did as he was told. At the end of the ten minutes he led the way back into the living-room. At his heels came the half-breed; Escobar followed next with Bandini holding a gun on him; Aunt Polly and Gipsy entered after the others. Aunt Polly's lips were twitching and it would have been hard to say whether she was on the verge of laughing or weeping.

"Rogue's gone," Cameo told them quietly. "He had the hunch that he could make it, and since there's been no shooting, I guess he did. He's off for Long Corbin and the rest of the boys. What's more, on his way he's going to set fire to the big haystacks; Long Corbin will see the blaze clean across the hills and—"

"They'll kill him!" cried Gipsy fearfully.

"Here's how he worked it," said Cameo, and smiled. "He knew they'd be on the lookout for Toroblanco's messenger to come out. So he got an old blanket and draped it over him, took an old hat and wore it like this fellow. I opened the door. You ought to have seen him swagger out! No slinking at all, right out the front door, and swore he'd have the horse of the first man he saw! He must have gotten away with it; I've been listening and haven't heard—"

But all heard now a sudden voice right at the door shouting urgently:

"Open! Open up! Hurry, Cameo! Let me in!"

Rogue Madden's voice! Madden already returned! Cameo jumped to the door and jerked it open.

A man was catapulted into the room. With such force was his entry made that he tripped and pitched forward and fell on his face. At first all thought it was Madden. But in another instant here came Rogue Madden following the other figure. As the door was closed Madden, struggling with an old blanket, hurled his hat far across the room and burst into such joyous laughter as had not been heard from him for many a day.

"Look!" he cried out. "Look and feast your eyes!"

He pointed at the man on the floor. That worthy sprang hastily to his feet and turned upon them the inflamed face of Toroblanco!

"It was too easy! Too easy," cried Madden, carried away into the ultimate ecstasy of delight. "The Bull Calf's own cunning defeated him. I walked out and the poor fish out there thought that it was the king's messenger coming back! I mumbled like a man with a cold, demanding Toroblanco. He had scattered his men all around the house, thinking we might make a break for it. I saw him on his big white horse, and went to him holding out a scrap of paper. It was the easiest thing in the world to grab the hand he put out. And, would you believe it, with a gun between his shoulder blades, he did every little thing I asked him! Oh, what a poor *bezugo* the man is!"

"Hooray! The war's over!" yelled Bandini, and flourished his weapon close under Escobar's twitching nose.

Of a sudden the trapped Toroblanco went mad. It had been one thing to march here with a revolver pressed against his back; he had been half stunned with amazement, too. But now to hear this laughter, to see the look in his old enemy Smiley's eyes, was too much for him. Fury mounted to frenzy, and though they sprang on him and brought him again to the floor, he had shouted out his commands to his men whom he named dogs and urged on to slaughter.

"Chop the doors down! Kill! kill! kill! I don't care if I die! Kill these—"

They silenced him, but already bullets began ripping into the woodwork; behind the shutters glass fell clinking.

Aunt Polly sprang up, stood a moment looking bewildered, then ran to her niece and threw both arms about her and began whispering frantically. Gipsy started and grew stiff from head to foot. In another second she cast Aunt Polly aside and ran to Madden.

"Quick! This way!" she cried excitedly.

They ran together into the gun-room and to a heavy chest of drawers standing in a corner. Madden shoved the unwieldy piece of furniture aside; behind it were all the rifles, a full half-dozen with as many full cartridge belts. Electrified, Gipsy gasped in partial explanation:

"Aunt Polly did it! It must have been while I was talking with Escobar! She hid them here just for a joke on them—"

Madden ran back into the living-room with an armful of rifles.

"We've got 'em licked!" he exulted. "Why,

there are only forty of the rabble, and there are four of us with the best that's made in guns and enough ammunition to fight an army! Let's give 'em hell, boys!"

They made swift short work of trussing up both Toroblanco and Escobar.

"This other bird," said Smiley, indicating the messenger, "has our parole. Open the door and let him go!—Stand aside, ladies!"

The door opened and the man scuttled through, carrying word that it was a question of rifles now. Through the open door Smiley and Madden began firing together. The erstwhile messenger, with a squeal of terror, vanished among the shadows. Bullets from the attackers tore into the oaken panel; shot after shot did Madden and Smiley pour out in hot reply. Bandini and Cameo ran to two windows and began pumping lead through the narrowly opened shutters.

"I—I knew it was the real thing when—" It was Aunt Polly speaking queerly while rifles cracked and the room filled with the smell of powder. "I knew it was the real thing when—But I was afraid I might be mistaken—and I didn't want the boys to laugh at me! So I told Gipsy and—"

Aunt Polly stopped abruptly. She settled down in a chair and that queer smile came back to her face. Even now how was she to be sure of anything? In her dilemma she did a very sensible thing. She simply fainted dead away.

Toroblanco's men withdrew under fire. But they returned with axes and set to work at three doors. The sounds of their labours drew such a spraying storm of hot lead upon them that again they broke and ran. This was not the sort of work they excelled at and even had they had their high and mighty colonel at their backs it is to be doubted that they would have held to it with much greater courage. They were in the open; their opponents were under cover. They fell back after each spasmodic attack for a parley, and each parley was longer than the one before.

Then came Long Corbin and his men, tired of waiting and beginning to think that something was wrong. Through the night cut that most welcoming of all sounds, the long, quivering, blood-curdling yell of a pack of cowboys. In the house there was a wild dance of joy, and back to Long Corbin's ears floated a chorus like an echo to the yelpings of his own following. There was a rush of hoofs, a sally, and a perfect pandemonium of shots and yells. Then sudden quiet settled down over this Rancho of Joyous Guard.

And upon the other Rancho of Joyous Guard, to which they made all possible haste to return, a veritable cavalcade of them, all was peace with a new golden gleam in the sunshine and all the little pearly-grey doves cooing.

Smiley Himself had his way. He announced that

his vacation was over. He had brought back with him across the border and in his own unofficial way two men whom he was very glad to have caged and upon United States soil. Only when the two had been sent ahead and under guard, did he tell Rogue Madden all about it.

"It was a frame-up on you from the jump, and for a while it came close to fooling your Uncle Samuel. Sooner or later they knew the game would be uncovered; you were to be left holding the sack. Wonder they didn't put you in the pen, or at least, pry you loose from your ranch to save yourself. Using your ranch in Mexico and your place up here as the two ends of the Chink-and-Dope trail, they were all for pinning the whole thing on you. But I've got 'em, my son; got 'em for something else, too." Smiley's old eyes grew grim and hard and savage. "Escobar is going to hang for a murder done up here behind the high fence; he killed a Chinaman. But, between you and me, what he really swings for, and he knows it, is for the murder of your dad, down in Sonora. Yep; he's the party. He and Toroblanco together were after the mines down there; that's what they wanted with the girl, by the way. That dame, Velvet Jess, she goes clear; I can't help that, but most likely I'll get her later on. But clear she goes now, because she's going to help me stretch Escobar. And Toroblanco? Behind the bars for a nice long stretch; crimes committed on U.S.

territory. Maybe I can hang him, too. Oh, sure, I'll try. So long, Rogue. And it's all right about that sorrel horse."

So Smiley made his adieux. And the days at the ranch ran by filled with strange, new glory. Rogue Madden had reformed; he told Gipsy so and she believed him and was satisfied and, judging from the soft lights in her grey eyes, happy. He told her all about Father Juan's learning English, and making that strange speech to her; and together they went to call on the old priest. And Madden, speaking in Spanish, made an announcement and asked something of him which made the old man's eyes twinkle. When Father Juan blessed them, Gipsy pretended that she had not guessed what Madden had said. But she was very rosy and very lovely.

Then in his exuberance Rogue Madden gave a party, invited his "Gloomsters" and made the Marlibones and the Aston Ferribees his guests of honour. Never did a man seem to enjoy himself as did Madden over the veritable banquet he had set forth. It began with cocktails; Aunt Polly had one. It ran on with plentiful wines. Gipsy and Aunt Polly quitted the table while the Marlibones and the Ashton Ferribees made merry in their exhilarated gloom. Gipsy, with a little proprietary air which had but newly come into existence and which suited her charmingly, Madden thought, called him aside.

“I am afraid, Roger,” she admonished him, “that they are really drinking too much!”

“Oh, a function like this one only comes once in a lifetime for those folk,” he laughed at her. “Wait for me in the garden; I’ll send them along pretty quick.”

She thought that he was a long time coming. After a while she heard the guests leaving; horses pawed in the yard and wagon wheels rattled. It was too dark for her to see them, but she heard their querulous and uncertain voices with Madden bidding them a hearty good night. The wagons rattled away into the night.

He burst upon her in the garden like a young storm wind. When she heard his rollicking laughter she had her swift suspicion of the lastingness of any reform ever to alter Rogue Madden.

“What is it?” she asked, commanding him in her new manner to behave himself and talk sense. “What have you done to them?”

“Oh, Lord!” he choked. “If we could only look into the future, Gipsy, my love. Say an hour or so, or a few hours. The poor things were muddled—they got mixed up!”

“Tipsy, you mean?” she said sharply. “I told you they were drinking too much—”

She had to put her hands on him and shake him with all the violence which she could bring to the occasion before she got it out of him. *Mixed* up! That was what he meant! Ferribee had driven home with Mrs. Marlborough Bowen, thinking he had his own wife with him and Marlborough Bowen, with Mrs. Ferribee dozing against his shoulder, had gone away in full innocence that he had eloped with another man's wife!

"Oh, Rogue!" cried Gipsy—when she had made a practice of calling him Roger.

They heard Aunt Polly laugh. She had been listening and did not in the least care who knew it.

"And, Gipsy darling," she said, coming to join them, "think of the terrible existence you are headed straight into! Despite all your old aunt's warnings, I've no doubt that before the end of the chapter you will stand up with this rascal, and Father Juan's question will be asked: 'Do you take this man—for better or worse—' "

"For worse!" said Gipsy, laughing.

Center Point Large Print
600 Brooks Road / PO Box 1
Thorndike, ME 04986-0001 USA

(207) 568-3717

US & Canada:
1 800 929-9108
www.centerpointlargeprint.com